I0726904

I Know a Few Dogs in Heaven

Steve Reece

Table of Contents

Acknowledgements

First and foremost, I must give thanks to the Almighty for His blessings and for allowing me to write day after day.

I am also extremely grateful to my editor, Will Davis, for giving me a chance and teaching me to build a newspaper.

Dedication

To Debbie. She asks me to write

Excuse Me While I Take Off These Cowboy Boots

Living in high cotton.

Life Is Taken One Step at a Time

There are steps a man takes through life's journey that are truly meaningful. Like when he walks up to receive a diploma, takes steps down an aisle with a bride, or steps up to face a judge.

Neil Armstrong took a small step he famously called a leap for all mankind. The most solemn steps are the 21 taken by guards at the Tomb of the Unknown Soldier, repeated again and again, forever, lest we forget.

Most of us took our first baby steps when we were around 12 months old while our eager mommies and daddies squatted on the floor, cheering and encouraging us to release the edge of the coffee table and wobble into their outstretched arms. Eventually, we became bold enough, and our parents were never prouder. Ambitious babies like to show off and begin walking upright as early as 9 months. Laid-back little people prefer to get around on all fours until 15 or 16 months, when they are much too large for a worn-out mother to lug them around.

I've wasted a lot of my own steps, forgetting why I walked into a room or searched for something in the same place repeatedly, knowing perfectly well I already looked in that spot. I waste steps searching for my phone while holding it in my hand or looking for keys still hanging in the lock.

And there's no telling how much leather I've worn out by walking away mad.

Depending on their occupation, the average person takes around 7,500 steps a day. That means if a person has a 30-inch stride and they are lucky enough to still be stepping proudly at the age of 80, they will have walked 110,000 miles. At a speed of 3-4 miles per hour, they have walked for at least 27,750 hours. This is equivalent to hiking 5 times around the globe at the equator. Nearly halfway to the moon. Or 19 round-trip flights across the continental United States.

The average schoolteacher takes 12,564 steps every school day. I now know why my old English teacher, Mrs. Brewer, was always in a sour mood with those big, fleshy feet bulging out of those hard, black-leather, old-lady shoes. I added a lot of mileage to her daily step total because she had to keep walking to my desk, positioned way in the back of the room, and rap it soundly with her cane to jumpstart me back awake. I was usually so bored and sleepy in her class; it was easy for her to sneak up on me, even with her noisy clomping all over the classroom.

If walking is your thing, then you should choose to be a waiter as a career with 22,778 steps per day. When a server tells you, "I love you to the moon and back..." they mean it. This is more than 3 times the normal rate at twice the pace.

It's a tough job. Please keep this in mind at tipping time. Don't ask me to walk a mile in their shoes because I can't take watching a bunch of strangers all eating at the same time. It reminds me too much of a herd of cattle chewing cud.

Being too busy making calls to have much time for taking strolls, call center associates walk a mere 6,618 steps each day. It must be nice sitting around all day, kicking back, and calling up people just to annoy them.

I do my share of walking, but not much stepping out. Not like back in the days when I would boogie out of some Atlanta disco early in the morning after getting down like John Travolta all night. The sun made me blind, and I was running late for work. I'd rush to my pickup, change out of my fancy Italian shoes into my muddy work boots, race to work, and clock in, raring to go. Jumping, fighting, kicking, and showing off fancy footwork all day. I like to think I can still do that, but I have no desire to strut down a road already well-traveled. That fire is out. The ashes are now cold.

I've never had to cover any tracks, but there are a few steps I've taken I wish I could backtrack. I've traveled down a couple of paths, I suppose I shouldn't have, but thank the Lord, He showed me the way back. I've left my footprints in many places on this planet Earth, but right now, these dogs are howling. Y'all excuse me while I take off these cowboy boots.

Our Hands, Everyday Miracles

Look at your hands. Those things at the end of your arms that you give so little thought to. Your dexterous, agile, flexible, strong, and sensitive hands tell the story of your life, whether they be gnarled and old, twisted, bruised and bumpy, or soft and manicured. They are always busy, regardless of occupation or age. From infancy to old age, our hands define us; they create the things we think in our minds and put them before us.

Even if calloused and rough from hard work, our hands can comfort our friends or even strangers. Even the most hardened worker can feel the softness of a baby as they hold them, dress them, and keep them warm and well-fed.

We touch the frightened faces of the dying, then put our palms together to pray for them. Our hands can heal the sick and comfort the lonely. You can press your fingers against a loved one's cheek and tell them, without words, how much you appreciate and care for them.

The sense of touch in our fingers lets us know whether something is hot, cold, warm, soft, smooth, or even nasty.

Our hands construct the world around us. They build our homes, buildings, roads, bridges, and businesses. They can hold a nail and then swing down a hammer on its head. Hands can saw, and hands can weld. With them, we weed our gardens, trim the lawn and build birdhouses. Then we can go inside and use our hands to write a little bird poem with a computer, a pen, or a dab of ink on the tip of a feather.

Do you want to show your wife or girlfriend you're proud of her in public? Simply grab her hand as you walk around the square. Want to show your buddy you're a true friend? The bro handshake is easy enough. Or, these days, maybe a fist bump. We can hold a baseball bat and somehow smack a speeding ball over a wire fence 100 yards away, or catch it just before it goes over.

Every day, our hands perform hundreds of wonderful things, all unnoticed and unappreciated.

My father's hands were work-worn, calloused, and often stained from hard work. Yet years of abuse never diminished the intricate details he put into his work. The hands that held me when I was a baby continued to serve him for nearly 80 years without a hitch, except for the time a cat bit him in the fleshy part of his hand between his thumb and his index finger. He nearly lost it due to the infection, but thankfully, he recovered, retaining the strong grip he was known for and continuing with his creations. More proof that our hands are miraculous.

My mother could hold a tiny needle and make things of great beauty. She could also grab a maple switch with equal ease and inflict great pain. And just by holding up one finger at the supper table, she was able to immediately command complete silence. By placing her hand in my dad's, she showed us she loved him.

My own hands are less calloused than earlier in my life when I spent years working with wood outside in the weather. I carry the scars of my guitar picking on the tips of the fingers of my left hand that will never go away, but I now use the hands of a writer, a bit softer. Somehow, my fingers instinctively know the keys to strike as quickly as my brain can conjure up the words. Along with the occasional typo.

When I was a kid, my Uncle Marvin lost his hands while working on the lines of Georgia Power. He was told the electricity was off, and he grabbed two live wires. The shock was so strong it completely knocked both of his climbing boots off his feet. I remember well how the tragedy affected the entire family. The relief of his surviving the accident was dampened by the loss of his hands. Even though I don't believe I could survive without the use of my own hands, Uncle Marvin has gone through his life undeterred in furniture making, driving, fishing, and anything else an ordinary man can do. But my uncle is not ordinary. Even though we now have amazing prosthetics that can do anything the human body can do, my uncle has stayed with the rudimentary claws he was given in place of his hands, and no one who knows him considers him to be handicapped. He was an inspiration to me growing up and always will be.

Unfortunately, hands can also kill, maim, and do harm to others. They hold pistols, knives, and rifles, steering wheels, and hypodermic needles full of dangerous drugs. They can shove someone off a cliff or push them down the stairs. We can ball them up into a fist and knock someone out for a ten-second count or just plain slap them silly.

In our hands, we hold the power to create a better world. The way you use yours is up to you.

English, My Mother Language

Humans are the only animals that have abstract thoughts, and language is an essential tool for abstract thinking. There are 7,117 different languages spoken across the globe, which used to be a major problem, but we now have translation apps that have improved over the years. I once deeply offended a Chinese lady I met in a restaurant after she translated my innocent English into vulgar Mandarin on a popular translation app on her phone.

According to the Bible, around 604 to 562 BC, a large Babylonian construction crew, supervised by Nimrod (who was the great-grandson of Noah), was building a tower of burnt brick that came close to heaven but didn't quite reach it. When it reached the astounding height of 5,433 cubits and 2 palms, which equals roughly 1.6 miles high, God saw his people still hadn't changed their sinning ways, but instead of sending another flood, he simply halted the project by giving everyone a different language and scattering them across the face of the earth. God was so angry that he also destroyed the tower.

According to linguists, there are two main hypotheses that explain the diversity of languages. The first is the belief that all languages originated with one language that spread due to early humans' nature of wanting to pack it all up and travel at the slightest notion. This is known as monogenesis. The second hypothesis, called polygenesis, holds that humans evolved in different parts of the world, and so did their languages. Each of the original languages was then split into numerous languages, until we ended up with the confusing mess we have now. I prefer the Bible explanation, the simpler, more reasonable version.

Many languages are useful in different ways. For instance, English, with 1,132 million speakers, is the global language of business. Some multinational companies, such as Airbus, Daimler-Chrysler, Nokia, and Microsoft, have even mandated English as their corporate language. It is also the standard language for aviation communications.

If you want to talk to God, the intonation of a Spanish prayer is considered incredibly beautiful. And Spanish is also especially handy if you like to speak with the señoritas. If you want to make love, the language of all the great lovemakers is obviously French. If you stub your toe, the utterance of a German word can fit nicely, but feel free to use a vocalization of your own invention.

The Oxford English Dictionary defines 171,476 words of the English language. More words than any other language. A language called Taki Taki has the fewest words, with 340. Not much to talk about, I assume.

There's a craziness in how English words are spelled. What sense does it make that there are so many ways to pronounce words ending with "-ough"? Such words as: "Cough," "tough," "through," "bough,"; and "dough." English comes naturally when you're a baby, but the language is considered extremely difficult to learn. You can see proof of this every day on numerous Facebook posts. I hope the writers' religion is more orthodox than their spelling.

Our language also has lots of silent letters, which causes stress for beginners. For example, words that begin with a silent "K," such as "knife" or "knock." The silent "H" at the beginning of "honor," the "P" at the beginning of "psychology," and "pneumonia," or the "B" in "thumb."

Just learning the nuances of our simple two-letter word "up" would be enough to make me give up. We look up. But we also wake up, break up, then make up. We mess it up, screw it up, and then fix it up. In the morning, we open up, then at night, we close up. You work up an appetite, so you fill up. You can walk up, speak up, find out what's up and stir up a little trouble. Word up.

According to the U.S. Census Bureau, of the almost 41 million foreign-born residents in the United States, only 15% speak only English at home. 35% speak a non-English language at home but also speak English "very well." This leaves 50% of these immigrants without any English-speaking ability.

Bad words are usually the first you learn when you teach yourself a second language. I know people who have lived in this country for over 25 years, and the only real English they know is cussing.

There is no excuse for not learning the native language. I taught myself a second language, so I know it can be done. If you want to live here, you need to acclimate. Of course, if you don't already know my mother language, you don't have a clue about what I'm saying…

There are many benefits to being multilingual. Your brainpower is boosted, and your memory improves. It also enhances your ability to multitask, sharpens your mind, and improves your first language. So "¿Qué pasa, señor?"

Southern Sayings Explained

So, in the interest of my Yankee friends and other confused Northerners, here is a short list of some Southern phrases to help them navigate their way through the South on their way to Orlando: "He's as drunk as Cooter Brown." When you hear someone refer to another person as "He's as drunk as Cooter Brown," you probably know that person is as inebriated as they can possibly be. That is, if you are from the South. What you might not know is that Cooter Brown was supposedly a real person who lived on the Mason-Dixon line during the Civil War and couldn't decide which side to fight for because he wasn't sure which side would win. To be safe, he came up with an ingenious plan to avoid being drafted by either army: to stay drunk throughout the conflict, rendering him useless as a soldier.

A different version of Cooter Brown's story says he was a half-black, half-Cherokee man who lived in an old Cajun fur trapper's shack down in southern Louisiana. He successfully drank his way out of military service, but by the time the war was over, he was a hopeless alcoholic, and he couldn't put it down.

Cooter's shack caught fire one night, and when they sifted through the ashes the next morning, nothing remained of his body. Not even a bone. The theory was that he was so full of whiskey he just completely burned up.

"He's got enough money to burn a wet mule." Back in 1929, Standard Oil Company got "madder than a wet hen" with Gov. Huey Long when he tried to pass a 5-cent tax on each barrel of oil to fund his welfare programs. A bunch of erroneous charges were put together against Long, which included him getting drunk at a party with a stripper, and they tried to have him impeached. But the good ole' boy Democratic governor didn't take it lying down. He said that the company tried to bribe legislators with as much as

$25,000 to vote him out. He called the amount "enough money to burn a wet mule," and it has been with us ever since. He ended up being assassinated in 1935.

"He could eat corn through a picket fence." The definition of this phrase is self-explanatory: it describes someone with an extreme set of wide gaps between their teeth. It isn't a very nice thing to say, but it is very colorful and expressive, so don't hold it against us. An example of such a person would be David Letterman. I could see that such a condition could be useful, especially if you want to only eat your corn one row at a time. Vertically.

"We're living in high cotton." This phrase doesn't mean much to those who aren't blessed enough to live in the South. To them, cotton is nothing more than the material their sheets are woven from, but there was a time when cotton was the main source of Southern wealth. Tall cotton bushes are easier to pick and yield higher returns. So, if you're living "in high cotton," it means you're feeling particularly successful or wealthy and probably can afford silk sheets.

"You look rode hard and put up wet." This may sound like some type of Southern sexual innuendo, but it refers to a person who hasn't had enough sleep or maybe has drunk too much. A good rider knows to walk his horse around to dry before being put into the stable. If this step is skipped, the horse will look sick and tired, much like a person who "got drunk as Cooter Brown."

Southerners love to use pigs in their conversations. These sayings include, "You can't make a silk purse out of a sow's ear." We might use this to describe a cousin's double-wide decorated with deer antlers. Or if we want to explain the obvious to someone, we might say, "It's as plain as a pig sitting on a couch." One of my favorite pig expressions comes from Mark Twain, who once said, "Never try to teach a pig to sing. It wastes your time and annoys the pig."

This simply means some people are just too close-minded to deal with. And then there's "She's as happy as a dead pig in the sunshine." This describes a blissfully ignorant person. It originated because when a pig dies in the hot sun, its lips slowly pull back as its skin dries out, giving the pig a nice toothy grin, still smiling on his worst day ever. Bless his heart.

Never Eat Anything Ugly

Food is the primary source of energy and building materials for your body, the most complex organic system on the planet. When we were embryos, our bones, organs, and skin were built from what our mothers ingested during their pregnancy. In the case of some of the baby boomer folks, a bit of nicotine, alcohol, drugs, and caffeine was also included in that diet. I'm not saying anything bad about baby boomer mothers. No one knew the dangers back then.

Hippocrates said 2,500 years ago, "We are what we eat." I know this to be true because I once dated a gal for a while down in South Georgia who had eaten nothing but fried shrimp for years. Three meals a day. In fact, she ate so much shrimp she started looking like one. Skinny girl with bugged-out eyes. Hollowed out cheeks. Sadly, she was sorely lacking in the tail fin area.

Another lady I knew strongly resembled a barnyard chicken, down to her mannerisms. She loved fried chicken so much that she applied for a job at the Big Chic. They put her behind the counter taking orders, and she would strut back and forth between the register and the sweet tea, making contented clucking sounds just like an old hen. Even bobbed her head. Wisely, she stayed out of the kitchen. She understood that the worst part about being a chicken is that you taste like one.

I really don't eat that many domesticated birds, and with this pandemic going on, I worry about eating anything that requires any finger-lickin', but chickens are jealous of my chicken legs.

I don't eat a whole lot of food; therefore, I don't look like a whole lot. My favorite chow is pinto beans, fried potatoes, cornbread, and other dishes of poor-country-folk food, which obviously doesn't do much in the looks department. I have heard, though, that grits can make girls awfully pretty.

This theory also applies to animals. My dog loves cat food. I can't keep him out of it. If it weren't for him, my cat food budget would be cut in half. I believe this is why he has taken on a feline attitude lately and has been walking around acting snooty toward me, just like one of my cats. When he snores, it sounds like a purr. And they have totally accepted him into their exclusive cat club. You should see the three on rodeo cat night when they tear up my house. I'm not included in their clique.

There are people who look like their pets, which I hope has nothing to do with what they eat. If you want to amuse yourself, you can Google this fact and find side-by-side comparisons. I once was doing some carpentry work in the home of a long-haired blonde lady. She told me in the kitchen what needed to be done in the living room. I was quite startled when I entered the living room and saw what I thought was the back of the woman's head I had just been speaking to. I said hi, and she ignored me, so I went straight to work. I nearly hammered my thumb when an Afghan hound jumped down off the couch where I thought the lady was sitting and came over to sniff my ladder. The resemblance was uncanny. I'm only like my dog in that we're both small but aggressive. Hopefully, that's about it.

Another phenomenon is that married couples tend to resemble each other over the decades. Scientists explain that years of shared emotions experienced simultaneously can result in similar wrinkles and expressions. This makes perfect sense, but I think an additional reason is that they have been eating the same food day in and day out since their honeymoon.

But there are some things we consume that seem to have no effect on us at all. Smart Water comes to mind. At $2.99 or more per liter, the only smart people I see are the ones selling it. I once drank a gallon of it and felt about as sharp as a spoon. Muscle Milk is another good example. I drank a bottle of that tasty stuff every day for a couple of weeks, but one look at me, and you can tell it doesn't live up to its name.

I'm always careful not to eat anything ugly. I need all the help I can get. This basically means I never touch anything that's in a Tupperware bowl in my refrigerator. I think I'll head over to the Dairy Queen and have a banana split.

In the Lines of a Face

A braham Lincoln once took a line from an old limerick and said, "As for my face, I do not mind it, as I am the one who is behind it." When it came to looks, our most recognizable president was no Ronald Reagan, our movie star president. You can clearly see the burden of war in the lines of Lincoln's sad face in the final photograph taken of him just four days before his assassination. Lincoln is proof that you don't have to be nice-looking to achieve great accomplishments.

It's been said that when a man turns 50, he will be wearing the face he deserves. All his life's struggles and achievements will be permanently etched into his face. And the less handsome a man's face, the more character it reveals. I can't recall how I looked at 50, so I can't say whether this is absolutely true. I do remember I had somewhat more hair on my head and less on my chin.

Although it covers only 4.5% of an adult's body surface area, the human face performs some pretty important functions, like tasting, smelling, eating, seeing, and speaking. Some lucky people can also add kissing. By comparison, a child's face occupies 9% of their body space, in proportion to their smaller size. That's twice the surface area of an adult face. You wouldn't know that just by looking at them. It seems like I would have noticed something like that before now.

We communicate much better when we are face-to-face because we can see and interpret each other's body language and facial expressions. This is much better than texting because you must resort to all caps when you need to shout. LOL, and OMG.

Sometimes, when meeting in person, you don't even need words. You can express a wide range of emotions with just your eyes. There is no questioning a "come hither" look from across a crowded room. Whereas a stern glare will have the opposite effect. If only looks could kill.

Other than the fact that I like to look at them, I don't profess to know a lot about women's faces. It's difficult for me to tell a woman's past just by looking at her. That could be because most of them are hidden behind a mask of paint and powder. But that's fine with me.

Makeup can be extremely beneficial. Go to the internet and look up some close-up shots of our most famous beautiful female movie stars, before and after makeup, and you'll see what I mean. And imagine what would have happened if Hillary had been elected president and was summoned to the war room in the middle of the night after she had removed her makeup. War can be ugly.

There are several folks who aren't too happy with the appearance of the mugs they were born with. Fortunately, modern medical procedures can fix that unsightly problem. The American Society of Plastic Surgeons reports that 1,811,740 people underwent cosmetic procedures in the United States in 2018. A lot of these people were women who had facelifts, but they hid them with makeup anyway. Of these, 213,780 patients shelled out the big bucks and transformed oversized beaks into cute little turned-up noses.

While not officially considered a part of the face, conveniently located just around the corner, we have the ears. Some people's ears are beautiful, but I've always considered our ears to be the part of our body that's the most oddly designed, aesthetically speaking. They are also the part of our body that's most difficult to clean because of all those weird little crevices you must dig into. An interesting and handy thing about our ears is that the spot where the top of your ear is attached to the side of your head is exactly horizontally centered with your pupils. And your pupils are positioned in the exact vertical center of your face. You look good behind those Ray-Bans because they are perfectly balanced and level, centered on your face and not sitting all askew because your ears are either too low, too high, or out of whack.

From the neck down, other than a wide variety of sizes, we are all pretty much the same. Our faces are what really distinguish us from each other. Our faces make us unique. It's how we are identified.

Handsome or pretty, or just downright butt-ugly, unless you have an identical twin or a doppelgänger somewhere on the other side of the planet, your face is one-of-a-kind. You can put makeup on it, shave it, tattoo it, or put on a jewel-encrusted N95 mask. It will still be just a face in the crowd.

Put Some Teeth Into the Wedding

Since I recently wrote about the trials of being single in the interest of fairness, I thought I'd say something about the institution of marriage. I've been married a couple of times, so I consider myself to be almost an expert on the subject, but still, I did obligatory research, and these are some of my findings:

According to government figures, there were 2,132,853 marriages in the United States in 2018. 65,036 of these knot-tying ceremonies were held in Georgia. I couldn't find any statistics on the number of marriages since the COVID disaster, but there's no doubt the number has dropped dramatically. A positive side of this is that when marriage rates drop, so do divorce rates.

There are one million divorces in the United States each year. This is nearly half of the number of marriages. "'Until death do us part" is the part of the wedding vow that is now largely ignored, as the average length of an American marriage is only 8.2 years. In 2018, Georgia had 26,550 divorces. This is a little better than the national average, but not much.

A few years ago, one of my sideline jobs was making wedding videos. Every wedding has its own unique story, and recording something so special on video is always challenging. You only get one chance for every shot. Of course, the bride is always the star of the show, and her mother is always the one in charge. The groom only becomes important when he's standing before the preacher.

Unfortunately, of all the wedding videos I've produced, I know of only one couple who're still together. Sometimes I could just tell when a blessed union wasn't going to last.

Once, I was commissioned to do a video for a couple who obviously had no business getting married. They had an extremely tumultuous engagement, fighting and arguing daily, and even the cops had to show up a couple of times. Still, they were convinced their love would overcome any of their differences and were determined to go through with it.

An important sequence of any wedding video is one with the bride and bridesmaids primping hair, piling on makeup, and generally having a good old time while getting ready for the big moment. The hero shot of this sequence is a close-up of the bride smiling into a makeup mirror. Well, this argumentative bride wouldn't crack a smile no matter how much I begged and explained the importance of it. I could've goosed her in the ribs, and it wouldn't have done any good. I assumed she was angry with her fiancé since she always was anyway.

This grouchy bride scowled throughout the happiest day of her life. But, in all fairness, she had every reason to. The ceremony began with the groom showing up 15 minutes late with two drunken groomsmen dragging their even-more-drunk buddy up to the altar. The bride had to keep a tight grip on him to keep him from falling over while he mumbled and slurred his vows, swaying left and right.

During the reception, as the newlyweds were having their first official married fight while performing their first official dance, the bride happened to smile sarcastically after an insult directed at her new husband. I then realized the real reason for her constant frown was that she was missing several teeth. Upper and lower. Front and back. She and her family had invested quite a bit of money in this big event, but teeth weren't on the budget.

My motto is "the show always comes first." Personalities, egos, or crybaby feelings come last. Even if it's a cheat, I always strive for the best look, so I took the frames of those fleeting seconds when she finally smiled during that most important dance, imported them into Photoshop, and tediously painted her missing teeth frame by frame. I then exported those frames back to the editing program, and the rest was magic.

I was a bit nervous as I sat with her on her couch as she reviewed my work for the first time on her big-screen TV. At first, she seemed quite pleased with everything. The music cuts fit perfectly, and with my use of effects, filters, and a couple of tricks I know, you couldn't even tell the groom was plastered on his butt.

When she reached the frames of her only smile, which I had rendered in slow motion, she stopped the video, rewound it, and replayed it three times without a word. I became extremely concerned that I had offended her by giving her computer-generated teeth and asked her if everything was OK. She responded with the biggest toothless grin I've ever seen. She was so happy; I could've gone on a honeymoon with her.

In case you're wondering, their marriage didn't even make it past the one-year mark.

Not Even Alexa Cares

The number of single people living alone makes up nearly a third of our population. You would think that there would be an entire line of products designed just for them, specifically food products. I'd have to eat four banana sandwiches a day in order to eat a whole loaf of bread before the expiration date. A better solution would be for one-third (in proportion to the single population) of all loaves of bread to be baked at half size. Most weeks, I end up tossing nearly half a loaf of stale crumbs to the birds from my back porch.

Same thing with bacon, cheese, lunch meat, and even oatmeal. I recently checked the date on an old oatmeal box I found in the back of a cabinet and discovered it had been there for two years. And that single-serving packet isn't oatmeal. I'm not sure what it is. The only things geared toward single folks are the vegetables in those cool little cans on aisle five at Ingles and a few tasteless TV dinners.

Once I get my groceries home and make the two trips necessary to get them inside, I must put them all away, then cook, eat, and clean up the dishes and the nasty kitchen. What a pain. I know from experience that two can eat more cheaply than one, and things go more smoothly when chores are shared. That isn't happening right now, but I'm working on it. The girlfriends I've had lately have all been bat-poop crazy, so I've raised my standards. This, in turn, has narrowed the field dramatically.

Two and a half million years ago, when humans first started eating meat, a man's days were filled with the accomplishment of only one goal: finding food. There was no preservation technology, so every meal had to be a fresh catch. He'd leave early in the morning and sneak up on wild cattle, young saber tooth tigers, or red deer and hopefully bring down a meal with a well-aimed spear. Then he would have to clean his kill with a sharp stone and drag the carcass back home. He then had to find dry wood and set it afire by creating a spark with a couple of rocks. After cutting and cooking the meat and consuming what was probably a tasty meal, he had to clean up all that mess. By then, it was time to rustle up some lunch. And when that was over: supper. If he had little cave babies crawling around in the dirt and a cavewoman constantly nagging him about a better and bigger cave, his stress level was even greater.

Out of curiosity, as a single man, I did a Google search and asked Alexa for "items for single people." The first item that popped up was a "boyfriend pillow." Amazon alone produced 38,000 results for this incredibly popular product. It is a pillow designed for single women with the same shape and size as a man's torso. It comes dressed in a shirt or pajama top, with only one arm permanently positioned in the shape of a warm embrace, where a lady can rest her head on a lonely night and feel wanted and loved. One size fits all. The cost of one of these comforting pillows is under $40, but for $10 extra, a lonesome lady can get one with bulging muscles if she needs to feel extra secure. Men can order a female version of the pillow, available with or without a blouse. There aren't any you can order that match my small physique. Sorry, ladies. But I'm sure any old Teddy bear will achieve the same results.

Another companion for a single gentleman is a product known as "Grow a Girlfriend." They advertise her as never complaining or nagging. Sounded like a good deal after what I've been through, and I was thinking about ordering one of my own, but I'm not quite ready to make that kind of a commitment. Besides, my new girlfriend would show up at my door at a height of only 2 inches. She would begin to grow six times that within 2 hours once submerged in water, but still, at only 12 inches tall, she would never be able to reach the sink. Another drawback is once she's removed from the water, she begins to shrink. She'd have to spend all her time in the hot tub.

In my extensive search, I also found many sites for singles looking for other singles. I've never tried one of these sites. I'm afraid I might be laying my charm on some stinky old man in dirty underwear posing as the girl of my dreams, trying to get my money. Other than that, I found

little with the key phrase "items for singles". Not even Alexa cares.

The Only Thing We Have to Fear...

It doesn't matter how brave you think you are; we are all afraid of something. Many people fear snakes and spiders, and some folks don't care to board airplanes or speak in public. I fear God and mothers-in-law. But most of our fears are unfounded. As Franklin Roosevelt said during his first inaugural address in 1933, "The only thing we have to fear is fear itself."

My dad learned this lesson well as a boy in the Georgia mountains, while FDR was still president and World War II was raging across the globe. His father had died the previous year, and he found himself at the age of twelve as the man of the house with five younger siblings. Times were hard, but my old man was harder. Fortunately, my grandmother was even harder than him.

Instead of school, my dad was forced to spend his days working at whatever an uneducated mountain boy could do.

But even the most menial jobs requiring little more than muscle were scarce. Still, with his charisma and salesmanship, he convinced nearby farmers and storeowners in Ellijay that he was the man for the job. Sometimes they didn't even know they had a job for him until he showed up with that Wayne Reece smile and pointed out that a pile of wood needed chopping or some boxes that needed to be stacked. They would hire him on the spot; he'd do the job and walk away with twenty-five cents and an invitation to return. I'm proud to say I got my strong work ethic from my father.

We all know about Georgia summers. It's so hot, even at the top of a mountain, it can be muggy and uncomfortable.

Hot and tired after a long day of lugging rocks out of a field, my dad was relaxing with the family after a supper of a bellyful of pinto beans sitting on the old rickety wooden front porch of their old rickety wooden shack, cooling off in the only way possible on a hot night in the middle of July. The night had a full, bright moon, as ours did a couple of weeks ago.

The family lived on a dusty dirt road directly across from a cow pasture where, rarely, a cow had been seen. My dad once told me he would sometimes cross the barbed-wire fence to hunt for rabbits, which were also rare. He said that on this particular night, while he was talking with my grandmother and enjoying the breeze, he saw her face suddenly freeze with fear as she looked toward the cow pasture. My dad then turned, and with the entire family as witnesses, they saw what appeared to be a simple brown coffin floating slowly across the pasture in the moonlight about three feet off the ground.

Everyone immediately bolted into the little shack they called home, with my dad in the lead. Not because he was the most scared, but because he was going for his .410 shotgun. By the time he returned to the porch, the "ghost" had disappeared. Nevertheless, the door was secured with a hook latch and heavy furniture, and my frightened ancestors sweated it out the rest of the hot night.

The next evening was a repeat performance. The moon was just as bright, and the air was just as still and maybe even hotter. The only sensible place to sit was on the porch. But this night, my dad was prepared, his shotgun at his side, ready to defend his family against that thing in the cow pasture they had seen the previous night. That thing that had been on their minds the entire day, and what had made their conversation so lively over supper. Of course, everyone had a different opinion of what the apparition was, but the final consensus was that it was not of this world.

Sure enough, out of the bushes, the ghostly, coffin-shaped box once more came slowly drifting out of the woods to the edge of the grass and stopped. No one said a word, but all jaws dropped. My dad bravely slipped off the porch with his shotgun and crept down the dirt road a few yards away from the "coffin," ignoring my grandmother's loud whispers to return.

He crossed the fence and hid himself lying down in a tall patch of grass. He tried to slow and quiet his excited breathing, but his heart was about to explode. He took off the safety and carefully took aim. When I mentioned to him that a shotgun shell wouldn't hurt a ghost, he told me he knew that but was hoping the sound of the blast might at least scare it away.

Then, while his sights were set on the broadside of the "coffin," it turned forty-five degrees away from him and silhouetted against a full moon, my old man saw the unmistakable outline of a brown cow with black legs and a black head. He laughed and fired a shot into the sky. The beast then slowly ambled away to saner pastures.

What's Going on Inside That Head?

Most people believe we use only 10% of our brains. This is a myth that has been debunked by studies using functional magnetic resonance imaging (fMRI), which show that most of our brain is active nearly all the time, even while performing simple tasks or sleeping. The percentage of brain use varies from person to person (I'm sure you've noticed that), and it also depends on what a person is doing or thinking about. Then there are those who have about as many brains as a box of rocks, but that's a different subject.

About 100 billion neurons (cells that communicate with other cells) make up 10% of the human brain. This fact is possibly the source of the 10%-use myth, which has been widely repeated in films, TV, and articles for decades. You can't believe everything you read.

Although the brain weighs only 2% of a person's weight, it uses 20% of its oxygen and calories. The brain is 73% water, and being dehydrated by as little as 2% can impair a person's ability to perform simple tasks that require motor skills, memory, and concentration.

While you are reading this, you are likely to hear your own voice inside your head. Just yakking away, sentence by sentence. And then, when you are finished with this column, that voice will continue, saying things like, "What was that I just read?" When you hear that voice "speaking" in your head, and even though you don't realize it, your larynx is making minuscule muscle movements along with it. Sometimes, my larynx goes a little too far, and I surprise myself and everyone around me by accidentally expressing my thoughts out loud, usually at the worst possible moment, like while I'm sitting in church or at a family gathering.

Except when we pray silently, we all believe that the voice(s) we hear inside our brains go unheard. That is about to change. The use of an electroencephalogram (EEG) can detect electrical activity in your brain by using electrodes attached to your scalp. So, while you sit there looking weird with wires coming all out of your head, scientists can detect the state of your brain. Experiments involving controlling video games using brainwaves are underway. Future useful applications of this technology include powering wheelchairs and replacing the mouse and keyboard. Experiments to determine someone's thoughts about a new product or a well-placed advertisement are also underway. No, thank you very much.

A computer has also been developed that can identify images visualized in your mind. So far, the machine that uses only fMRI data has limited capabilities. It has learned only a few specific images, such as a screwdriver and other simple items, but its inventors are excited. This technology has also revealed a surprising discovery: the same thoughts across different human brains are neurologically similar and yield the same readings. The computer has been correct 100% of the time in capturing the imaginations of human subjects.

As far back as 2015, a computer at a Japanese Institute was able to predetermine rock-paper-scissors game choices made by the players even before they moved their hands. And in another EEG experiment, a computer attached to a certain area of the brain was able to "see" words two full seconds before the words were uttered.

In 2008, researchers predicted with 60% accuracy whether a volunteer would push a button with their right or left hand.

What was notable about this experiment was that the scientists were able to predict 10 seconds before the subject felt they had made a decision.

An interesting use of all this mind-reading technology is in the security field. It is now possible for investigators to use fMRI to identify recognition in the brain to determine whether a criminal recognizes a crime scene or a murder weapon. Security measures that use EEG also include using "pass thoughts" as an alternative to passwords. This method is touted as being significantly better than previous high-tech methods such as retina scans, fingerprinting, and voice recognition. I'm not sure what's to stop someone from hacking into your brain and stealing your secret pass thought or PIN.

With brain-scanning technology rapidly becoming more and more accurate, debates will undoubtedly pop up over when and how it should be used. In the application of criminal law, some say not using brain scans on suspects prevents the wrongly accused from proving their innocence. Others say involuntary brain reading of criminals violates the 5th Amendment's right not to self-incriminate.

In India, thought identification has already been used in criminal law. An Indian woman was convicted of murdering her ex-fiancé by poisoning him after an EEG of her brain showed that she was familiar with the ghastly deed's circumstances. After the scan, she had no defense.

Sometimes you just need to keep your thoughts to yourself.

Goats Don't Care How I Smell

Possums don't mind it much either...

Why'd the Chicken Cross Rumble Road?

Why a little brown chicken crossed the road off exit 181 to live beneath a pear tree at Rumble Road BP is still a mystery to all of us who knew and loved her. Sadly, she recently passed away, and in her memory, this is her story:

Seven years ago, while I was working at Rumble Road BP and checking the parking lot, a hen walked over the hill from the direction of the interstate and right up to me. More surprising than that was that she started following me around, contentedly clucking away. I called this new friend Ms. Rumble. Before Ms. Rumble, I knew nothing about chickens, only that they ate chicken feed and laid eggs. We didn't sell chicken feed, so I gave her a hot dog, and she tore it up.

She wasn't allowed inside the store, so she would wait for me outside by the front door unless a pickup truck would pull up to a pump, and she would scamper out and perch on the tailgate while the driver pumped their gas. Ms. Rumble had a big thing for trucks, and when delivery trucks arrived, she'd jump up in the back with the delivery man, sit on a box, and watch him scamper up and down the ramp.

She roosted in the pear tree next to the peach stand and would come down in the mornings and eat mealworms from my hand. She'd even leap up and take them from my fingers. Boy, I sure was proud of that. She barely weighed two pounds, but she was feisty. A hawk once swooped down on her, and the hawk barely made it out alive. For that reason, I didn't really worry about the hawks. I would come to regret that later.

Incredibly, one sunny morning, while Ms. Rumble was enjoying a tasty peach and I was smoking a nasty cigarette, a rooster walked up to us from the same exact direction Ms. Rumble came from two months earlier. Now I had two chickens following me around. I used to consider myself to be quite the chick magnet, but suddenly, I found myself becoming quite the chicken magnet. Due to the way he sounded when he crowed, I named this rooster Willie (after Willie Nelson).

Willie and Ms. Rumble soon fell in love and went on their honeymoon in the woods across Lee King Road. After a week or so, I found Ms. Rumble under a bush, sitting on a pile of eggs while Willie was pecking in the dirt nearby. Soon, I had 12 chickens following me around. I named all the chicks, like Cowboy and Lucille and such, and they would sit on my lap under the pear tree while I patted their pretty little heads.

Ms. Rumble proved to be quite a prolific hen. I estimate that at least 300 of her chicks are spread out across the South. In order to obtain a miracle chick from Mrs. Rumble's brood, you had to promise me you would never abuse or eat it, and you also had to show me a picture of where you would be keeping it.

We lost Willie when a hawk came down upon him one day in a flash of feathers and talons. It was all I could do to kick that hawk off him. I buried poor Willie out behind the storage shed beneath a smooth, round stone, and my sister and I quickly put together a makeshift chicken coop beneath the pear tree and herded the remaining chickens into safety. A friend brought us a new rooster, and soon Ms. Rumble was back in the chick-making business. Our chickens were quite the hit with travelers, especially the kiddies. Many Yankees who had never seen a live chicken would stand next to the ever-expanding coop and take smiling selfies with them.

Roosters came and went for various reasons. The latest rooster, Waylon (after Jennings), came to us because he was making so much noise in Forsyth that they passed a law banning roosters. His owner called us in desperation, and we took in the beautiful black-and-red exiled bird.

After many years, the old pear tree had to come down, and the decision was made to take the chickens out to my sister's country house, where, sadly, Ms. Rumble died a couple of weeks ago. We all miss her, but none of us nearly as strongly as Waylon. He grieved at her passing so much that he couldn't be alone at night, and my sister had to put him in a dog cage inside her home for a few nights. This was the same rooster that raised so much racket he caused a city-wide rooster ban, and I can only imagine the noise in that big old house at 3:30 a.m. The problem was remedied when three good-looking hens were purchased, and Waylon is now back to his flirtatious ways.

May you rest in peace, Ms. Rumble. I'm going to miss your contented clucking.

When the Chickens Come Home

Now that spring is just around the corner, when you look out your window, you probably assume that the redbird, the robin, or even the sparrow are the most populous birds on earth, but you would be wrong. That honorable distinction goes to the Gallus domesticus, otherwise known as the domesticated chicken. It's difficult to know exactly how many of these tasty birds are roaming the earth because they're running around everywhere in all directions. But according to government statistical websites, there were 66 billion chickens in the world in 2016, which is well more than double the number of chickens that were scratching our planet just twenty years ago. In 1961, it was estimated there were 0.0024 chickens per person worldwide, which is equivalent to one chicken for every 400 people. Today, there are 8.82 chickens for every person on the planet.

In America, the number rose from 14 birds for every person to 30. We love our chicken, and we can get it at almost any interstate exit from the world's largest chicken franchise, KFC, to Popeyes Louisiana-style, which I'm eagerly looking forward to arriving soon next door to the Walmart. What a convenient location!

The problem is that the National Center for Health says nearly 75% of American men are overweight or obese, and about 2 in 3 women are in the same condition. A study found that, compared with those who ate no chicken, people who ate at least 20 grams of chicken per day had a significantly higher body mass index. If we like it, we're not supposed to eat it. If we're supposed to eat it, I generally don't have a taste for it. Y'all can have it.

The most numerous wild bird species ever known before the lowly chicken took the crown, the Passenger Pigeon, probably numbered a maximum of 5 billion. This was also a delicious bird that could fly at 62 mph, but it went extinct in

1914 due to the high demand for its flavorful, cheap meat and habitat loss. I don't see that future for our modern chicken. They're hatching them faster than we can eat them, and they can live in anyone's yard. I know of some just down the street.

The chicken is not only in our pots and frying pans but also in our language. If you call someone a chicken, of course, you're calling them a coward. To say the cost was "chicken feed" means it didn't cost that much, but we all know that chicken feed is no longer cheap. If a person's bad karma kicks in, we say his chickens have come home to roost.

Any food whose flavor is hard to describe is usually said to have the taste of chicken. If a picture hanging on a wall is tilted, we call it "cockeyed." If a man's wife has a sharp tongue and a nagging nature, we refer to the poor guy as "henpecked." Military rank can be a "pecking order" describing the hierarchy of a flock of hens. If a momma is over-attentive, she could be called a "mother hen." Then, later on, after her babies have flown the coop, she may come down with the "empty nest syndrome." And a bully thinks he is the "cock of the walk."

And every day, all of us, like chickens, scratch out a living, but if you do good and work hard, you can save up a "nest egg," and if you work even harder and save even more, you are "feathering your nest." Maybe you'd rather not work and invest instead. In that case, be careful "not to put all your eggs in one basket." And never, never count your eggs before they have hatched. Don't forget; sometimes things can become "as scarce as hen's teeth," and that will cause the price to go up accordingly.

And then sometimes a person may just need to get away, and we learn he has "flown the coop," and maybe we say he made a "bird-brain" move. Or it could be he is just running around "like a chicken with its head cut off."

A stern boss is sometimes referred to as having a "hard-boiled" personality. Some of those incarcerated in jails and prisons can be considered "bad eggs." A few times, I have decided not to perform certain dangerous feats or attend a social event like a blind date and "chickened out."

I can no longer think of myself as a "spring chicken," but I'm hatching an idea that might give me a little something to crow about if I don't wind up with an egg on my face. It's possible that by asking the right questions and committing to a lot of thought, along with a generous government grant, I could crack the riddle of two of the most perplexing questions known to mankind: Which came first, the chicken or the egg? And why did the chicken cross Rumble Road?

If You Feel Froggy, Jump

An army of tree frogs once invaded my living room during a hurricane late one September night when I was in Florida. I say an army because that is the proper way to refer to a group of frogs. I looked it up. We experienced four hurricanes back-to-back in 2004, starting with Hurricane Charlie on Aug. 13 and ending with Hurricane Jeanne on Sept. 26. In between, we had Francis and Ivan.

You have two options when you are faced with a storm as deadly as a hurricane. Evacuate or hunker down. I'm the hunker-down type. When the radar showed Charlie approaching, I checked my hurricane emergency kit, got milk and bread at Publix, and stood in the long line for plywood. We then rode out a rough storm that tore up the yard and blew off shingles. Then we had to endure the inconvenience of being without power for a couple of weeks, like with every other disaster. It was like camping at home. You've been there.

When the next two storms hit, I once again went through all the proper procedures for hurricane preparedness as the government pamphlets advised, but by the time Hurricane Jeanne came around, I was tired of it. I was tired of the lines and lugging plywood and a ladder all around my house.

After three hurricanes, the plywood I had purchased for Charlie was now warped and buckled from the hard rains and unusable, and you couldn't drag me to Home Depot to go through that mess again, so I decided to slap some duct tape on the glass instead. I had seen that done a few times before, so I figured there must be something to it. After all, it was duct tape.

Everything was ready in the food department, and we had plenty of candles and batteries. I felt like we were well-prepared for round 4. My ex-wife wasn't so sure and set up a place for her and the kids in her large walk-in closet, which, for her, was never quite large enough. I decided to bed down on the couch, which was more than fine with her during that stage of our marriage.

After everyone was settled in, I went out to the backyard and immediately noticed how fresh and clean everything felt. It had been raining all day, and we were in between the bands of squalls that had been passing for hours. The wind had slowed a bit, and the howling had ceased for the time being. I could hear the tree frogs chirping sweetly from somewhere nearby.

The tree frogs in Florida are among the strangest creatures on Earth. The only time I've ever seen them was after a rain. Where they hide in between rains, I have no idea. But once the drops start falling, here comes the army. Many times, I've had one plop from a wet tree limb onto my windshield while I was driving through a residential zone. All frogs are slimy, but tree frogs are like slime with legs. Powerful legs.

I felt satisfied that everything was secure and went inside to take my place on the couch. It felt so good outside, I decided to go for it and left the sliding glass door wide open to let some of that fresh air into the house. It needed a good airing out anyway. I had the Weather Channel on, and they were saying that the category-three storm was going to get worse, so be sure to do this and do that, and, more importantly, stay tuned. I set the sleep timer for 30 minutes, took off my shirt, and took on a reclining position. I was enjoying the nice breeze blowing into my living room, and I soon passed out as the wind picked up.

They say when you have a heart attack, one of the symptoms is that there will be a sensation in your chest that you've never experienced before. Well, a tree frog plopping down in the middle of my chest while I was sleeping was such an experience. And in my dreamy state of mind, I believed I was having a cardiac arrest and reached for my heart. I instead grabbed a tree frog. Still dreaming and without my glasses, I thought it was my heart that I took from my bare chest and held above me like an Aztec priest offering a sacrifice. When I discovered that it was a frog, along with about 500 more hopping all around my living room, I nearly had a real heart attack.

My ex-wife was freaked out about slimy animals in the house but by the time she emerged from her closet, I had discovered the best way to capture the little buggers was to catch them in my ball cap and toss them out the door, and unless she reads this column (she won't), she will never know how bad that hurricane really was.

My Uncle's Monkey

Back in the early 1940s, there was once what some called a zoo just outside a little town in North Georgia. It wasn't much of a zoo. The only animals they had were a bunch of monkeys packed in a few cages and a pair of possums that didn't get much notice. Even so, people would come from all over the county to be entertained by crazy monkey antics and pet the possums on the head.

I have relatives that come from that mountainous region, and a great-great-uncle of mine, Uncle Rudy Leeroy Reece, now long gone, pulled off one of the most heinous crimes ever committed in that part of the country and got away with it. He was well-known as a prankster and would do anything for a laugh, like standing on the downtown corner after a rainstorm and fishing from a puddle in the street, pulling out a dead fish he had pre-hooked every time a car would pass. I've also been told he once switched the outhouse and the well structures behind the local Baptist church, and a man fell into the well after a lengthy wait for the sermon to finish, but that's a little too much to believe.

According to an old legend passed down to me through my family, one night after the town was sound asleep, Rudy snuck into the zoo, picked out a monkey he especially liked, easily broke a padlock, and soon had an excited furry passenger sitting next to him in his rusty pickup. Rudy calmed the monkey down with bananas and apples he had ready just for that purpose. The curious monkey took great interest in the contents of the glovebox, which included a bottle of moonshine whiskey that they both enjoyed on the bumpy ride out of town to Rudy's farm. The ape didn't appreciate the taste of alcohol at first, but Rudy showed him how it was done, and the monkey was a fast learner.

Once at the farm, the now drunk and sleepy monkey was secured in a pen, where Rudy proceeded to shave him completely bald with a set of sheep shears. The monkey later fell asleep in Rudy's arms after he passed out in the hay. It's hard to imagine what a shaved monkey might look like cuddling with an old mountain man, but once you have that image in your head, it isn't easy to remove.

There were so many monkeys in his charge that the zookeeper didn't notice at first that one was missing when he arrived the next morning. It wasn't until he found the broken padlock lying in the dirt that he did a headcount and discovered one missing. He immediately drove to the sheriff's office to report the stolen animal, and the sheriff assigned his only deputy to the case.

While the deputy was performing his investigation, Rudy and his monkey were busy having a breakfast of bananas and apples, and fast becoming good friends. Rudy thought the ape was the funniest thing he had ever seen in his life and told him so. The monkey thought the same of him, and they shared a few laughs. After a fresh slug of moonshine, Rudy loaded his new buddy back into his truck and headed to town, bursting out laughing every time he looked over at his seatmate and driving off into the ditch a couple of times. It was still early for the town, and the streets around the courthouse were pretty much deserted when Rudy eased into a parking space and quietly removed the monkey from his truck. He then sat him on a low-hanging branch of an old oak tree and gave him an apple, which the monkey threw back at him and took off for higher branches. Rudy laughed at him and went to the café across the street, where he could watch the ape while he had a cup of coffee and a peach-fried pie.

It didn't take long for folks to start opening stores and shops and walking around here and there, which drew the attention of the hairless monkey who was familiar with people and liked them because they always threw peanuts into his cage. He made a couple of fancy swings out of the tree and bounced to the sidewalk beside a pair of elderly ladies who started screaming at the sight of what they thought was an alien from space.

A couple of years earlier, the whole town had heard Orson Welles' radio broadcast of "The War of the Worlds," when many people panicked, thinking the Earth was being invaded by extraterrestrials, so the ladies naturally thought an invasion was happening right before their eyes. So did everyone else within screaming distance. Meanwhile, Rudy was thoroughly enjoying the bedlam watching from the café window.

It was soon discovered that the alien was the missing monkey, and the deputy captured it and returned it to its cage. But that night, Rudy returned to the zoo and rekidnapped him. This time, they say he took him to Atlanta, where he had even more fun. But that's a little too much to believe.

I Know a Few Dogs in Heaven

King was only 14 in dog years, and I was only 9. When his ears were standing up, he looked a little like a German Shepherd, but he was still just a mutt I happened to love dearly. He was never trained because he never needed it. He was a good dog who always knew what to do and, more importantly, what not to do except for that one time when it cost him his life.

King had a bad habit of sleeping on the warm concrete of the driveway of our little house, and one early morning my dad didn't notice he was there and, in his rush to get to work, backed over him with his old Ford pickup. Hearing a yelp, he jumped out and found my poor pooch lying in a heap, apparently deceased. As was his habit, my old man was running late and didn't have time to do much with the dog except to put him under our little house, intending to bury him in the backyard when he got home from work.

It was summertime, and my siblings and I didn't even think about getting out of bed before 9 a.m. This was two and a half hours after my dad had left for work, and somehow King had time to recuperate. When we ran out into the yard, he was right there with me at first, romping and playing like he always had. We didn't have trees in our yard, and no sticks were available, so I had him fetch a rock I was throwing out in the street. Like most dogs, he usually resisted somewhat when I tried to take something from his mouth, but suddenly, he put up no fight, showed no signs of wanting to repeat his favorite game, and lay down in the dirt like he was sick.

This was when my dad was single, and we were cared for by a couple of different babysitters that summer, who usually stayed inside, taking it easy while my brothers and I did whatever we could get away with outside. I went in and told the lady, who didn't speak much English, that I thought my dog was sick, and she suggested a little water might perk him up and gave me a plastic bowl.

When I went back out with the water, King had crawled back under the house and wanted nothing to do with it or me. I couldn't coax him out, and he growled when I reached in, so I just sat down in the sunlight in the dirt next to our house and waited for a miracle that never came.

When my dad finally returned home that afternoon, he was surprised to see King was alive. He told me what had happened and reached under the house and grabbed King by the collar. The dog was howling in pain as he dragged him out.

There were no veterinarians in our little town that I remember. Usually, my dad was the one who did whatever he could to help any local animals with their injuries or sickness. I remember many times when I watched him stitch up a dog or a cat that had been laid open after a fight, using an ordinary upholstery needle, pouring whiskey over the wound. He told me there was no hope for the dog.

He went inside, brought out his .410 shotgun, and placed it in the gun rack fitted to the back window of his pickup. He then went to the backyard, grabbed a shovel, threw it into the truck bed, and lowered the tailgate. He grabbed a blanket from behind the seat, and we gently placed King on it and eased him up into the back of the truck. I kept a close watch on my dog as we drove to the woods, looking through the back glass beneath the shotgun. I wondered if he knew what was coming as I did. Only I really didn't know.

When we got to a clearing in the woods at the end of a long dirt road, we laid King on the ground. He was in obvious pain, and I knew there was no hope. I heard my dad load the .410 and closed my eyes, waiting for the blast. But instead of pulling the trigger, he nudged me with the stock of the shotgun, told me that it was my dog, and gave it to me. So, looking down the barrel of a shotgun through the tears of a little boy, I put my beloved King out of misery.

Isaiah prophesied in the Good Book that in Heaven, the wolf shall dwell with the lamb, and the leopard shall lie down with the young goat. And even though some folks don't believe animals have souls, I'm sure my old buddy King is up there somewhere.

Sometimes, a Man Needs to Fish

He was an old man then, but he wouldn't be considered old at all by today's standards. He loved all animals, and whenever he came across one that was hurt, he never hesitated to alleviate its suffering, even if it increased his own. He once picked up a cat that limped up to him, and while he was inspecting the sore leg, the cat bit him on the fleshy part of his hand between his thumb and forefinger and left a wound that soon became infected.

It was an ugly injury that kept getting worse, and even though his wife kept telling him to go to the doctor, he thought she was saying he was off his rocker, so he never went. Besides, he thought he was as good at doctoring himself as he was at doctoring hurt animals.

He poured peroxide on the two punctures that were beginning to become full of pus, grabbed his fishing gear, and headed to the Cherokee Reservation for some trout fishing. In the dead of winter. He told me he liked fishing on the reservation in the winter because he would be completely alone. There weren't any tourists poking around making messes. Nothing but the sound of perfect quiet. And even though his eyesight was rapidly fading, the beauty of the Great Smoky Mountains always brought him back.

He had a 1970 Ford van outfitted especially for his fishing trips. He'd slept comfortably many nights in that van. The cupboards were well stocked with canned sardines and crackers just in case he didn't catch any fish, but he always did.

He believed the proper way to catch a trout was to get in the stream with him, even though I heard him say the mountain water was so cold it once turned his boxers blue. By the time he made it to the mountains, snow was on the ground, and ice was on the rocks, but that didn't stop him from tying a rooster-tail spinner on his fishing line and trudging downstream through a frigid creek.

He had caught his daily limit of ten fish early on his third day and was on his way back to camp when he slipped and fell on ice as he was climbing out of the water, scraping a leg against a jagged rock and causing a deep gash. He knocked off his wire-rimmed bifocals into the water during his stumbling to stay upright and could barely see them as they sank into the water and disappeared. He sat on a rock for a few minutes, caught his breath, and washed the cut leg with creek water.

He limped back to his van and soaked his leg with the peroxide he had brought along to medicate his infected hand and bandaged it with a ripped t-shirt secured with duct tape. He then pulled out his knife and cleaned his fish. He had been eating trout three times a day, but not even a bad fall could dampen his appetite for rainbow trout fried over a campfire.

Despite the pain, he fished for two more days, always catching his limit by day's end. He spent his last night in the camp burning up with a fever that soaked his mattress.

When he woke the next morning, his hand was throbbing, and he could barely walk. He knew he had to get home fast. He dragged himself around the campsite, making sure his fire was completely out and covered. When he finally pulled himself up into the cab of the van, you could see no sign that he had spent the last five days there. He had even swept the tire tracks behind his van away with a pine branch.

He sat in the van, shivering with fever, and waited for the old motor to warm up. It was only a five-hour drive. He could make it. He squinted through his legally blind eyes and drove slowly out of the woods.

It was a rough trip. By the time he pulled into his driveway, he didn't have the strength to make it to the front door. His wife saw him sitting in the driver's seat with the door wide open and ran out to help him inside. After scolding him for not taking better care of himself, she rushed him to the VA hospital.

He called me a month or so later. He said, "Son, we live in wondrous times. The blind can see, the deaf can hear, and the lame can walk. The doctors fixed up my hand, repaired my leg, and I had laser eye surgery!"

I congratulated him on his progress, and he said, "Not only that, but I also bought the best hearing aid money can buy. I can hear anything!" I told him I thought that was wonderful and asked, "What kind is it?" There was a pause, then he answered, "Uh, a quarter past four."

Even Dogs Can See We Have a Problem

We have so much junk and trash we even have it in space. NASA now says it tracks over 500,000 pieces of "space junk" that can travel at speeds up to 22,300 mph. This is much faster than a speeding bullet, which comes out of a muzzle at a mere 1,700 mph. Besides having the potential to do catastrophic damage to working satellites, this debris is especially dangerous to the International Space Station and other spacecraft carrying humans. When there is a collision between two pieces of space junk or defunct satellites, thousands of new pieces of junk are created. Some fall back to earth. Scary thought.

Every material thing we own or will ever own, including our bodies, will one day either rust, rot, fall in a heap, burn up or corrode. It's only a matter of time. As you drive around in that nice vehicle past those rusted-out old cars piled high in a junkyard, you can be sure the one you are now driving will one day end up on top of that heap. That new car smell is the first thing to go, and it is all downhill from there.

According to statistics I found on Google, the average American produces about 4.4 to 5 pounds of trash every day. If you do the math (which I did), you'll find that it comes to over 728,000 tons of refuse in this country per day. That's a lot of garbage trucks. Unfortunately, a large portion of this trash doesn't end up in a garbage truck or even a trash can; it ends up on the roadside.

When I opened my front door this morning to let my little pooch, Muchacho, out for his first order of business for the day, he immediately went into attack mode and ran out to protect me from a large plastic ice bag that had blown into my yard. The wind was causing it to flap a little bit, so he must've thought it was still alive. It probably had flown out of the bed of some passing redneck's muddy pickup, just-a-gettin'-it, roaring down Lee King Road.

Muchacho growled at it as I picked up the bag, and we went to the mailbox, where there was an empty Wendy's Frosty cup, some napkins, a few cold fries in a bag, and a water bottle lying next to the post. There was ketchup and mustard spattered on the post, so I cleaned it off with one of the napkins I found on the ground. I figured someone had hit it with what he had left of a cheeseburger, and some animal ate what bounced off. Good shot, dude.

I checked my mailbox and added what was in there to my armload of trash, coaxed my dog away from sniffing the post, and disposed of the trash properly. The only good thing about all this was that it gave me a legitimate excuse to be even grumpier than I already was.

Later, as I drove down my curvy little road, which is always as pretty as it can be, I noticed my neighbor picking up trash that someone had tossed in her yard overnight. No doubt she is as tired of the ritual as I am. I'd be willing to bet that the people who are tossing all this trash out their car windows are doing it from trashy cars. I suppose that's how they live, and they're used to it. I'm fairly sure the inside of their cars is a reflection of the inside of their homes. Normally, they would've tossed that Wendy's bag into the back seat, but the window just happened to be open.

Once in Alabama, a car was behind me at a stop sign, and I noticed in my rearview mirror a bunch of guys tossing trash out their windows from a recent fast-food purchase. I couldn't contain myself, so I opened my door a little and rudely yelled back at them, "Y'all clean that crap up!" The driver didn't appreciate my approach, and he responded by giving me an obscene middle-finger gesture that had to be at least 12 inches long. His four buddies quickly joined in, ready for action, shouting profanities and ready to whoop my you-know-what. By then, I knew I had been at the stop sign long enough and raced off, leaving them in their pile of trash. They chased me all over Opelika until I somehow managed to escape them. The trash was still there the next day, so I did the right thing and cleaned that crap up myself.

It might take a while (it takes a thousand years for plastic to decompose), but Mother Earth eventually reclaims everything. Meantime, y'all quit throwing your trash out of your car windows.

Life Among the Gators

The other day, I typed the word "tall" into my phone, and it was immediately auto-corrected to "y'all." I guess it's a Southern thang. There are many things that make the South unique beyond the way we speak. Even though we have a gift for combining words into one, such as making "you all" into "y'all," "are not" into "ain't," and "y'all ain't" into "yain't," we are blessed in countless other ways. We have grits, collard greens, and peach cobbler. Then we have our manners, our football teams, and Waffle House. Limited space prohibits listing all the advantages of living in the South.

A much shorter list would consist of the negative aspects of southern living. This list might include the heat, hurricanes, and driving on one inch of snow. There's also taking 30 minutes to say goodbye, getting stuck behind a tractor, and small-town gossip. And then there's the unlikely danger of an alligator attack.

There have been many movies that used thousands of alligators as extras, and even some as stars. There wasn't one Tarzan movie produced that didn't feature at least one gator peering with yellow eyes just over the waterline, even though alligators don't live in Africa. They live in Mexico, China, and the Southeast United States, where we live.

Some say there are alligators living in the sewers of New York City. According to this urban legend, these monsters were purchased by families who went south for the winter, bought a gator, and, once home, flushed the babies down the toilet. Who needs an alligator crawling around the apartment? Due to the lack of sunlight, these subterranean monsters are supposedly albinos and grow to huge proportions because of the endless supply of city rats.

Don't be alarmed. These prehistoric reptiles might appear scary, but they aren't as mean as they look. We fear the things we know little about, and the American alligator (alligator mississippiensis) is one of the least understood of all creatures. They are usually thought of as aggressive, life-threatening man-eaters, but they just want to be left alone. According to the Florida Fish and Wildlife Conservation Commission, even though Florida is home to more than 1 million of these reptiles, the state averages just six bite victims per year. Between 1948 and 2020, gators killed just 26 people in the state.

Having lived in Florida, I know a little about this distant cousin of the domesticated chicken. Florida is not a place where you just jump into any old pond or lake willy-nilly. During my years there, I lived just a few miles from the Wekiwa Springs State Park. The kids loved swimming at the park, but with my skinniness, I could never handle the cold. As you would assume, it was also a great place to fish, and we had a special bank we would sit on just across the bridge from the bait shop. We were used to the gators that liked to share the spot with us. They also knew where the fishing was good.

Early one Saturday morning, I loaded up my tackle box and a couple of my young'uns and headed to our usual spot with hopes of catching some lunch. We were starting to get a few nibbles when the quietness was rudely interrupted by a woman excitedly yelling to her friend in a Yankee accent to come to see the alligators. After watching the sleeping gators for a few minutes, one of the ladies decided they looked hungry, went back to her car for a loaf of bread, and started tossing pieces of white bread to the beasts. One piece even landed on a gator's snout. Suddenly, she slipped from the bank down into the water during one of her hardest throws. Even though the gators completely ignored her, fishing for the next two weeks was ruined due to her frantic screams. Her friend was running around in small circles, also screaming loudly.

There was no danger of her drowning, and the gators were utterly bored with her, so I laid down my pole and helped the terrified woman back up the steep bank. Due to my small size, this was no easy feat on my part with this particular-sized woman, and although, according to her, I saved her life, I really didn't.

In Georgia, a quarter of a million alligators are lurking in our dark waters, including rivers, lakes, and even cow ponds. If you want to experience the thrill of alligators swarming completely around a rented motorized metal boat while you're trying to hook a bass, that can be achieved at Georgia's famous Okefenokee Swamp, which is only three and a half hours from where I'm sitting right now. There are an estimated 10,000 to 13,000 gators blending in among the rotting plants, perfectly camouflaged in the murky waters of the 684-square-mile National Wildlife Refuge. Little dogs like my Muchacho aren't allowed near the swamp for obvious reasons.

Gator courtship has already begun, and they're out and about looking for a date. Y'all better watch out!

Legend of the Goat Man

Most of those born since the 70s have probably never heard of the "Goat Man," a colorful part of Georgia's past who became famous by herding goats back and forth from Iowa to Florida, creating traffic jams along the old Dixie Highway for three decades.

The locals would always know his approach long before his arrival because of the odor attributed to his sleeping with goats. He once wrote, "The goats don't care how I smell or how I look. They trust me and have faith in me, and this is more than I can say about a lot of people." Even with his stench, he was a sensation to the crowds, spicing up his sermons with colorful stories.

He survived on donations and goat milk. People lined up to pay for photos with a celebrity and to buy his junk. In later years, he sold postcards and prints. You can still buy his postcards on eBay for around $20. He didn't have to spend much on the goats because they'll eat anything, which also helped keep the roadways clean.

When folks in small southern towns smelled the Goat Man coming, schoolteachers would dismiss classes, workers would abandon jobs, and entire families would rush to meet him. The Goat Man, whose real name was Ches McCartney, would've gone viral overnight if the internet had been around.

McCartney had to sell his horses during the Great Depression and had to use goats to plow his fields. The goats became his close companions, and after he lost his farm, he piled chairs, licenses, plates, tires, and other junk on a wooden wagon and set off for Florida with around three dozen of his closest friends, some pulling his wagon.

He trekked up and down Old Dixie Highway. Always in Florida by winter. He had a wife while on the farm and then two more while on the road. They all decided that life with a man who liked to sleep with smelly goats was not for them. He somehow convinced these ladies to bear his children, but no one is certain how many times they went through that ordeal.

He traveled to forty-nine states but couldn't herd goats across an ocean, so he skipped Hawaii. He was on The Tonight Show with Johnny Carson and shook the hand of presidents. I couldn't find documentation that he showered before these appearances, and wondered what the presidents and Carson thought when they got a whiff of Bouquet of Goat.

Then, in 1969, the highways got too crowded, and crime too bad, and the Goat Man sadly had to park his wagon and corral his goats. He even bought a little house, but after it burned down in 1978, he and one of his sons bought an old, converted school bus and parked it near Jeffersonville.

But in 1985, he got the itch again, hitched up the goats, and headed to California, hoping to meet actress Morgan Fairchild.

He was reported missing and was found in a California hospital after being mugged on the side of a road. His friends pitched in and flew him home. His wandering days were finally finished.

They put him in a Macon nursing home, where he became a local celebrity. He made his final journey in November of 1998. This time without the goats. His obituary was published in The New York Times. Some say he was 97, and others say he reached 103.

Earlier in that year, his son was found shot dead at his home in the converted school bus. His murder remains a mystery.

McCartney's eccentric life has inspired writers, documentary makers, artists, and musicians. Some say he influenced Flannery O'Connor's writing. There is even a Facebook group dedicated to sharing his stories, memories, and pictures. If you're curious, go here:

https://www.facebook.com/groups/TheGoatMan.

I was too young to appreciate it, but I once saw the Goat Man as a boy during a family trip from Oklahoma to Georgia while packed with four siblings in the back seat of my old man's '55 Plymouth in the middle of a hot Georgia July. Plymouths didn't come with A/C back then.

We were chugging slowly around a mountain curve when suddenly, there was the Goat Man trudging uphill with his parade of goats on the shoulder of the two-lane road. I remember there was a goat riding on top of his pile of junk.

My dad slammed on the brakes, and those of us in the back were slammed hard against the backs of the seats in front. Plymouths didn't come with seatbelts back then, either. My old man leaped out, and I quickly followed. I couldn't understand then why my dad was so enthused about shaking the hand of a man who had to be the smelliest man on earth, but in my defense, I didn't realize I was inhaling the odor of a legend.

No, I Am Not My Dog's Daddy

A dog used to be just a dog. You could toss him a chicken bone beneath the supper table, chase him out the back door, and be done with it. We never worried about feeding dogs chocolate when I was a kid. I remember a cocker spaniel we owned who ate a whole bag of M&Ms and still survived. (don't try this at home) There were no leash laws in our little town back then.

Occasionally, a loose dog would get hit by a car, but only because it was dumb enough to chase it, but that was about it. Most mutts I knew had enough sense to stay out of the street on their own if a car was headed their way. There was a rabies vaccination law that everyone pretty much obeyed, but that was about it. It was never a big deal for our neighbor's dog to wander over to our porch for a little rub on the head. No one freaked out and called 911 or animal control.

But times have changed, and even dogs have a new norm. Nowadays, people consider their pets to be their children, calling themselves "daddy" and "mommy" to 4-legged animals who probably think we are all nuts, and I would have to agree.

My dog, Muchacho, bears no resemblance to me nor to anyone else in my family. He has never once celebrated Father's Day by giving me a cheap tie or a homemade card, nor even serving me breakfast in bed. To Muchacho, it's just yet another day of me keeping him out of trouble and the cat food. I'm not his daddy, and he doesn't think of me like that. I am what we used to call his "master." My job is to tell him what to do and what not to do. His job is to do it or not do it. I'm not trying to be politically incorrect, but y'all, please don't say I'm the parent of a pooch. I am the proud father of 5 humans, and I'm satisfied enough with that.

Of course, like everyone else, I spoil my dog. Muchacho has an impressive wardrobe that includes Georgia Dawg jackets and overcoats, a snowsuit, and even an ugly Christmas sweater with a matching Santa Claus hat he likes to wear to holiday parties. He has more toys than I ever dreamed of having as a boy. There are three different types of dog treats in his special place in my cabinets. I won't get into medical and grooming expenses. All this isn't cheap. I should be able to claim him on my taxes even if I'm not his daddy.

Americans spent $72 billion on their pets in 2018. By comparison, federal funding for assistance to homeless people is expected to be only around $3 billion in the fiscal year 2021. I'm not saying our beloved furry creatures don't deserve everything we do for them but imagine if those numbers were reversed. Maybe a few folks currently sleeping on concrete could get a house where they could have their own little puppies for their children.

And let's not forget the homeless strays that wander our streets, scrounging for food and have no place to sleep. According to the Humane Society of the United States, there are about 70 million of these animals living just out of our view. Of these, only about six to eight million enter our nation's 3,500 shelters each year. Even if we had ten times as many shelters, these unfortunate creatures would still have to be adopted, and these days, adopting a pet is no easy feat.

No longer can you just go to the local pound and pick out any old mongrel you take a liking to. Like everything else these days, there are hoops you must jump through. Just because you completed an application does not guarantee you will take home a critter. And Humane Society rules won't even allow you to adopt one as a surprise gift for your loved one, because the recipient must meet face-to-face for an interview. You don't necessarily get to pick out the one your heart desires. They match the pet to you. And if you currently own a dog or cat that lives outside, you can't adopt. I don't know what you would do if you needed a junkyard dog. And on and on.

I'm thankful I have a little pooch I can talk to, even if he never answers. He isn't much for keeping me warm on a cold Georgia night because he's only big enough to cover just one of my feet, and he howls like I'm beating him to death whenever I play my harmonica, and as a son, he isn't. But as companions, we're together to the end.

Nothing Can Eat a Ghost

And I've never seen Bigfoot.

Not of This World or Any Other

If life exists only on Earth in this great, vast universe, that means we humanoids are as good as it gets. Now that's a scary thought.

Last year, there were nearly 6,000 UFO sightings reported in North America. That comes to nearly 16 a day. UFOs are all over the place, but mainly in California, Washington, and Florida. Extraterrestrials think people in those states are more interesting to study than we simpler folk who live in places like Georgia and Alabama. If they only knew.

Georgia has had its share of strange objects in its skies, though. Two years before becoming our governor, Jimmy Carter was standing outside a small restaurant in Leary when he spotted an object changing colors from red to white and to blue. After that scary experience, he announced, "If I become President, I'll make every piece of information this country has about UFO sightings available to the public and the scientists." Well, I don't remember that ever happening, but I do remember him being attacked by an angry rabbit after he became president.

According to the National UFO Reporting Center, the most recent UFO sighting we've had in Georgia occurred just the other night between 9 p.m. and midnight on July 22 in Cumming. It was reported to be a circular, lit craft emitting beams of bright white light onto the surrounding clouds. This supposedly went on for a full 3 hours. Why isn't the video of this incredible event being shared all over Facebook and YouTube? If I saw something like that, my phone would be out in a heartbeat. A video like that would go viral overnight. Last April, the Pentagon officially released three videos that appear to show unidentified flying objects moving rapidly while being recorded by infrared cameras. This is an unprecedented move by the government. Two videos contain pilots reacting in awe at how quickly the objects are traveling. President Trump wondered if the footage was real and tweeted that it was a hell of a video. So much has happened since April that I had forgotten this earth-shaking news story that lasted for about one day.

Personally, I believe that within the infinity of the universe, there are probably other beings out there, but I doubt that extraterrestrial beings are buzzing around above us. And with our current behavior, I would be highly embarrassed if visitors from another world were actually watching us. I sure hope they aren't hovering over Portland, Chicago, or Macon. We would be the talk of the galaxy.

Another doubt I have is the existence of ghosts. One in five Americans has seen a ghost. This can't be true. That equals 82,500,000 ghosts. The population of Georgia is only

11,000,000. I don't believe in the existence of ghosts for one simple reason: Ghosts don't eat anything, and nothing can eat a ghost. What good are they if they have no position in the food chain? They don't fit within the circle of life, even if they are dead.

I am also a non-believer in the Loch Ness Monster, the elusive Chupacabra, and Bigfoot. I recently visited the Bigfoot Museum up in the mountains and walked out less convinced than when I walked in. On top of that, they didn't have anything my size in their t-shirt selection.

Although a large bear was recently spotted in Monroe County, we haven't as yet had a Bigfoot sighting in these parts. The nearest sighting occurred way back in 1957 by a young boy in Macon. It was in the middle of the day, and the lad was so shaken after he saw the monster he ran out of the woods crying like a baby. The sheriff was called, and he said, most likely, it was a bear or someone pulling a hoax in a suit. The boy's parents disagreed, and that was the end of it. Bigfoot became disgusted with the whole affair and moved on.

Even less convincing to me is the existence of Chupacabra. Its name is a combination of Spanish words meaning "goat sucker" because it supposedly sucks the blood from its victims. Now that's nasty. There have been a lot of supposedly unretouched photos posted on the internet of this ugly creature, and most of them look like underfed dogs with a bad case of mange. Maybe I'm just an old cynic, but come on, y'all.

There's always a reasonable explanation for any strange phenomenon. For example, my dad once thought he saw a casket floating slowly three feet off the ground across a cow pasture on a hot summer night. After his initial heart attack, he figured it out to be a light brown cow with black legs and a black head, taking a leisurely midnight stroll in the pale moonlight.

There's no Escaping the Gremlins

Sitting in traffic on Interstate 75 North, headed to Ingles, at a standstill in the fast lane near the Juliette Road exit. I notice cars in the middle lane are moving at a brisk pace, so I make the only logical decision and cautiously begin a slow merge to join those who obviously know the best lane for quick travel.

After several uncaring Yankee drivers speed past, I finally get a break from an elderly man who can't quite keep up with the pace. I look over my right shoulder, make my bold move, and the old man, now back three car lengths, sticks up a bony middle finger directly at me. I nod in acknowledgment of his courtesy, and suddenly I see red taillights before me and slam the brake pedal in the nick of time. Middle-lane traffic is now creeping along at two mph. This is a signal for vehicles in the lane I just left to pick up speed, moving so fast it would be dangerous for me to return. I remain where I sit, trying not to look as dumb as I look.

Now standing at the rear of a crowded, slow-moving checkout line in Ingles, clutching a bag of hot dogs and a can of pork 'n' beans. If we were socially distancing, I'd be standing in the middle of the Corn Flake aisle. I rarely use self-checkout anymore because I don't know if there are any germs on those screens, and I don't see many disinfectants applied to those money-taking robots that feel the need to tell me every move to make a simple purchase. The cashier at the next register is clicking along, sliding groceries under the laser light, and shoving them into the bagging zone. Disinfecting the conveyor belt like a pro. I make what I consider to be a sensible decision and do a quick line hop.

The customer finishing up at the register in my new line sticks her card into the reader while I wait at the rear, uncharacteristically patient and content with my new position. Then the world suddenly grinds to a halt because of a defective chip on a credit card. Reinserting the card over and over does nothing to correct the issue, but that doesn't stop the lady from trying. Meanwhile, the cashier of the line I just escaped from is now checking out the customer who was previously behind me.

I finally get home and drag a garden hose across the yard to water the only scraggly rose bush I have left. I walk a straight line, but the hose has no concept of straightness. It finds the only stump in my yard and wraps itself around it, stubbornly refusing to release its grip, resisting my tugs and curses. I want to roll the stupid thing up and throw it in the trash.

I then decide to finish a little project I've been putting off and pull an extension cord from the toolbox in the back of my pickup. It comes out a tangled mess, knotted up in a wad. I didn't store it away like that. I always neatly roll up my cords and stack them away in an orderly, military-style fashion. I disengage the impossible knots, and while I'm dragging it to the table saw, the cord decides to take its own crazy route, twisting around a yard gnome, a water spigot, and my poor rosebush. It takes a path no sane man could duplicate. It makes me want to toss the whole mess.

Deciding not to wait until the last minute, as I do every year, I decided to inspect my decorations for the upcoming holidays. I reach high in the back closet and take down a worn-out cardboard box, inside of which I find the mother of all messes: a twisted, tangled, knotted-up collection of Christmas lights.

I am not a deranged madman who tied those tight knots in those strands of pretty, little twinkle lights. I distinctly remember laboriously removing those delicate illuminations and packing them away systematically sometime back in late February. After struggling with just one knot, I decided it was more economical to buy new sets of lights than to untangle that crazy mess. Now the garden hose, extension cord, and Christmas lights can all have a festive time tying each other up in the trash can for all I care.

I don't believe in gremlins or other such nonsense, but there seems to be something mischievous going on in the world. Maybe it's just a part of life that no matter what we do, there will always be obstacles. Because without conflict, there would be no story.

Again, sitting in traffic on Interstate 75 North, this time headed to Walmart, completely stopped in the fast lane near the Juliette Road exit. This time I think I'll just stay put and see what happens.

Implosion of the Big Bang Theory?

While it might seem that most Americans are somewhat knowledgeable of science, according to a National Science Foundation study, 25% do not know that the Earth revolves around the sun, and an even larger percentage have no idea that the Earth's core is hot. A market research firm found that only 66% of millennials firmly believe that the Earth is round. Research also shows that 40 percent of Americans believe the Earth was created some 6,000 to 10,000 years ago, in direct contrast to the evidence scientists have been giving us for decades.

Raised in a Baptist church where my mother made my brothers and me sit in the front pew where the good Rev. Lemmon could keep an eye on us, I was early educated on how the earth was formed. In the Bible that I had earned for never missing a Sunday School class for an entire year, I read that "In the beginning, God created the heavens and the Earth." And He saw that it was good, and that was good enough for me.

Then along came my 6th-grade science class teacher at Will Rogers Elementary School, who surprised the class by telling us that, no, the truth was that everything in the universe began with a huge explosion called the Big Bang.

At that age, I was fascinated by explosions, and I figured God probably was too, and it made perfect sense in my adolescent mind. My devout Christian mother didn't think it made one bit of sense. She gave me the Big Bang on my young behind when I repeated to her what I had learned in class that day. She also called the school administrators, but as I recall, all it did was increase her anger.

The Big Bang theory was developed around 100 years ago by a Catholic priest named Georges Lemaître. In a nutshell, Lemaître theorized that the entire observable universe was compacted into an infinitely tiny speck that grew to the size of a grain of sand at the beginning of time. Then roughly 13.8 billion years ago, that grain of sand suddenly exploded with an unimaginable force. No one can say exactly where this explosion took place or why it ignited in the first place. Scientists agree that before this occurred, everything was empty space at nearly absolute zero. They have never explained how all the empty space got there or how that tiny speck of sand came to exist in the first place.

The Big Bang theory remains the leading explanation for the history of the cosmos. At least until recently.

Even with rampant ignorance, civilization has somehow managed to achieve wondrous things over the past few decades. Less than a century ago, no one knew there was anything past the Milky Way. We knew nothing of other galaxies. Now we have the James Webb Space Telescope, which can see what the universe looked like around 250 million years ago, back to the era when the first stars and galaxies began to form. NASA says the telescope is orbiting the sun 1 million miles away from Earth. It took 30 days to reach its destination.

Some scientists studying the awe-inspiring images from the Webb telescope are extremely surprised that many show phenomena that don't quite fit the accepted theory of the beginning of history. Things like the number of galaxies, galaxies that are extremely smooth and surprisingly old. Much older than what was predicted by the Big Bang theory. Reportedly, the hypothesis they have defended for decades as unquestionable truth is now being overturned by new unquestionable data. One theorist said, "Right now, I find myself lying awake at three in the morning and wondering if everything I've done is wrong." There has always been dissatisfaction with the Big Bang theory, and now the James Webb Space Telescope has contributed to the debate, potentially changing everything.

If you ask an atheist how creation occurred, they will inevitably point to the Big Bang. It's a convenient answer for non-believers in God. If the theory is disproved, I'm sure they'll be content to wait for the new explanation that will be presented to us as truth and will be taught to our kids in the sixth grade as such.

You don't see me in church much, but I believe God made the universe and everything in it, including us. If He started it all with a huge explosion, I wouldn't be surprised. What better way to begin such a beautiful creation?

I'm just a regular guy. I can't wrap my head around the fact that the universe is infinite and goes out into the vastness of forever. That it has always been infinite and always will be infinite. Just thinking about it makes me feel smaller than the tiny speck of sand that scientists say started the whole thing.

If It Wasn't for Bad Luck...

Depending on how you look at it, a Croatian man known for escaping death, Frano Selak, can be described as either the world's luckiest or unluckiest man. It has been claimed his luck began in 1962 when he was on a train that crashed into a river, and he was pulled to safety while 17 of his fellow passengers perished. The next year, he was somehow blown out of a plane door and miraculously landed in a haystack while 19 of his fellow passengers crashed to their deaths.

Three years later, he was able to swim to shore after a bus he was riding ended up in a river in an accident that took the lives of four others. In 1970, he survived a car fire by managing to escape before the gas tank exploded. In 1973, a broken fuel pump shot flames through the vents of his car, leaving him completely bald. And it gets better. Or worse... After he was hit by a bus in 1995, sustaining only minor injuries, he avoided a head-on collision with a truck on a mountain road by crashing into a guardrail that failed to stop his car. Luckily, Selak was driving without a seatbelt and was ejected from his car onto a tree branch, where he watched his car tumble 300 feet down.

Then, two days after his 73rd birthday, he won over a million dollars in the lottery. It could be argued that this good fortune was negated by the fact that he also married for the fifth time on the same day. Sadly, Selak's luck finally ran out in 2016 when he died at the age of 87.

I've had my own share of luck playing the lottery. All bad. I've played poker with my soldier buddies while in the army and learned early on that, unless someone's cheating, luck goes around the table. And I've been both unlucky and lucky in love.

An incredible stroke of good fortune happened to me back when I was working in Orlando, building props and sets, and I was overdue for a vacation. It was finally summertime, and I had been planning on taking a 2,000-mile road trip with my family to Guadalajara for months. Even though we had saved as much as we could, we still needed my last paycheck to go on our dream vacation. The plan was to leave at 6 a.m. on the first Saturday in July, after I got paid the day before.

I'm not sure why I did it, stupidity, I suppose, but for some reason, after I got paid that Friday, I tossed my hard-earned check onto the dashboard as opposed to putting it in the glovebox as any sane person would do. Back in those days, my then-wife drove the nice car while I drove the beat-up pickup truck with no air conditioning, which meant my windows pretty much stayed down.

You may not know about Interstate 4 in Orlando, but I can tell you it sucks, especially on a hot Friday afternoon. I was approaching downtown, feeling pretty good about everything, even though it was stop-and-go traffic, when I suddenly got a lucky break and hit the speed limit. But my luck quickly changed when the wind at my speed caused my check to fly off my dashboard and out the window. I watched it in my rearview mirror spin around a few times before it disappeared beneath the car behind me.

I immediately pulled over to the shoulder, but my check was gone. I finally gave up and sadly drove home to face my eager family with the depressing news that we wouldn't be able to leave until next Monday afternoon at the earliest. I escaped my wife's disappointment in me by doing what

I usually did: I went to take a nap. Just as I was dozing off, she interrupted me, handing me the landline phone and saying it was "some woman." I could tell by the tone in her voice that she was still upset, and I didn't blame her. The woman calling asked me if my name was Steve Reece and said if I could give her the address on a check she found floating down in her yard, I could have it. It turned out that the check had somehow gotten caught in an updraft and traveled 12 miles from downtown Orlando to within 2 blocks of my house. I rushed to the lady's house, and she told me that while she was pulling into her driveway, the check landed right in front of her car, and she looked up my name in the phonebook. My wife was still glaring at my lucky self when we left for Mexico on time the following morning.

All in all, I still consider myself extremely lucky and blessed to be free, doing what I love in the greatest country in the world.

Thinking About Living Forever?

The Bible says that before Noah rescued his family and two of every animal from the Great Flood, people lived for many hundreds of years. Tradition, legend, and the Bible all say that Noah's grandfather, Methuselah, lived to be 969 years old. But when mankind became corrupted in the period preceding the flood, God said: My spirit shall not abide in man forever, for he is flesh; his days shall be a hundred and twenty years (Genesis 6:3). Since that time, few have attained such longevity as 120 years. Nowadays, the average person is expected to live around 78 years. And it doesn't matter how young you are, that's not long.

A French supercentenarian, Jeanne Louise Calment, lived 122 years and 164 days, making her the longest-lived person since Biblical times. Born on Feb. 21, 1875, her age is well documented, appearing in fourteen census records. In 1995, at the age of 120, she was declared the oldest person ever to have lived.

There is a person still alive today who was born nearly a year before the Wright brothers made their historic flight at Kitty Hawk. She is Kane Tanaka, who was born prematurely in Japan on Friday, Jan. 2, 1903, the seventh child of her parents. As of today, Kane has lived 118 years, eight months, and 14 days. Every single person who was born before her, and many since, has passed on. She says she wants to live at least to the age of 120 and credits her faith in God, lots of sleep, hope, eating good food, and working out mathematical problems for her longevity. By comparison, it has only been 117 years, eight months, and 30 days since Orville was strapped into that rickety contraption of an airplane and astounded the world by flying 120 feet before returning to earth in 12 seconds. Kane has witnessed many changes in the world.

Scientists struggle to understand how centenarians can achieve such longevity. The centenarians themselves usually have vastly different success stories. Some attribute their long lives to healthy diets, while others chalk it up to social support or religion. All these factors surely have an influence, and I might investigate them.

There are many animals whose lifespans exceed ours by many years. The Aldabra tortoise lives for an average of 150 years. One tortoise named Adwaita lived for 250 years before it died in a zoo in 2006. A tortoise named Jonathan recently made it into Guinness World Records as the oldest known living land animal at 187 years old. A koi carp named Hanako lived until 1977 after swimming around for 226 years. And there are whales alive today that were splashing around in the ocean during the Battle of Gettysburg when Lincoln was president.

There is also a species of tiny jellyfish known as the turritopsis dohrnii, which scientists say can technically live forever. A researcher said that when the creature experiences starvation, physical damage, or other crises, instead of dying, the animal somehow transforms all its existing cells into a younger state. Of course, these immortal jellyfish are being studied rigorously for their secret.

The naked mole-rat's life is extended by, of all things, breeding. Like ants and bees, these rats designate a queen, and she is the only one who bears young and, for some reason, lives many generations longer than her subjects. Scientists are also experimenting with mutated worms and are saying they hold great promise for aging therapies much in the way human immunodeficiency virus (HIV) and cancer are currently being treated.

Sadly, the animals we love the most die in a few short years. Although some old dogs can live up to 20 years, the average life span of a dog is between 10 and 13 years. Fortunately, American scientists are currently conducting a trial that could extend dogs' lifespans by two to four years simply by giving them a pill. An indoor cat can last between 10-15 years. Outdoor cats survive only 2 to 5 years. Long live outdoor cats.

There are plants that can live for thousands of years. A quaking aspen colony known as Pando in south-central Utah is 80,000 years old. The plant covers 108 acres and weighs around 6,600 tons, which makes it the heaviest known organism on the planet. A seagrass colony in the Balearic Islands of Spain has been on Earth for 100,000 years, never leaving the place where it was born. It remains in the same exact spot where it will eventually die, which some say, due to climate change, won't be long.

I'm not sure I care to live forever. Not on this earth, anyway. After such an extended stay, I'd tire quickly of listening to the same old classic rock songs and Christmas carols year after year.

Working On My Bucket List

During the Middle Ages, execution by hanging was commonplace. The condemned person would stand on a bucket that would be kicked from beneath him by his executioner. Hence the term: "kick the bucket," which now means to die. In 2007, a new phrase entered the American lexicon: "Bucket List," which came from a film starring Morgan Freeman and Jack Nicholson about two strangers who meet in a hospital room and make a list of things they want to see and do before they die. They then set out on an adventure only a billionaire could finance.

Since the movie's release, many folks have made their own bucket lists. A few squeamish people won't use the term because it reminds them of their own mortality, so they might say something like "Meaningful Life Goals." Should you decide to make such a list, be sure to do it yourself rather than letting your spouse do it, or you could end up retiling the shower or cleaning up the mess you made on the back porch.

One popular item on people's lists is to traverse the Appalachian National Scenic Trail, which runs through 14 states from its southern terminus at Springer Mountain, Georgia, to its northern terminus at Katahdin, Maine.

A friend and I both had the hike on our bucket lists, and we once decided to complete the journey in sections. I went crazy on Amazon. A new tent and sleeping bag followed by cooking equipment, utensils, plates, bowls, etc. A canteen, water purifying kit, canned food, and a bunch of Sterno canned heat. All these mostly unnecessary items were neatly arranged in a fancy backpack, along with enough clothes for a week. The load on my back weighed around 45-50 lbs. I also purchased a pair of fancy hiking boots guaranteed to give me a blister.

To get to the beginning of the world's longest footpath, you must first hike 8.5 miles to Springer Mountain from Amicalola Falls. At the top of the falls is a sign which clearly reads "A.T. Approach Trail," with an arrow clearly pointing to the bottom of 425 strenuous steps. We were dropped off at the top of the falls and took off on the adventure of a lifetime.

By the time I reached 100 steps down, I knew that lugging 50 lbs. of gear was a horrible idea. When we reached the bottom, my skinny legs were rubbery. It was all I could do to keep from toppling over under the weight. There was a ranger at the bottom of the stairs, and I swayed from side to side as I asked him if he knew where the approach trail was. To our surprise and dismay, he said it was back at the top of the stairs. When I complained that the sign pointed down to the bottom of the stairs, he said, "Whatever. You have to go back to the top." I knew I couldn't go through the ordeal of those stairs again, especially going up instead of down, and asked him if there was another way. Of course, there was: a climb. Duh.

After groaning for a few minutes about the wasted 425 grueling steps we had just made, we went to the other side of the falls, and with my wobbly legs barely making it, I pushed myself back up to where we started, with my hiking buddy leading the way. I was keeping up pretty well, but halfway up, I had to stop and throw up on a rock. After that, I stayed in front so he could make sure I didn't fall off the mountain.

I was feeling better when we reached the top of the climb, and the scenery more than made up for my dizziness. We continued to trudge up and down the well-worn path one painful step at a time. Going down a path is just as difficult as going up.

Finally, we came to a camping spot, and it was the end of day one, and time to roll out the sleeping bag. Hallelujah. Unfortunately, we had to pitch our tents on the side of a steep mountain, and I spent the night fighting gravity inside a slick-bottomed tent. It took us a couple more days just to reach the first shelter past the start of the Trail, and we decided to return to civilization. I decided then and there to scratch the AT off my bucket list. Ain't no way I'm going through that again.

I've been to a lot of places. I've jumped from airplanes and even once rode a bull in a Mexican rodeo (another thing I won't do again). If I told you all the things I've experienced, you'd think I was bragging, so I won't. There are still a few things I'd like to do, though. Such as going into space. I'm working on that one.

The Legend of the Great Hill Place Ghost

Ashort distance west of Bolingbroke lies a pile of burned-out rubble. It is all that's left of Great Hill Place. When it was placed on the National Register of Historic Places in 1973, the home was described as an almost perfectly intact plantation complex sitting on 350 acres. There is now little left but ruins.

Built in the early 19th century, the structure was enlarged in Victorian style for his retirement home by William M. Wadley in 1874. Originally a blacksmith, Wadley became a railroad executive of the Central of Georgia Railway and was president of the Central Railroad.

Great Hill Place was once a magnificent home featuring 13 fireplaces. It is also rumored to be haunted. According to many believers, the ghost of a young girl named Rulie has often been seen by former residents of the home and neighbors who live nearby. One of these neighbors is Mr. Lance Hill, who lives with his wife, CC, on Red Oak Road, which is the original wagon road that led to the plantation before they built I-475. He said that the ghost was of a seventeen-year-old girl who committed suicide over a boy. Lance told me that when he moved into his house, he was told that Rulie walked up and down the road, but like most people, he didn't believe in ghosts. He does now. He said that he'd seen Rulie twice. Once was around midnight one night in the 1990s when his chihuahua, Butter Bean (who used to love to eat butter beans out of the garden), suddenly went crazy yapping, and when Hill opened the front door, the dog dashed out the gate into the driveway and started running around an apparition wearing an antebellum dress spinning around, looking at Butter Bean. She soon disappeared, and Butter Bean ran back inside. It was a vision Lance said he would never forget.

CC told me she also had a ghostly experience when she was awakened one night by a spirit hovering over her bed. She said she immediately broke out in a cold sweat, and being a religious woman, she kept calling out to Jesus over and over, and it eventually dissolved away. Her husband slept through the whole ordeal.

I consider myself to be a man of the twenty-first century, and I told the Hills that I meant no offense, but I've heard these types of stories before, and before I become a true believer, I need concrete evidence. That's when CC invited me into her home. They live in a nice, warm, cozy house. Nothing scary about it at all. That's how I felt until she showed me a spot on the living room wall that had been hit by lightning during a summer storm. Just beneath the window to the front yard is an image of a terrifying face that looks so real it almost appears to be a photograph. On a table near the image lay a large cross, I assume, meant as protection. As I said, I don't believe in ghosts, but the hair on the back of my neck was standing straight up.

I know in my heart that it's purely coincidental that such an image would appear from a lightning strike, and it would be a shame to wipe out a piece of art created by nature itself, but I suggested to CC that it would be simple enough to get rid of it with a brush and a can of paint. She said that was true enough, but she liked it. As freaky as it is, so do I.

After I hastily made my way back out into the yard, Lance took me to an old shack just next door that all the local kids call the Spook House. Supposedly, sightings of Rulie have been experienced there, also. Its name fits it perfectly. Lance said it may or may not have once been a slave house. It is a solidly built structure, but there's not much left. I then got the idea that it would be the perfect place to do a little ghost hunting, and since it's Halloween week and after listening to the convincing stories told by the Hills and other interviews

I've done about Rulie, I asked Lance if I could come back on Saturday night around midnight and hang out for a few hours. He said I was welcome anytime.

Since Butter Bean seemed to interest Rulie, I decided to take my own chihuahua, Muchacho, along for the adventure and to give me protection just in case I needed it. We arrived at a quarter to twelve on the darkest road you've ever seen until the moon started shining eerily through overhead branches. I stayed until 2 a.m. and gave up. The only time I got freaked out was when Muchacho started whining like he saw something. After fumbling with my flashlight for a few seconds, I discovered he was excited over a scent he had discovered on the right front tire.

Lake Lanier's Curse

Georgia is the largest state east of the Mississippi River, and until Texas became a state in 1845, it was the largest in the Union. Georgia has 159 counties, outranked only by Texas, which has 254. They say the reason our state has so many counties is that our Georgian forefathers reasoned no man should have to spend more than one day on horseback to reach the courthouse. I've always liked that explanation because it sounds so sensible.

Since this is Women's History Month, I would also like to mention that the only county in Georgia named after a woman is Hart County, for Nancy Hart, a patriot who fought against the redcoats during the Revolutionary War. She must've been quite a lady. I'm going to see what I can read about her. Even larger than the Everglades, the largest swamp in North America is the Okefenokee. And Florida also has nothing on Georgia when it comes to alligators, either. I know this from experience at both locations.

There are more than forty lakes in North Georgia, all of them manmade. The landscape of Georgia's mountains was changed forever when the state decided to dam the region's rivers to meet the water supply and power needs of metropolitan Atlanta. Land that was first owned by indigenous tribes and later by generations of hardworking farmers has been lost forever.

When Lake Lanier was created in the 1950s, entire towns and communities completely disappeared, and more than 700 families were displaced. Some of them had to be forcibly relocated. When contractors arrived at the home of seventy-eight-year-old Eliza Brock, they were met with a shotgun in their faces. Unfortunately for her, she was disarmed, and her farm place became only a memory submerged 80 feet down in cold waters.

The land they flooded was once rich and fertile, with lush vegetation, a healthy game-animal population, and nice little communities like Castleberry Bottom. Picturesque farms had been owned by the same families for generations, and although it was impossible to put a price on them, the government reportedly offered $30 per acre.

The homeowners were led to believe they were being paid a fair price for their land, schools, churches, and homes. Still, it was hard for them to negotiate generations of hard work and memories. Their roots were deep, and many families later reported they deeply regretted their decision to sell. They jammed the roads and bridges that day back in 1956 and watched as their history vanished beneath rising waters. Whatever they had left behind was slowly being washed away.

Anything deemed to be dangerous in the water was demolished by the Army Corps of Engineers. Trees were uprooted and loaded into the back of trucks. Anything made of wood, such as barns or homes, would float in the water and endanger watercraft, so they were torn down and hauled away. Bridges were also somehow relocated. Those Army Corps of Engineers boys were smart even back then.

Before they built the Buford Dam across the Chattahoochee River to create Lake Sidney Lanier, they brought in busloads of schoolboys to dig up the graves in the cemeteries. Many graves in the old cemeteries were unmarked, and the capabilities to identify unmarked burial sites didn't exist 70 years ago as they do now, and several bodies were left behind. Some of these graves dated back to pre-Civil War days, and Indian burial grounds were largely ignored. Due to the possibility of bodies floating free from their now-watery graves, an Army official said it was probable that unanticipated finds of human remains would be possible.

For this reason, many people believe the lake is cursed. It is a lake built over an underwater ghost town. There have been eerie reports of arms reaching out and grabbing swimmers, trying to pull them under. Divers have claimed to reach out into the darkness and feel an unmoving arm or leg. Some people say they have heard church bells from a sunken church. And there have been sightings of catfish as big as a small car.

Shortly after the lake's creation, in April 1958, two women were killed in a Ford sedan when it went over a bridge railing and ended up in the waters of Lake Lanier. Since that night, many have seen the "Lady of the Lake" as she wanders the bridge late at night, restless and caught between two worlds, wearing a beautiful blue dress.

Although Lake Lanier is the fourth-largest lake in Georgia, it is the one with the highest death count. Since its formation, the lake has claimed over 500 lives, with 27 bodies never recovered. Countless rescues have been made over the years. Fishing is a pastime I greatly enjoy, and even though they might have giant catfish up at Lake Lanier, I think I'll just stick to wetting my hook at Indian Springs, where there's less danger, fewer ghosts, and hopefully a lot more fish.

Is There Something Out There?

If you think you had a wild childhood, you did not unless you had YouTube, Facebook, or TikTok. Today, we have internet challenges for kids that can spread worldwide in seconds, but most are harmful or dangerous ideas. There were no such challenges when I was a teenager. We had dares—dares that rarely put anyone's life at risk.

Some challenges help our society, like the ALS Ice Bucket Challenge. This challenge went viral in 2014 and required pouring a bucket of ice water over your head while being filmed to promote awareness of ALS, once commonly known as Lou Gehrig's disease.

A participant "tagged" three other people on social media. Once a person was tagged, they had to also stand in a shower of ice water or give up a hundred bucks to the ALS organization. The ALS Ice Bucket Challenge raised $115 million for ALS awareness, research, and care. Sadly, at least two deaths were linked to the challenge. One participant kicked the bucket after jumping feet-first into ice water.

Another beneficial challenge was the Trash Tag Challenge. This one encouraged internet users to clean up a large pile of trash and post before-and-after pics. I like this one. We should do something similar on one of our many group pages in this area. This would be better than users constantly whining and complaining about the long wait times at Chick-fil-A and McDonald's.

A similarly-named challenge was the Trash Bucket Challenge. The challenge involved video footage of people in parts of Europe throwing their corrupt politicians into trash dumpsters. This was not strictly legal, so I will refrain from saying if it was for the public good or not. Still, many social media users enjoyed the clips, which quickly went viral.

A cute video challenge trending on Twitter had parents throwing cheese at their babies to stop them from crying. By all appearances, this trick worked every time. The babies were too surprised to continue their squalling. I do know from experience that if you squirt some Reddi-Wip into a crying little squirt's mouth, it will result in an instant smile. The benefit of this method is that they don't have to take it off the top of their head to enjoy it.

And then there was the Coronavirus Challenge. This crazy challenge involved placing your tongue on a door handle or a public toilet bowl and giving it a good old-fashioned lick. At least one person was reported to have gotten a good taste of COVID-19 after creating his video and getting only a few likes.

I am sure you remember the Tide Pod Challenge. It all began because the pods, created in 2012, resembled candy. By 2017, poison control centers reported over 7,000 cases of young children eating them because they thought they were a delicious sweet. Six children died. Former Senate Minority Leader Chuck Schumer said he saw one on a staffer's desk and wanted to pop it in his mouth.

Unsurprisingly, hundreds of online Tide Pod memes were soon created. Many showed diverse ways the pods could be used for food and gave cooking recipes. They do look tasty on a cake. Soon, not-so-smart teenagers and even-less-smart adults everywhere had bubbles blowing out of their noses as they vomited up on camera—fun times for all.

During a recent presidential campaign in Taiwan, three people had their stomachs flushed after the pods were handed out as freebies. The victims ate what they thought was candy. One victim was an 80-year-old man, and another was an 86-year-old woman. They are expected to recover.

I confess that I also know the taste of soap. Whenever my momma overheard a bad word coming from my dirty mouth, she would slice off a chunk of Ivory Soap for me to chew and think about what I said.

The biggest stunt we ever pulled when I was a youngun was "ring the doorbell and dash." I tripped over an elderly man's rose bushes as we dashed and got caught once. I struggled free from the headlock, but he called my dad, and I was put on a week's restriction. The fun was worth the punishment.

No video camera was rolling, but my brother, John, spray-painted a patrol car late one Halloween night. That trick would've gone viral.

The police officer was sitting in his car when he saw John creeping around his bumper in his mirror. John was having a good ol' time snickering and spraying away until reaching the driver's door. The officer popped open the door, and John was soon handcuffed.

After leaving him in jail for a few hours, my dad brought him home to a well-deserved butt-whooping and grounded him for life. The sentence lasted about a month.

John got a job selling the "Grit" newspaper to pay for the damage to the government vehicle. It took him quite a while to pay off his debt, but in the meantime, the whole family really enjoyed reading the "Grit."

What's That in the Darkness?

What kind of world would it be if there wasn't just a bit of weirdness? I'm not referring to the weirdness of beings such as ghosts, Bigfoot, or the Chupacabra that we all love, but rather the things we come across in the daily news. It seems that every day, there's someone somewhere capturing a new image on a security camera or a phone camera that just can't be explained.

Such as the image captured inside the fence at the Amarillo Zoo out in Texas in the early morning hours of May 21. The now-nearly-famous creature seen in the zoo's grainy security photo stands upright, much like Bigfoot, but appears not to be nearly as large. Michael Kashuba, director of Parks and Recreation in Amarillo, said, "We'd love to hear feedback from the community on what they think it might be. It's a unique picture, and we're excited to see what the community thinks. The photo is absolutely real." But is the creature? For now, it is known as the Unidentified

Amarillo Object (UAO), and the city of Amarillo is asking the public to submit ideas for what the mystery figure could be. If you want to make a guess, just search for the Unidentified Amarillo Object and take a gander. It's all over the internet and should be easy enough to find. If you know anything about its origins, please let me know right away so I can get some sleep.

In other news, a hospital worker filmed a long-lasting soap bubble floating down a hospital corridor as if it had a mind of its own. While watching the video, I kept expecting it to pop at any second, but it never did. It just kept bobbing and weaving, floating up and then slowly back down. Occasionally, it speeds up and then slows back down again. Even more amazing was how the bubble could go around corners, never touching any obstacle as it continued its search for something unknown. Weird is all I can say. In the video's description, the hospital worker claimed it had finished its journey at the nurses' station. I assume it hung out for a while before taking off again. I never saw it pop, even though a normal soap bubble usually disappears in less than a minute. They say you can add glycerin to soapy water to create bubbles that last for several minutes, but I've never heard of one with a built-in GPS system.

In yet another strange clip, there is a man sleeping on his couch who is suddenly awakened by a loud banging that sounds like it's coming from the next room. He gets up to investigate what you might assume is a ghost, but then suddenly, out of nowhere, we hear the Amazon Alexa, in a voice, we're all familiar with, say, "She was my wife."

The confused man beats it back into his living room, where Alexa appears to try to strike up a conversation with its tiny little speaker, claiming, "You took her from me," and "I found her here…my wife." I've heard of a few cases of Alexa being hacked, but I've never heard of one being involved with a poltergeist before.

Alexa is like a spy that I willingly placed in my home to listen to everything I say, just to give me the temperature outside and to call my phone when I have no idea what I did with it. If you own one of these gadgets, you've probably grown used to it answering questions that weren't asked. I used to think this was a harmless glitch, but if I were the guy in this video, I'd probably find another place to live.

Cameras are everywhere. Ring cameras on nearly every front door, dashcams sticking to nearly every windshield, and trail cams are watching more than just grazing deer, it seems. There are some strange things in this old world, and some of them are bound to end up on video.

As a videographer, I know how easy it is to fool someone into thinking what they're watching is real, but some of these videos just can't be faked. Just ask the government. A military database of UFOs (now called unexplained aerial phenomena – UAPs) now includes around 400 separate incidents, up from 143 in a report released just a year ago. The 2021 military report said that no evidence of aliens had been found. Scott

W. Bray, the deputy director of Naval Intelligence, told congressional lawmakers that they still haven't uncovered anything "non-terrestrial in origin," but there are many incidents that can't be explained. None of these so-called UAPs have made any attempt to communicate with American flyers, and we haven't tried to talk with them either. What would we say?

It's the Little Things That Give Us Hope

And there's good news coming out of Florida.

Hoppin' John and Skippin' Jenny

While most of us are still reeling from the effects of Christmas dinner, which came way too soon after that fine Thanksgiving dinner, it is now time to start thinking about another traditional meal for New Year's Day. Around here, folks say if you want to make a lot of coin during 2022, then you must put away as many black-eyed peas as you can. Black-eyed peas symbolize coins, and some cooks will even drop a dime or a quarter in the pot while they're cooking, and whoever ends up with the coin in their bowl will have the most luck in the coming year. Just add a couple of ladles of black-eyed peas, flavored with ham hock, fatback, or sausage, over a bowl of steaming-hot rice to create a dish that helped make the South famous: "Hoppin' John." My Aunt Shirley's recipe calls for adding a couple of spoons of chow-chow on top. Good eatin'.

Of course, if you want some dollar bills to go along with all those coins, you'll need to eat something green like collards, turnip greens, or mustard greens; it doesn't really matter which. Some people like to substitute chard, kale, or cabbage for the greenery. Personally, I don't think the color is quite right, and the taste surely isn't.

If you really want to get rich, that's easy enough; just help yourself to a couple of big ol' slabs of golden cornbread, which, as we all know, symbolizes gold. If you happen to be lucky enough to have any Hoppin' John left over, then have another bowl on January 2 when it becomes known as "Skippin' Jenny" and even tastier than it was the day before.

One of the reasons some people in other parts of the world aren't as prosperous is because they don't observe the same New Year traditions we do, except for Cuba, where they have a version of Hoppin' John using black beans, and they call it "Hoppin' Juan." That is, if those poor folks can afford a bowl of rice and beans.

In Spain, they have a tradition of eating one grape for every second during the last 12 seconds of the countdown to midnight for good luck. Then, with a mouthful of grapes, when the last page of the calendar flips at 12 a.m., they share sloppy kisses with grape juice running down their chins and necks. I know from experience this can be quite fun. In fact, it's so much fun that the tradition, which started at the beginning of the 20th century by a grape grower who came up with the genius idea after a bumper crop of grapes, has now spread to nearly every Spanish-speaking country, including Mexico.

While we in the United States celebrate the New Year in normal ways, like shooting off fireworks and pistols into the night sky, dropping big balls mounted high in the air, and maybe drinking a little too much, other folks around the world put out the old and bring in the new in interesting ways we might think are a bit strange.

For instance, in Romania, farmers spend the first day of the new year trying to communicate with their livestock. If they're successful in carrying on a conversation with their cow or pig or whatever, it is believed that the farmer will have a prosperous next twelve months. In Denmark, folks save up unused plates throughout the year to smash against the front doors of family and friends on New Year's Day. The bigger the pile of broken crockery you find on your welcome mat, the more luck you will have. Danes also have an unusual custom of leaping off chairs during their celebrations, symbolizing leaping into the new year. And it might be a good idea to steer clear of streets in South Africa where they indulge in the strange tradition of tossing old furniture out of upper-story apartments.

If you live in Georgia or Alabama and you really like to party, you might think about making New Year's Eve reservations in Columbus, where after it becomes 2022 in the Eastern Time Zone, you can easily make a quick trip of less than a mile across the Chattahoochee River and do it all over again in Phenix City, Alabama where they party down in Central Time style.

"Times gone by" is the meaning of the title of the song we traditionally sing at midnight on New Year's Eve: "Auld Lang Syne," written by a Scottish poet in 1788. I'll be up late this Friday night singing this song and making sure 2021 is really gone, witnessing the Forsythia Ball make its annual drop at the Courthouse Square. My weather apps say it might rain and be chilly that evening, but I don't care; I'll be wearing my new long johns I got from my Aunt Shirley for Christmas.

Tallapoosa Will Drop the Possum

We have been celebrating New Year's Day for at least four thousand years, and the day has evolved into eating black-eyed peas, making useless resolutions, nursing hangovers, and watching the Rose Bowl parade.

When I reminisce about the past twelve months, I promise myself not to think about bad things. I'm going to think of good things like drones, digital dinners, and wedding ceremonies over Zoom. I'll remember healthcare workers, first responders, and essential workers who are real heroes. And I'll recall that wearing sweatpants and sloppy tees became acceptable fashion choices all day, every day, anywhere, and everywhere.

It was a rough year, but good things did happen. McDonald's gave us the recipe for the Sausage & Egg McMuffin, and Burger King released their secrets for the Whopper. Now we can create our own unhealthy fast food in the comfort of our home kitchen. I wish I could've done that in 2019.

Even the recipe for KFC's legendary and highly secret 11 herbs and spices is also easily downloaded. Colonel Sanders would choke on a wishbone. I'm still waiting for the list of the well-guarded ingredients in Coca-Cola.

In 2020, we celebrated milestones creatively with drive-by birthdays, drive-by anniversaries, and Zoom parties. Our favorite musicians turned to social media and gave us concerts from their homes.

The year 2020 wasn't all bad. Eminem celebrated 12 years of being sober. Miley Cyrus also got on the bandwagon that year. She joined Brad Pitt and numerous other stars who had given up that hard Hollywood party life. That was a good thing.

And who can forget the 103-year-old grandma who celebrated beating COVID-19 with a can of Bud Light? Or did those drive-in theaters make a comeback? (With Bluetooth.) Or how about when "Tiger King" brought together an entire nation?

And you may remember where you were this year when a rocket constructed by Elon Musk's SpaceX launched two Americans into orbit from United States soil for the first time in nearly a decade. We are now looking at humans returning to the Moon's surface by 2024. This time, NASA promises a woman will be part of the crew. High-heel footprints on the moon. I like it.

There had been some surprises that year, other than the election results, like the man who walked into a Walmart store in Tennessee at 6 a.m. on Dec. 11 and paid off nearly $65,000 to cover the cost of all the current layaway items in the store. Even more surprising is that the man wished to remain nameless. A true Secret Santa.

In other 2020 Walmart news, a dog went missing from her Alabama owner's backyard and then, three weeks later, wandered into a Walmart store with her tail wagging and casually walked up to her owner, who was working at a checkout line. The pooch had never been into that superstore before. The owner's coworker said it was overwhelming to watch the reunion and that they were in disbelief.

In other animal news, a deer charged a hunter during November, snagged his rifle strap on its antlers, then ran off into the woods with the weapon. Fortunately, the gun was unloaded, and both hunters and deer were uninjured. Another hunter reported spotting the buck more than half a mile away with the rifle still dangling from its antlers. He was trying to get it loaded.

Y'all know there's always good news coming out of Florida, and this year was no exception. It was in the papers that a Lee County man rescued his recently adopted puppy from the jaws of a hungry alligator. The gator was dragging the dog under the water, but the man jumped into the pond and pried open the beast's jaws, freeing his pet with his bare hands. His hands were all chewed up, but the dog only had one small puncture wound.

And then there was the Florida couple who are grateful to a "Christmas angel" who found their bag containing

$250,000 of jewelry that had fallen out of their trunk, and they tracked them down to return it.

One of the most recognized New Year's traditions is the dropping of a giant ball in New York City's Times Square at the stroke of midnight. Millions of people from around the world watched the event, which began in 1907. Now at least

207 cities across the country mimic the celebration. In Georgia alone, 12 cities (including Forsyth) drop something to start the New Year off right. In Unadilla, they drop a hog. In Tallapoosa, they drop Spencer, the famous possum who is suspended inside a wire ball wrapped tightly with Christmas lights. The ball is kept low most of the evening of Dec. 31 so people can take selfies with him. Then at 11:30 p.m., he is raised high above spectators and then slowly lowered to bring in the new year. Spencer is a real possum that someone found dead in the woods a few years ago. They had him stuffed and then wrapped him up inside a weird-looking Christmas ball. Don't ask.

A Special Kind of Day

February 2 is a day that should be acknowledged for being exactly halfway between the first day of Winter and the first day of Spring. Today is also known as Candlemas Day, a celebration of the return of light, and many people have even left their Christmas decorations up until today.

Some Christians take a candle to their church on Candlemas Day to be blessed and will use their blessed candle on special occasions throughout the year.

February 2 is also the feast of the Presentation of Jesus, which commemorates the occasion when Joseph and Mary first took the baby Jesus to the Temple of God, and the purification of the Virgin Mary is observed on this day as well. Today's date cannot be considered ordinary on anyone's calendar. Best of all, Christmas can now be declared officially over.

There are 45 days from Feb. 2 until March 20, the first day of Spring, but there is a furry creature living in a scaled-down antebellum-style mansion at the Dauset Trails Nature Center in nearby Jackson who might have given us hope of an earlier spring this morning at 7:30 a.m. That is, if he didn't cast a shadow. If he did, we could expect six more weeks of misery. I'm referring to the famous Gen. Beauregard Lee, Georgia's own weather-predicting groundhog whose bragging rights of 60% accuracy far exceed his Yankee counterpart, Punxsutawney Phil, up in Pennsylvania, who can claim mere 30% accuracy. Ike English, the Dauset Trails director, told WMAZ in an interview a couple of years ago that Waffle House hash browns and Indian Springs water keep Gen. Lee predicting the weather with such mastery.

There has been more than one General Lee. All of them have had the unusual talent of forecasting the approach of Spring.

The first General Lee, who emerged in front of large crowds every Groundhog Day at the Yellow River Game Ranch near Lilburn from 1981-91, was Gen. Robert E. Lee. He had an exceptional 94% accuracy rate but was forced into retirement after he became too old and too fat to perform his duties. A monument was erected at the ranch at his retirement in honor of his outstanding meteorological service to the southeastern U.S. When the ranch closed suddenly in 2017, the general's current successor was taken to Dauset Trails.

Some believers trust the shadow of a groundhog even more than the local "weatherperson." You may have wondered how it came to be that folks put such faith into the largest member of the squirrel family to determine whether they needed to keep the long johns handy or prepare to kick the dogs out from under the covers. I decided to find out what's behind this strange tradition, and according to an overload of reliable information online, the practice dates back to 4th-century Greece, when Christians believed that a sunny Candlemas, 40 days after Christmas, meant 40 more days of snow and winter. A lot of people seem to know this fact, but no one has an explanation as to why Christians would think such a thing.

German woodsmen later noticed that if a hedgehog crawled out of its burrow and cast a shadow on Candlemas Day, it was a sure indication that an early spring wasn't something to be counted on. After this discovery, they kept a close eye on the prickly creature on Feb. 2 every year, and the practice quickly spread throughout Europe.

Later, when German immigrants settled in Pennsylvania starting in the 18th century, they were disappointed to learn there weren't any hedgehogs on this continent, so they resorted to using the available groundhog to continue their time-honored tradition. Apparently, the American rodent was well suited to the task, and the immigrants came to rely on its yearly predictions. I assume they chose the groundhog because the animals have the same last name, even though they aren't at all related.

In 1887, a newspaper editor in Punxsutawney, Penn., needed a story and brainstormed the idea of forming the Punxsutawney Groundhog Club, and he somehow sold his plan to local businessmen and groundhog hunters. On Feb. 2, the founding club members hiked to nearby Gobbler's Knob and conducted the first official proceedings of the first Groundhog Day. The participants were disheartened when the sleepy groundhog predicted a long winter that year.

The dignitaries who preside over the yearly festivities every year these days in Punxsutawney are known as the "Inner Circle" and wear fancy top hats during the proceedings. They preside, speaking Pennsylvania Dutch dialect and claim to converse with Punxsutawney Phil in the language of "Groundhogese" before a throng of tens of thousands of cheering spectators.

Of course, it's ridiculous to place any faith in the predictions of a rodent that lives in a hole in the ground, but like my Aunt Shirley says: "It's the little things that give us hope."

The History of Presidents Day

Among the many things that Americans have contributed to the world is the concept of the presidency. Before George Washington's election, most countries in the world were ruled by monarchs. Some with absolute power who answer only to God.

There is a myth that our first president turned down the offer of a crown during the Revolutionary War. The myth stems from a letter sent to Washington from Col. Lewis Nicola in 1782, who wrote, "I believe a strong argument might be produced for admitting the title of king, which I conceive would be attended with some material advantages." Nicola had no crown to offer, but the legend persists because it makes Washington appear noble.

There are numerous myths, stories, and legends regarding this remarkable man. One of the most enduring is that his dentures were made of wood. In truth, they were constructed of human teeth and, more than likely, horse and cow teeth, ivory, and metal alloys. It's possible some thought his choppers were wooden because of the brownish stains from daily use.

The best-known legend about our first president is the tale of his admitting to cutting down his father's cherry tree. He was given a hatchet as a gift when he was six years old, and he used it against the tree. His father became extremely angry upon discovering the ruined tree and confronted young George, who famously replied that he had indeed cut down the tree and could not lie. Even though the often-repeated tale demonstrates Washington's honesty, the story itself is a complete lie, invented by the first Washington biographer, Mason Locke Weems, whose bestseller, written immediately after the president's death at the age of 64, depicted Washington's high virtues intending to give young people of the United States stories that would influence them to achieve high moral standards. Such as those demonstrated by the Father of our Country. It didn't matter that the stories were false; they were inspirational.

Although silver dollars weren't minted in the United States until 1794, the claims that Washington once skipped one for a mile across the Potomac River in his youth continue to this day. This tall tale probably originated with his step-grandson, George Washington Parke Custis, who once related that the General hurled a piece of slate about the size of a dollar across the Rappahannock River in Virginia. This is a bit more believable as the Rappahannock is a narrow river. And that powdered wig you thought he always wore? Nope. That was his real hair that he kept long, powdered white, and tied in a ponytail. The images I found of George Washington in his youth depict him as a redhead. Even though the six-foot-two-inch general lost more battles in the Revolutionary War than he won, his winning strategies at the Battle of Trenton in 1776 and Yorktown in 1781 proved Washington to be a capable leader.

More places have been named after him than anyone else in our country's history, with the Census Bureau listing 94 locations with just his name and 127 including those places whose name is within a longer name, such as Washingtonburg, Pa. Even though never a president, Benjamin Franklin comes in second with 89, including 31 cities and many counties. Five thousand settlers once created the State of Franklin, or "Frankland," in a wild, mountainous area in what is now eastern Tennessee, just after the Revolutionary War, but the land was later ceded to the State of Tennessee. President Abraham Lincoln ranks third with

70. Cities such as Lincoln, Neb., and Lincoln, Ala., are named in his memory.

The anniversary of Washington's birthday, Feb. 22, 1732, was the first federal holiday to honor an individual's birth date when in 1885, Congress voted to give a day off for all federal workers on Feb. 22. The date was changed in 1971 when the Uniform Monday Holiday Law moved it to the third Monday in February after an executive order from then-President Richard M. Nixon. The name "Presidents' Day" is not an official moniker but became popular due to retailers having sales in honor of both Washington's and Lincoln's birthday, which is on the 12th of the month. Right after Lincoln's assassination, there were several attempts to get his birthday observed as a federal holiday but all failed. Presidents' Day is now recognized as a holiday to honor all American presidents.

This year, Presidents' Day will be observed on Monday, Feb. 21. The banks will be closed, the mail won't run, the kids get to stay home from school, and many federal workers will be enjoying the last day of a three-day weekend. Meanwhile, the rest of us will carry on and go to work like it's an ordinary day, but with the added inconvenience of finding someone to watch the kids and the temporary absence of several government services. That's okay, though. Most of our presidents deserve such an honor.

It's Valentine's Day, Baby!

Valentine's Day has always been a special day for me. While it's true that I'm a romantic at heart, it's mainly because I was born on Feb. 14, and I must confess I was born north of the Mason-Dixon line. It absolutely wasn't my fault, but there are those in my family who won't leave the place of my birth alone.

Around the time of my earthly debut, my daddy was a mountain-boy Airman with just a single stripe on his sleeve, and in order to get another, the Air Force insisted that he further his education by taking some courses at the now-defunct Chanute Air Force Base just outside of the desolate town of Rantoul, Ill. In the meantime, my mother, just 17 and pregnant, was in Georgia, waiting for her new husband to come home.

From what I've been told, about nine and a half months into her pregnancy, my mother couldn't take any more loneliness and decided to take a 4-day train ride all the way from Georgia to Illinois. In the middle of winter. Into the land of snow. Just to be with my dad.

Shortly after her arrival in Illinois, I made mine.

You would think, after all those days of being jostled around on the cheap seats of a bumpy cross-country train, that her labor would be quick. But my birth didn't come easy for my mother on that freezing Valentine's Day in the middle of nowhere. Hours later, as she held me in her arms, she weakly hissed at my father, "Don't you ever give me another Valentine's present!" Just one week later, our little family was back on that train, this time southbound, headed back to Georgia.

Several years later, when I had a whole houseful of babies of my own, I needed a copy of my birth certificate and called up the Champaign County, Ill., courthouse to have one mailed to me. While I was on hold and waiting for the clerk to look up my record, I casually mentioned to her I had left Rantoul when I was just one week old; I've never returned, and I was wondering how it was there. Have I been missing anything all these years? She told me that leaving that hellhole was probably the smartest thing I'd ever done. To this day, I've never returned to my birthplace. I have visited a few other hellholes, though.

Being Valentine's baby can have its benefits. Usually, once people find out I was born on that special day in the middle of what's always a dreary month, they automatically assume I'm a sweet guy. Well, I guess I am. Can't help it. Just don't nominate me for the Most Romantic Man of Monroe County. Not that I could even come close to winning, but if I did, my buddies, brothers, and nephews would never let that one go.

One of the most romantic men ever was Saint Valentine himself, which is probably why our holiday of celebrating love is named after him. Claudius II, the Roman emperor from 268 to 270 AD, decided that soldiers were better fighters without wives and families and decreed marriage was against the law for young men and women. Valentine thought this was a ridiculous law, so he defied old Claudius and continued to marry young soldiers in secret. When word of his crime got out, he found himself behind bars with the promise of a quick beheading.

According to legend, while he was in prison, Valentine fell in love with the beautiful young daughter of his jailer and composed the very first Valentine's Day greeting. After writing her a letter proclaiming his undying love, he signed it "From your Valentine," an expression still on nearly every Valentine's Day card. Unfortunately, their relationship never got past the letter-writing stage. You could say he lost his head over that young gal. There are a couple of men called St. Valentine and some confusion, but this is the one who should win all the Most Romantic Man prizes.

Valentine's Day is big business, with 62% of Americans observing it in some fashion. Of course, candy, greeting cards, and flowers top the list, but then there's the dude who makes the rest of us look bad by taking his lady to El Tejado for tacos and strawberry margaritas.

Obviously, sales will be slower this Lover's Day due to the ongoing pandemic. Even so, according to the National Retail Federation (NRF), $21.8 billion will be spent in 2021. And that's with 74% of Americans saying the pandemic will directly impact their romantic plans. The NRF also says that this year, most couples will buy gifts for each other online. Makes sense to me. Most of them met online anyway.

A Blue Moon for Halloween

This month, a "blue moon", the second full moon in a month, will be shining brightly on Halloween night. As a special treat, this spooky spectacle will be visible to the entire world, something that hasn't happened since 1944.

The philosopher Aristotle believed that full moons caused insanity in individuals by providing light during hours that would otherwise have been dark. Until 1700, many believed the moon influenced rheumatism, epilepsy, and a myriad of other diseases. Ancient legends say that people can become violent or even turn into wolves during a full moon.

A word rarely heard these days is "lunatic," which is derived from lunaticus, meaning "moonstruck." Lunatic was once commonly used in legal terminology, but now the phrase "person of unsound mind" is used in its place. I can only assume it's politically correct, even though it takes longer to say and write. They have also replaced the term "asylum" with "mental hospital."

I am a non-believer in ghosts and other unproven phenomena, and the idea that the moon could somehow affect human behavior seemed to be bunk, but after some research, I'm starting to think there might be something to what I previously thought to be pure nonsense.

While most scientific studies show no correlation between the full moon and human behavior, police departments and prisons around the world regularly beef up patrols and vigilance during a full moon, especially in the summer months.

A spokesperson for an English police department said, "Research carried out by us has shown a correlation between violent incidents and full moons." Another officer continued, "From my experience, after over 19 years of being a police officer, undoubtedly on full moons, we do seem to get more people with strange behavior - more argumentative." A study by Professor Michal Zimecki of the Polish Academy of Sciences argues that a full moon could affect criminal activity and health. Also, a three-month study in 1998 conducted on 1,200 inmates at the Armley jail in Leeds, England, showed a rise in violent incidents.

Locally, a trio of deputies at the Monroe County Sheriff's Office told me that crime does indeed increase around the time of a full moon. One deputy said he believes that since it is a brighter sky, more people are outside with a tendency to drink more. He also said the moon provides just enough light to see something to steal but not light enough to see who stole it. Monroe County deputies plan to be out in extra force this Halloween for the safety of trick-or-treaters.

This year's Halloween will be different than any we've ever experienced. Are the plastic Halloween masks the kiddies wear considered safe enough for going to strangers' houses for that meager handful of candy, or will that mask need to be covered by yet another mask? I've grown accustomed to seeing strange masks when I shop the aisles, and I doubt a mask on top of a mask would seem that odd anymore.

Some folks have been building apparatuses described as "candy chutes" that dispense sweets to trick-or-treaters from the socially acceptable, medically approved, and CDC-advised distance of 6 feet. The candy givers will be wearing masks and frequently sanitizing their hands. The chutes are simply decorated shipping tubes or PVC pipes angled downward toward the little open hands. I've only had one trick-or-treater tap on my door in the five years I've lived next to the deep dark woods, so I'm not going to worry about it too much. If some little ghost happens to show up, I guess I'll have to give up that peanut butter cup I've been saving in the fridge.

Halloween is not only a holiday for donning some stupid costume and sneaking all the Snickers out of your kid's candy bag the next day, but also famous for pranks committed in the dead of night. With this year's holiday falling on a Saturday right before Election Day, I'm sure some pranksters will be having a great time. I expect a lot of political signs will be switched around in people's yards, and there are going to be some incredibly angry voters on the morning of Nov. 1. This isn't a prank I would do personally.

I'd be too worried my neighbor would retaliate with the old, flaming dog poo bag on my front porch trick.

Although there's a black cat silhouetted against a big yellow moon on nearly every Hallmark Halloween card, full moons occurred on Halloween only four times during the previous century. The last time a blue moon appeared on Halloween was in 1974. You should take time out from your coronavirus-style Halloween activities to view this rare occurrence. It's still 2020, so who knows what you might see on this once-in-a-lifetime Halloween night?

Halloween Has Lost Its Meaning

Scientists estimate that there are 15 dead people for every person alive on the earth today. Death is so widespread that we even have a holiday in its honor. This coming Monday, Oct. 31, the day dedicated to remembering all deceased people since the beginning of time and one of the world's oldest holidays, Halloween, will be celebrated.

Few gives thought to those who have gone on before us on this day devoted to them. Most of us try not to dwell on thoughts of our own mortality and have turned what started as a somber day in the first millennium A.D. into a cute holiday that is completely at odds with its original purpose. When I see someone walking around in a sexy avocado costume, my mind goes to tacos. Not death.

Irish and Scottish immigrants fled famine in the 1840s and brought Halloween to America. They spent the evening before All Saints Day conversing with the dead. Now we have trick-or-treating and encourage our children to put on adorable little costumes and go door-to-door, filling decorated bags with sugary sweets that we know aren't good for them.

Halloween is not just for kids, though. More than 5.3 million American adults plan to dress up as a witch. Most of them will be women. Nearly two million grown-ups will go to a party dressed as a vampire, while 1.2 million will spend the evening as a cat. Dogs will get in on the action as pumpkins and hot dogs. My own pooch, Muchacho, will be begging for treats this year, wearing a little sombrero and serape. My solid black cat, Noche, needs nothing.

Like Christmas and all holidays, Halloween has gone full-fledged commercial. This year's spending will break records during the post-pandemic holiday season. At least $2.9 billion is expected to be spent on costumes, with $700 million on pet costumes. To the delight of the dental industry, $10.6 billion will be spent on candy.

I was never much into putting on a costume and drawing attention to myself. I'm shy like that. But once, so long ago, my oldest son was still in diapers, I gave in to my wife and agreed to go to a costume party. Fittingly, she decided to go as a witch and spent nearly all of my paycheck on makeup, nail polish, the hat, the broom, and the works. I admit that when she was finished, she looked hot. Better than she usually did. But I kept my thoughts to myself.

When she finished destroying the budget, there was nothing left for my costume, so I had to resort to creating one out of whatever I could find. We lived ten miles from the middle of nowhere in the Alabama woods, and resources were few. I didn't want to go, but while changing my little boy's diaper, I suddenly had an inspiration.

If you think Pampers are bad now, back then, diapers were a real mess. Made of cloth, they weren't just rolled up and thrown away. You had to clean them out in a toilet, wash them, and then reuse them after you hang them outside on a line. So, while I was gagging over the changing table, it came to me that I could rip up a dozen or so baby diapers and make the perfect mummy costume.

I had my wife wrap me in 3" strips of genuine diaper cloth from head to toe, fastening them wherever needed with diaper pins that she tucked beneath the folds. To ensure the cloth was tight, all I had on beneath was my whitey-tighties. Afterward, I put on my cowboy hat and my glasses, and man,

I looked good! The babysitter acted scared when she arrived, so I knew I'd be a hit.

We kissed the boy, jumped in my pickup truck, and headed slowly to town. I drove below the speed limit so folks would be sure to notice a mummy driving a '52 Chevrolet Thrift Master with a good-looking witch snuggled up next to him.

Things were going well at the party until near the end, when everything began to unravel. I was dancing with my arms in the air when I noticed a loose piece of diaper cloth hanging from my arm. From there, it only got worse. Soon, I didn't have enough hands to keep everything together and convinced my wife we had to make a hasty exit before my face and other areas became exposed. We made it to the truck, and everything was fine, except that every time I changed gears, another rag would come untied. We were only about five miles from the house when my old truck started sputtering and then suddenly decided not to go another inch without fuel.

My witch-wife was following close behind, cursing my every step as I stumbled down that old dirt road on that Halloween night with a full moon shining, hanging on to all I had left.

Veterans Are Worth Honoring

In 1918, on the 11th hour of the 11th day of the 11th month, an armistice was declared between the Allied nations and Germany, ending World War I. The following year, President Woodrow Wilson proclaimed November 11 as Armistice Day to honor the American soldiers. November 11th became a federal holiday in 1938 and was later renamed Veterans Day, one of our most solemn holidays.

The men and women in our Armed Services can attest that freedom does not come free. Many heroes had their freedom stolen by becoming prisoners of war. The story of the American POW is an inspiring chapter in our nation's history.

An estimated 20,000 Americans were held as prisoners during the Revolutionary War. For many, their miserable lives were spent in the lower holds of British prison ships. Those who died were simply tossed overboard or buried in shallow sand. After the Revolution, many were enslaved by the "Barbary pirates."

During the War of 1812, Americans were again held in prison ships until they were taken to England and thrown in stone prisons like the infamous Dartmoor. Prisoner Charles

Andrews said, "death itself, with hopes of a hereafter, seems less terrible than this gloomy prison."

The Civil War had more prisoners of war than any other conflict in history, with 194,000 Union soldiers and 214,000 Confederate soldiers captured. Around 30,000 Union troops died in Confederate prisons, and 26,000 Confederates died in Yankee camps. Near the end of the war, the Andersonville camp, barely 75 miles from Forsyth, had few supplies and high mortality rates. Although the Confederate camp was in existence for only 14 months, Andersonville is blamed for 43 percent of all Union prisoner-of-war deaths.

During the two years of U.S. involvement in World War I, around 4,120 Americans were held as prisoners of war. In World War II, lack of medical attention was common, as well as malnutrition among the 94,000 POWs in Europe. When the war was ending, many prisoners were forced to march for weeks as the Germans tried to flee the advancing Allied Forces.

The Japanese captured nearly 30,000 Americans, who suffered some of the highest death rates in history at nearly 40 percent. The Japanese were especially brutal to prisoners of war, and many were crowded into "hell ships." Those that survived these torturous journeys were often forced to work as slaves in Japanese mines, seven days a week, with little food. Their lives as POWs meant forced marches, solitary confinement, and barbaric punishments.

The harsh treatment of American POWs during the Korean War rivals the evilness exhibited by the Japanese. More than 7,100 Americans were captured, and over 2,700 are known to have died while imprisoned.

During the Viet Nam War, at least 766 American heroes are known to have been prisoners of war. Of these, 114 gave their lives. The torture of prisoners was common, and since the North Vietnamese claimed the Americans were not prisoners of war but rather political criminals, they didn't follow the rules of the Geneva Convention. The length of time these prisoners were held was extensive, with some living in hell on earth for more than seven years.

One of these prisoners was the late Senator John McCain III, who was held for 5 ½ years as a POW in North Vietnam after being shot down in his Skyhawk dive bomber in 1967. He received little care for fractures in both his arms and right leg and endured unbelievably cruel treatment. Tony Orlando, a well-known entertainer and champion for American veterans, said that he recently met McCain when he first publicly performed "Tie a Yellow Ribbon" at a show with Bob Hope in Dallas to welcome home returning POWs from Vietnam in 1973.

He said he noticed former POW McCain sitting still during the show, seemingly unfazed by everything going on. Concerned that the Navy pilot didn't enjoy the show, Orlando approached him afterward to see if there was a problem with the performance. McCain told him he enjoyed it immensely, but the only thing he could move was one toe, which tapped inside his boot throughout the entire show.

When Orlando performed during Monroe County's Bicentennial celebration on Sept. 25 at the Fine Arts Center, he not only wowed the audience with a spectacular performance but also impressed them with his fierce patriotism and love for our country. There wasn't a dry eye in the place when he introduced former Georgian POW Colonel D.W. Waddell, who made his way down to the stage. Waddell was shot down over North Vietnam in an F-105 and, like McCain, spent time in the Hanoi Hilton.

This is a big week for Tony Orlando, who is helping host Veterans Homecoming Week in Branson, Missouri. He started the event nearly 30 years ago, and Branson is now a destination for many veterans. Orlando plays an important role in many veterans' organizations and said his causes can be supported at www.tonyorlando.com.

A Crisp Salute to Our U.S. Veterans

Today is Veterans Day, 2020. Veterans Day was originally called "Armistice Day," and the date of Nov. 11 was chosen to commemorate the signing of the armistice with Germany that ended hostilities during World War I. The war was to end all wars. We all know that didn't happen.

We are living in unstable times. But when in history have times ever been stable? There have been only 230 years without a war over the last 3,500, and I'm sure during those few years of peace, there were some yahoos rioting and tearing up some city somewhere.

God created many rivers, but not one fence or wall. It is man's invention to separate the world into nearly 200 countries, with each one willing to go to war with the next at the slightest provocation. Responsible citizens across the globe feel they owe their respective countries fierce patriotism. They teach their children the unique culture and ideals of their nation, then send them off to die for those ideals, waving flags and singing songs as their children march to the horrors of war.

They give up their money through taxes to build bigger, better, and smarter weapons. They live with the guilt of the deaths of innocent people because these deaths were necessary for freedom, religion, or greed. Hiroshima comes to mind, as well as the Wounded Knee massacre. Humans seem to have a need to kill other humans.

I have a friend who immigrated from Russia. He is a friendly, funny guy whom everyone likes and will do anything to help anyone. He loves America so much that he learned English and became a citizen. We are about the same age, and one day we discovered he had been a paratrooper in the Soviet Army during the same time I had been a paratrooper in the U.S. Army. We talked about what would have happened if, as sworn enemies, we had met face to face on an ugly battlefield as opposed to sitting on a barstool next to the beautiful Atlantic Ocean in Daytona Beach.

God alone determines our birthplace and heritage. We are born where He chooses; there's nothing we can do about it. For that reason alone, my friend and I would've both had a duty to try to kill each other. We didn't discuss who would have won the war. War these days would leave no winner.

If we had faced off in a field of battle anytime between the 17th and the 19th centuries, we would've been standing face-to-face with loaded muskets in long rows of fellow infantrymen in line formation. I can only imagine what went through the minds of those unfortunate soldiers positioned at the front as they awaited orders to fire. A lot of prayers go up to heaven just before any battle begins.

These shootouts could last for hours, and they say the results were always unpredictable. I could have predicted them easily. It's obvious that whatever side had the most men with the most musket balls would win the battle. Maybe a little core math before the mayhem could've prevented a lot of deaths.

American Indians taught our American Revolutionary soldiers the benefits of stealth, camouflage, surprise, deception, and other tactics that used terrain as cover and confused the British, who knew only how to fight like gentlemen. They considered guerrilla warfare to be crude and ill-mannered. Brits still consider us to be coarse and quite boorish.

Wars are extremely profitable to the handful of people who provide the terrible products of destruction. The Lockheed Martin Corporation is the largest defense contractor in the world, raking in nearly $45 billion in 2017 in arms and defense contracts. Boeing comes in second at half that amount. Also profiting are 51 members of Congress and their spouses, who own between $2.3 and $5.8 million in defense contractor stock. According to reports, in a review of financial disclosures filed with the Senate on December 13, 2019, it was revealed our own Senator, David Perdue, is a major investor in a pair of defense companies while serving on the Senate Committee on Armed Services. God was good to me before I was even born. I feel so blessed he made me a red-blooded American. I thank Him for making me a proud Southern man whose ancestors were a bunch of moonshiners from the Appalachian Mountains as opposed to being the grandson of some Russians who produced illegal vodka somewhere in the Siberian Mountains.

I realize we must defend ourselves and our way of life, or everything will be gone. I'm extremely thankful to my dad, my uncles, my cousins, my brothers, and all veterans who sacrifice for us. I salute them on this solemn day. But while we must be willing to die for our freedom, we also must be willing to kill. I wish we knew another way.

Freedom Is Not Free

When the American Revolution had been won, and the veterans of the world's first army of free men returned to their families, there were no parades welcoming them home on Main Street. No speeches from courthouse steps praising their bravery or thanking them for their sacrifices.

A quarter of a million American men fought against the world's greatest army to gain our freedom for little material gain. Lowly privates were paid $6 a month, equal to $160 in today's dollars. That was considered a lot of money in those days, except that the Continental dollar was practically worthless. These men weren't in it for the money or fame. Only generals and leading officers became famous and honored as heroes, with few exceptions.

America's earliest disabled veterans received small pensions, but those who survived unscathed received nothing. Many reached old age and died without ever being recognized for their role in creating what would become the world's greatest country. Finally, in 1832, Congress voted to award pensions to most surviving soldiers, marines, and sailors of the Revolution, regardless of rank, financial distress, or physical disability.

Many wars have come and gone since then. We've even had a war with ourselves, leaving more than half a million Americans dead. Three hundred of whom are resting forever in our own city cemetery. While Union veterans enjoyed federal benefits for their military service during the Civil War, as former enemies of the United States, Confederate soldiers were denied benefits. In 1958, Congress at last pardoned all surviving Confederate soldiers and allowed them benefits. By then, ninety-three years after Lee handed over his sword to Grant, there was just one remaining:

Walter Washington Green Williams of Mississippi. Walter, also known as "Old Reb," finally received every benefit Union soldiers had enjoyed since 1865. Unfortunately, he died the following year, reportedly at the age of 117.

Greater respect was given to returning soldiers following World War I, known then as the "Great War." On the 11th hour of the 11th day of the 11th month in the year 1918, hostilities were temporarily halted between Germany and the Allied nations bringing the war to a close. The following year, President Woodrow Wilson declared November 11 to be Armistice Day in the United States, as did many other countries, including Great Britain, France, and even Germany. The last surviving American veteran of the First World War was Cpl. Frank Buckles, who passed away on February 27, 2011, at 110 years old. Buckles was buried at Arlington National Cemetery with full military honors, and President Barack Obama paid respects.

A little over two decades after "the war to end all wars," on December 7, 1941, the United States again entered a conflict even more terrible than the previous. Sixteen million Americans answered the call to fight for freedom. No one really knows the exact number, but it is estimated that there were around 407,000 American military deaths during World War II.

Veterans from this horrible war are now in their 90s or older. There are now fewer than 167,284 alive today that we will be able to honor this coming Veterans Day. Sadly, around 180 of these heroes are dying each day. Private First-Class Lawrence Brooks, who was the oldest veteran of World War II, died on January 5, 2022, at the age of 112. Brooks had been drafted into the Army when he was 35. After his death, actor Gary Sinise posted a tribute on Twitter, and President Joe Biden called him "truly the best of America." Brooks was known as the last American man born in the 1900s decade, as well as being the oldest living man in the United States at the time of his death. He was laid to rest at the Mount Olivet Cemetery in New Orleans.

After World War II, November 11 was recognized as a day of tribute to veterans of both wars; then, in 1954, the United States designated the holiday as Veterans Day to honor veterans of all U.S. wars.

We now have around 18 million American veterans. They have survived World War II, the Korean War, the Vietnam War, the Grenada Invasion, the Gulf War, the War in Afghanistan, the Iraq War, and numerous other interventions and conflicts.

War can take a toll on those who serve. According to some statistics, veterans are at a 57% higher risk of suicide than people who have never served in the military. Nearly 4 million vets suffer from PTSD & depression, and 3.8 million have a service-related disability. About 40,000 homeless veterans are without a place to sleep on any given night. You've seen them walking the streets of our cities.

Hopefully, when we pause to think about those who served our country this Friday morning at 11 a.m., we will remember that many are still sacrificing and could use a little help. They put their lives on the line for us.

Turkeys are Infrastructure

Thanksgiving is upon us again, and during this time of year, a discussion about turkeys seems appropriate. A lot of doomed turkeys have been working on their bucket list lately, but two lucky 40-pound birds got off scot-free thanks to the pardon they received from President Biden last Friday. "Peanut Butter and Jelly were selected based on their temperament, appearance, and I suspect, vaccination status," Mr. Biden said in a ceremony held in a Rose Garden ceremony. "Yes, instead of getting basted, these two turkeys are getting boosted."

"Turkey is infrastructure," Biden continued as he stood with the birds. "Peanut Butter and Jelly are going to help build back the Butterball." Peanut Butter (this year's National Turkey) and Jelly (the alternate) heckled Mr. Biden during his eight-minute speech by gobbling loudly, showing little respect for the president nor appreciation for their pardons. The pair will live out the rest of their lives at Purdue University in West Lafayette, Indiana, once home to both Neil Armstrong and Amelia Earhart.

Presidents have been receiving these birds as gifts for many years, starting with President Lincoln, who didn't officially pardon one but told the White House to spare a turkey at the urging of his rambunctious son, Tad, who had grown fond of the gift. President Kennedy was given a live turkey with a sign hanging around its neck that read, "Good eating, Mr. President." Although he also did not officially "pardon" the turkey, he announced he would not be eating it. Three days later, he was assassinated in Dallas.

The official turkey pardoning at the White House began in 1989 under President George H.W. Bush, who pardoned "Liberty" and "Freedom," so named in the wake of the 9/11 attacks. There are always two turkeys, and they are always named in pairs, such as Mac and Cheese and Tater and Tot, all spared by President Obama. President Trump gave pardons to Drumstick and Wishbone, and later Corn and Cob. Most of us eat pretty much the same meal on Thanksgiving Day. I know this to be true because I see all the same dishes posted on Facebook every year. There may be some variations in the sides and in the dressing (or stuffing—think Yankee food), but we all generally stick to tradition.

Some vegetarians use recipes that call for "Tofurky," which is tofu "turkey." I imagine they generally don't go back for seconds, as most of us do. Y'all go ahead and help yourselves; I'll pass on anything that has tofu in it. And in some parts of Pennsylvania, folks call their dressing "filling" and mix it up with mashed potatoes of all things. I've even seen some so-called cooks add black olives to the mixture, thus ruining an otherwise delicious dish.

Eighty-eight percent of Americans eat turkey on Thanksgiving Day, which comes to around 46 million platters of the tasty bird. When Christmas rolls around just over a month later, we eat another 22 million turkeys for our festive meals.

You can cook a turkey in a slow cooker, an air fryer, or a convection or normal oven. You can also smoke it, deep fry it in a pot of peanut oil, or roast it on a spit as the Pilgrims did. It doesn't really matter. Turkey meat is delicious no matter how you cook it. White or dark.

The bird that graces our holiday tables each year is indeed a uniquely American species, native only to the Americas. According to a myth, the turkey nearly landed a spot on the Seal of the United States due to a suggestion by Benjamin Franklin, but he criticized the design of the bald eagle on the seal in a letter to his daughter, saying it looked more like a turkey than the majestic eagle.

There are some who say that, second to the sloth, the domesticated turkey is probably the dumbest animal on the face of the earth. The explanation is that they sometimes drown during a rainstorm because they just like to stare straight up at the sky while it's raining. Scientists say this is due to a hereditary condition called tetanic torticollis, which occasionally causes them to stare upward into space. Not necessarily looking at anything, just staring stupidly. I've seen people do that, also.

Then there are others who argue that turkeys are getting a bum rap. Even the name turkey is synonymous with an inept, slow-witted person and is a stereotype that needs to be changed in these days of equal fairness for all.

According to an Oregon State University poultry scientist who has studied turkeys for over 30 years, it's time the big birds get a little respect. He did agree that turkeys look stupid, especially when they're running. The scientist said, "I work with the animals, I talk to them, I observe them to be sure of their well-being and find out how they do when they are stressed -- you get attached to them. I'm an advocate for turkeys. Except on Thanksgiving..." No doubt.

Holidays Coming, but No Gifts?

Halloween is a holiday that all ages seem to enjoy. Especially the kiddies. But it seems some folks in a school district up in Michigan think the excitement children have over the scary holiday makes it difficult for them to learn, so their elementary schools won't be celebrating Halloween this year. They are concerned that some young children are overwhelmed and sometimes frightened of the costumes. They also said there are families that don't participate in the festivities, and it just isn't fair to them.

The school district wasn't only just spooked by Halloween; they also say that some parents don't feel comfortable with their children celebrating "love," so they're dropping Valentine's Day from their calendars as well. They say that while some students bring Valentine's cards to school, others do not, and it's an inclusivity issue that sometimes leads to drama and teasing. You know, like the way it is every day in any school. The district promises to offer other alternative days throughout the school year that are full of good, clean, fun, and learning. Other Michigan schools have joined the movement, and some are even eliminating Christmas observances. It's been a tough year for kids. I say let them have a little fun.

We didn't have much when I was young, but at least we always had some sort of Christmas. Our biggest Christmas was the year my old man went to the local thrift store and bought a bunch of used toys. Most were broken with missing pieces, but that didn't bother us one bit on Christmas morning.

My most memorable Christmas is remembered not due to any wrapped gift but because of a major butt whipping I received at 3 a.m. on Christmas morning when I was around nine years old in Oklahoma. Like all children that age, I took forever to fall asleep on Christmas Eve, and once I did, it was a fitful sleep; I woke up every time I heard the clock chime on the hour. Finally, I couldn't take it anymore and decided to sneak into the living room and find out what Santa had left for me.

Obviously, I didn't want to wake the rest of the family, so I grabbed a towel from the bathroom, which happened to be colored orange, and draped it over our only lamp before turning it on. With the crackling sound of rustling paper from me checking labels on presents combined with the orange glow emitting from the towel-draped lamp and reflecting on the hallway wall, my old man naturally assumed the Christmas tree had caught on fire, and our little wooden cracker box of a house was going to burn to the ground on the holiest day of the year.

Of course, he immediately leaped out of bed and aroused the whole family, running into the living room in his boxer shorts, shouting, "Fire! Fire!" I jumped up guiltily, holding one of my sister's presents in my hand while the rest of my family rushed in, and suddenly, I was in the center of a hostile group. I won't go into all the details of my punishment, but I will say I was the one chosen to clean the kitchen and dishes after the year's biggest and messiest dinner.

We all know once Halloween arrives, the countdown begins. And this year, there are fears that stress will be even greater than in previous seasons due to shipping concerns. Our network of ports and trucking companies moving goods around the world is in a mess, and the disruption to supply chains is getting worse, making products more expensive and causing shortages. We're used to shortages after more than 18 months of pandemic life, but now even Black Friday is at risk. This is problematic for retailers and holiday shoppers. Those in charge say pressures on global supply chains have not eased, and they do not expect them to change anytime soon. The latest problem is a terminal in China that has been shut down since August because one of its workers tested positive for COVID-19. The cost of moving cargo in a 40-foot container has climbed 360% since last year, sending consumer prices increasingly higher.

Our president recently announced that the Port of Los Angeles has increased its ship processing to 24 hours a day, seven days a week, to help ease the massive backlog. At the LA port alone, ships with nearly 500,00 containers, equaling about 12 million metric tons of goods, are sitting with anchors down, waiting for an open spot on the docks. The situation is the same in nearby Long Beach.

In Savannah, ships can be seen waiting to unload containers as far away as Tybee Island. Most of the containers are from China, filled with Christmas gifts just waiting to be bought. Personally, I think I'll check out what gifts are available from the local thrift stores this year. Like my dad once did.

Christmas in the Trenches

Christmas is supposed to be a time of peace on earth, but unfortunately, this has rarely been the case. Since 1776, the United States has been involved in war for 92 percent of its history, which comes to 225 Christmases out of the 245 years since our country's birth. We started it off with the Christmas of 1776 when General George Washington led his army across the frozen Delaware River on his way to victory in Trenton, New Jersey, surprising the British and reviving the cause of the Revolution.

Just before Christmas, on Dec. 23, 1777, while the Revolution was at its lowest point in the war, 12,000 soldiers, craftsmen, women, and children, marched with Washington to Valley Forge, Pennsylvania, without proper food, shelter, or clothing. Suffering from constant hunger and cold, 1,000 soldiers died from starvation and disease over that winter. Washington later wrote about the march, "To see men without clothes to cover their nakedness, without blankets to lay on, without shoes by which their marches might be traced by the blood from their feet, and almost as often without provisions as with, marching through frost and snow and at Christmas taking up their winter quarters within a day's march of the enemy..."

In keeping with the spirit of Christmas, the War of 1812, the war in which the British had the audacity to burn down our White House and other important government buildings, came to an end on Christmas Eve in 1814, when a peace treaty was signed in Belgium. Unfortunately for the British, it took nearly two months for news of the treaty to reach the United States. Meanwhile, British forces attacked the City of New Orleans and were completely decimated by inferior American forces led by General Andrew Jackson, 18 days after the signing. In the initial attack, which lasted a little more than 30 minutes, the British suffered around 2,000 casualties, while the Americans had roughly 70.

Christmases and wars came and went, and in the destroyed South during the later years of the Civil War, the presents were few, and many southern children went without. Some parents told their children the Union blockade was keeping Santa out, while others gave the excuse that Santa had been shot by a Yankee. For a Christmas present in 1864, President Abraham Lincoln was given the city of Savannah, Georgia, by General William Tecumseh Sherman, who had spared the city from fiery destruction after destroying everything else in his path during his march from Atlanta. In addition to the city, Lincoln was given 150 heavy guns and 25,000 bales of cotton and was extremely grateful for the yuletide gifts. He had a use for the guns, and I suppose the cotton could've been used in the manufacture of blue uniforms.

A Christmas miracle occurred at the outset of World War I on the Western Front. Fighting was so intense when the killing first began during the "War to End all Wars" that armies soon ran out of men and ammunition and breaks in the fighting would occasionally occur.

It was during one of these such lulls, five months after the outbreak of the war, 100,000 frontline French, German, and British soldiers began an unofficial impromptu truce resulting in widespread ceasefires and crossed into "no man's land" during the week leading up to Christmas Day of 1914 to share the holiday with their enemies.

The trenches of both sides were close enough that opposing soldiers were within earshot, some combatants were separated by less than 100 feet, and the truce amazingly began when some unknown British soldier shouted out to an unknown German soldier, "Merry Christmas!" and then suddenly an unofficial Christmas ceasefire went up and down the lines until by Christmas morning the racket of war was muted on the battlefields. No machine gun fire or the whiz of bullets. No grenade explosions. No screaming from men dying agonizing deaths.

Infantry troops of both sides mingled, chatted, and laughed with enemies like old friends, exchanging souvenirs such as buttons and hats. Prisoners were swapped, and burial ceremonies for infantrymen on both sides were held. They even played soccer on fields that, just hours before, were used for battlefields. Men who had been trying to kill each other stopped shooting long enough to sing a few Christmas carols. Even the artillery went silent after months of constant shelling.

Of course, you can't have a decent war with such goodwill towards men, so a few Scrooge generals put out orders forbidding fraternizing with enemy troops. There was also a young corporal in the Bavarian Infantry who opposed the truce: Adolf Hitler.

This Christmas, there are around 173,000 U.S. military personnel deployed worldwide in 159 countries, away from their families, protecting our freedoms on the holiest of days. And there are the homeless vets who once fought our wars, wandering the streets of our cities, and who are just as hungry and cold as those soldiers at Valley Forge. Remember them this Christmas Day.

Better Go Get Him, Boy!

Grandma can't reach her toenails.

Grandma Was a Mountain Woman

My grandmother was born with an unusual birth defect, which was having no toes on either foot. She was forced to wear high-top lace-up boots because shoes won't stay on your feet if you have only heels. They were always black. Nothing stylish for her. She would fill the boots' toes with rags, newspapers, or socks so they wouldn't flop around when she walked. Or ran. She once told me that when she was younger, she could climb trees and outrace the best of them. She married a moonshiner up near Ellijay who, oddly enough, had six fingers on each hand. This physical feature probably freaked out many eligible mountain bachelorettes but not my grandmother. I bet he would've been a heck of a fiddle player, but unfortunately, his art was making moonshine whiskey, and he ended up dying in a Gilmer County prison at the young age of 33 in 1943. He had a twin brother, my great uncle, who was killed in Atlanta at the age of 25 when his whiskey still exploded, but that didn't stop my grandfather from pursuing his illicit profession for even a second. It was the only thing he knew how to do to make money.

People can make a lot of money producing moonshine, but going in and out of prison can be expensive, and my grandfather died, leaving my grandmother penniless and with seven hungry children, ages from a few months to 12 years. She literally had nothing but a borrowed shack with a dirt floor. My dad was the oldest and had to drop out of school while in the 6th grade to become the man of the house. Three of my uncles, all in grade school, also had to drop out to help feed the family.

The family moved around to numerous places for a couple of years and even once lived in a shack in an abandoned chain-gang prison camp. The older boys did whatever odd jobs they could to keep the family alive, working for farmers and construction companies. My grandmother put in pitiful gardens; she scratched into the rocky earth. There were no fertilizers or chemicals, or fancy tools for her. She was lucky if she had a hoe.

Her fourth son died by electrocution when a bare electrical cable brushed across the top of his head while he was crawling beneath a building in Ellijay. He was doing construction work at only eight years old. Child labor laws existed in the Appalachians during World War II, but were largely ignored. Our family is still upset over this incident that occurred many decades ago. My Aunt Shirley says the supervisor of that project needed to be horsewhipped for sending that boy into those unsafe conditions.

Winters can be extremely harsh in the north Georgia mountains, especially for a starving family. After two or three years of pure misery, burdened with grief and six remaining children, my grandmother had to leave the mountains she loved and move south to yet another shack near Hiram. One that at least had the floor.

My older uncles and my dad had to keep working whatever odd jobs they could find, but she insisted the three younger ones stay in school until they graduated. To her and her three oldest sons' credit, they did. My father eventually joined the Air Force and became a technical sergeant and an educated man. My dad, uncles, and my aunt all did well with their lives and became respectable members of their communities, and their children have also done well.

This is being written while I'm sitting on the balcony of an amazing cabin next to the Cartecay River near Ellijay, just down the road from where a poor family nearly starved to death. They would have been amazed at the luxury I'm living in. I'm sure they would have considered me to be incredibly rich, which I'm not, by the way.

I miss my grandmother dearly. She was truly an inspiration and the strongest person I have ever met. Anytime I feel like I'm beaten down, I only need to think of what she went through and realize my problems amount to nothing.

We Rarely Travel on the Chosen Path

It doesn't matter your religion or even if you believe in nothing at all; we are all miracles. The odds of you being uniquely you are 1 in 10, followed by 2,685,000 zeros. There isn't a name for a number that high. If there is, I couldn't find it. This is also the best reason not to use your birth date as a Powerball number.

During the last 50,000 years, 108 billion humans have been born, and here I am, somehow alive during one of the strangest times in history, in the year AD 2020, in the unique position of being in the middle of Monroe County, Georgia, living on Lee King Road. Who would've thought such a coincidence could possibly occur?

The latest scientific studies show the Earth is 4.543 billion years old. The universe is constantly expanding and changing due to the Big Bang, which started it all, but no one seems to know who ignited that grand explosion. This is an extremely sensitive matter for some creationist proponents who claim the earth is merely 6,000 – 10,000 years old. I won't argue for or defend either side; I only know what I read online.

Scientists also say the universe appears to be almost 28 billion light-years in diameter. Past that, they don't have a clue. Probably just more universe, but maybe that's where Heaven sits, waiting for us.

Either way, somehow, everything has clicked perfectly into place, and now we have nearly 8 billion souls walking around messing it all up as only we can do. Our tiny planet went through a series of impossible coincidences millions of years ago and became the only life-sustainable planet (as far as we know) within this incredible vastness of space. Even the moon is positioned at the perfect distance. But that coincidence is just too great. Someone had to plan that one. Very few of us are where we thought we would be 20-25 years ago. Most of us are where we are due to a succession of unforeseen circumstances, fate, or coincidences beyond our control. We rarely travel down the path we planned. Life changes in an instant, and you do what you have to do on the day it is required. And this is where you ended up. Your life is the result of a series of causes and effects. Some of us are better off, while most of us probably think we are not.

A famous coincidence occurred on July 4, 1826, on our nation's 50th Independence Day, when two founding fathers, former presidents, and fast friends, Thomas Jefferson and John Adams, died just hours apart. Another founding father, after whom our own county was named, President James Monroe, also died on July 4, 1831. We should send up a special fireworks display at the Rec Center next year in his honor.

Strange presidential coincidences also occur between John Kennedy and Abe Lincoln. There is a long list of similarities between them, including that both were shot on a Friday, both were shot in the head, and both were shot in the presence of their wives. Lincoln's secretary, named Kennedy, warned him not to go to the theatre, and Kennedy's secretary, named Lincoln, warned him not to go to Dallas. Both of their successors were named Johnson.

A seemingly impossible series of coincidences occurred to Robert Todd Lincoln, son of President Lincoln. The first was when his life was saved when he was pulled to a train platform after falling onto the tracks next to a moving train, less than a year before his father's murder. His savior happened to be the brother of the assassin, John Wilkes Booth, Edwin Booth. He was also on the scene for two other presidential assassinations. In 1881, Lincoln was at the Washington railroad station with President James Garfield when a disgruntled office seeker shot Garfield in the back. He was also with President William McKinley when he was shot by an anarchist in 1901. Lincoln later wryly remarked that there was "a certain fatality about the presidential function when I am present."

There are some things that just can't be explained. I don't mean UFOs, ghosts, or Sasquatch. I'm referring to the incredible little coincidences that occur in everyday life. Like when you're thinking of someone and out of the blue, they give you a call. Or you can be thinking of a question and suddenly hear it answered on the radio, on TV, or from a friend. Or all the times you and someone else say the exact same word at the exact same time.

It's an interesting and incredible universe around us. I have no idea what life is about, and I doubt anyone else does, even if they claim they do. I have no clue why things happen. But it doesn't bother me; I'm just rolling with the flow.

The Cold Hard Truth About Lies

Everyone lies for so many different reasons, it's impossible to make a complete list. The most common motive for lying, of course, is avoiding punishment. Staying out of trouble is usually the primary motivator for big lies, regardless of a person's age. Like lies that help avoid a speeding ticket, even though you knew you were doing 84 mph, or telling the boss you had a flat tire. Most serious lies involve a threat of serious harm if the lie is found: the loss of a job, freedom, a relationship, a person's reputation, or even the loss of life. And even though they can't get in much more trouble, a person in prison who admits to their guilt is rare indeed. The lying never stops.

Other reasons for uttering untruths include protection of ourselves and others, maintaining our privacy, avoiding embarrassment, and common everyday politeness. For instance, we've all sat down before a plate of something we'd rather not eat, and yet when we're finished, we can't stop complimenting the cook on how delicious it was while praying we're never invited back to dinner.

The most common lie is the response we all give when asked how we're doing. "I'm fine" is rarely a truthful response from anyone. With all the craziness and bad going on in our lives, not to mention the day-to-day aches and pains, how can any of us be fine? And yet we smile and continue to do our best. Lying flawlessly when necessary.

There have been some whoppers told throughout history. Some that changed the world significantly, such as the one the serpent told Eve in the Garden of Eden, when he told her that she would not die if she ate the forbidden fruit, that her eyes would be opened, and that she would be like God, knowing good and evil. Since Eve wanted wisdom, she believed the serpent's lie, ate the fruit, and then gave some to her husband. And now we all return to the dust from whence we came.

One of the earliest lies recorded in American history was the claim that George Washington could not lie. Up until I was a grown man, I believed the tale of young George admitting to his father that he indeed cut down the cherry tree with his hatchet because he didn't have it in him to say something that wasn't true. I was quite disappointed to learn the story was a myth invented by a bookseller named Mason Locke Weems, who was simply supplying Americans' demand for facts about the great general after his death while making a few bucks on the side. The cherry tree story was only one of the myths published in Weems's biography of Washington, the first written about our first president.

Another falsehood most people still believe is that Christopher Columbus discovered America. We all remember that in "fourteen hundred and ninety-two, Columbus sailed the ocean blue" on his way to "discover" a new continent, even though he was one of the last to set foot on this land, 500 years after Leif Eriksson came here with a band of daring Vikings. Some scholars say there are signs that long before that event, travelers arrived in the Americas from China by boat, and it is highly possible that people came here from Ice Age Europe. But still, Columbus is the one with the big holiday, and cities, schools, and streets are named after him. And don't forget there were people already living here, which to me makes it a difficult place to "discover." There is currently a large opposition to Columbus Day because of the scores of indigenous people who were wiped out by diseases brought by early European settlers and were inflicted with war, colonization, enslavement, and torture. Some cities and states now celebrate Indigenous Peoples' Day in its place. And some places, like Chicago, have removed statues of the explorer after loud protests, while others, still believing the lie, are suing to have them brought back.

People often lie to themselves. We often say, "I'm entitled to one mistake." Not true. Everyone makes mistakes, but we are not entitled to them. Another is believing that "it can't happen to me." Yes, it can. Crazy things happen to ordinary people all the time. These events can occur at any time, anywhere. You can read about them every week in the incident report section of this newspaper. And young people carry the belief that they will live forever.

We were all raised to always tell the truth, but there are times when it's best not to. Like those situations when it's best to be polite instead. I know from life experience that it's impossible to be a gentleman and not lie. For instance, I know what to say if a woman asks me if a certain dress makes her look fat. The truth is that it's sometimes just common sense to tell a bald-faced lie.

A Gringo Gets in Trouble

At the time, I was pretty much by myself, recently divorced, living in Los Angeles, building movie sets during the day, and playing my guitar alone at night. There are many things to do in L.A., but I wasn't doing anything other than working.

Sometimes I needed a little help. In California, back in those days, if you needed a day laborer, all you had to do was go to any lumber yard and take your pick from the crowd of Mexican men always eager to work, standing at the edge of the parking lot. Anytime I stopped to ask for a man or two, eight or nine would leap in the back of my pickup, and I would have to eliminate those I didn't need. It was "pick and choose" back in the days when people wanted to work.

Immigration laws weren't as strict in the 80s, and employers weren't required to ask for proof of legal status, and it's possible that I might have inadvertently hired a couple of undocumented immigrants. It wasn't as big a deal as it is now, and rarely was anyone questioned on their immigration status.

I had a big project, and I went to load up my truck with as many laborers as I could carry to work with the carpentry crew. This time, they didn't run and jump in my truck as they usually did, but stayed waiting in the shade while one of the men sauntered up and asked how many men I needed. I told him all he had. He dropped the tailgate, the men loaded up, and he jumped in front with me. He said his name was Jesús, but he was known as Chuy. The men in the back were all related to him. Cousins, brothers, brothers-in-law. All migrants from Guadalajara, Mexico. Chuy was their spokesman because he was the only one who spoke any English at all, which wasn't much. He said that he came to the United States through a cut in a barbed-wire fence and then across the Rio Grande but had since secured a visa. He was sure proud of that.

Chuy and his crew were an exceptional team, and we became good friends. It was Christmas, and since I had no one to spend the holidays with, he invited me to spend Christmas Eve with his family. After that, I became inspired to learn my friend's language, purchased the local Mexican newspaper, and started looking up the words one by one in a Spanish/English dictionary, writing out the definitions ten times each. I got to where I could communicate with my newfound friends and became quite obsessed with their culture. Their music was beautiful. Their food was tasty. The señoritas are amazing.

One day, Chuy suggested that I go to Mexico to meet the rest of his family. The idea was intriguing. I was between projects with a pocket full of money, so I decided to go for it.

I found a cheap camper top that fit my truck and outfitted it with enough supplies for a month-long trip of a lifetime and headed south. I was ready with my old, bulky Canon camera that used 35mm film. The Mexican border patrol agents acted like they were happy to see me coming and excitedly waved me into their country as I barely touched the brakes.

It's 1,850 miles from L.A. to Guadalajara, and I took my time, meandering through the desert and taking what I considered amazing photos of adobe ruins. When I arrived in Guadalajara, the traffic was crazy, and nearly every intersection had a roundabout. After a couple of days of that mess, I learned that I could ride the bus anywhere in the city for only a nickel, so I took to using public transportation and became pretty good at it.

The Mexican buses were always crowded with people carrying packages and whatnot. And at the stops, there was always a horde, and people would push themselves to pack into an already overcrowded bus. It was part of the excitement of being in a foreign land.

One day, while standing in the middle of a crowd, the bus stopped at the curb, and I was shoved from behind into the back of a woman wearing a homemade skirt with a piece of elastic around her waist, holding it up. Somehow, the catch on my belt became entangled with the woman's skirt, and as she went up, her skirt stayed down. All I could see was white. She immediately spun around, thinking I had pulled down her skirt, and while pounding me on the head with her huge purse, she was calling me words I had never found in my dictionary. To free her skirt from my belt, I had to unlatch it, which caused her to think I was removing my pants, and the situation rapidly intensified. Somehow, I escaped her brutal blows and took the next bus, making sure this time, I stood at a safe social distance.

Crazy Happens While You Sleep

Over 70% of American adults report not getting enough sleep at least one night a month, and 11% say they are sleep-deprived every night. Americans of all ages from all walks of life suffer from sleep-related problems, including insomnia, restless legs syndrome, narcolepsy, and sleep apnea. A lack of sleep can affect every aspect of our lives, including our work performance, relationships, mental health, and ability to maintain our lane while driving.

For a motivated person with goals and deadlines, sleep can seem like a great waste of time, taking up a third of our already short lives. Considering this, I searched the App Store for sleep learning aids.

For $22.99, I found that I can achieve self-made success while enjoying a good snooze. Not only that, but there are also apps for learning to build my self-confidence, manifest love, boost my mental power, and, of course, learn another language with all the work done by my sleeping, unconscious, yet tired brain. I got excited and started imagining what I could achieve, all from the comfort of my own bed, sound asleep with Muchacho curled up at my feet.

Fortunately, before plopping down that kind of money, I had the good sense to do a little online research and discovered that while learning during sleep is undoubtedly possible, what we learn while we sleep is inaccessible while we are awake. I was so disappointed because it seemed like such a bargain.

But the human brain is never at rest, not even while sleeping. Now you might think that's an exhausting thought. Maybe you're a person who turns problems over and over in your mind while waiting for sleep, but then you hear, "Sleep on it. Things will look better in the morning." You roll your eyes when you receive this advice, and while you certainly don't want to wait until tomorrow, your brain does solve problems while you sleep. This is much better than getting up in the middle of the night to resolve an issue. You'll end up exhausted the next morning and still no closer to a solution. If you must get up in the middle of the night, there are better reasons.

More proof that our brains never stop is people who talk in their sleep. Sleep talking can involve complicated monologues, total gibberish, or mumbling. This is a common phenomenon, formally known as somniloquy, and is reportedly more frequent among young folks. But an old man rambling on while asleep is not unheard of. Sleep talking can come on at any time. It usually doesn't last long, and the one-sided conversations can range from a single unintelligible mutter to a long, hostile, angry speech peppered with curse words. Research has shown that people who talk in their sleep often shock their sleep partners with speech they would never use during waking hours. Scientists say swear words occur 800 times more often during sleep conversation than they would normally in a person's daytime discourse. A recent study found that in 10 percent of cases, sleep speech is rich in swear words and negative content. This may be because the outburst probably happened in response to a bad dream where anything goes.

If you ever wake in the morning and are shocked to find cracker crumbs, food containers, or candy bar wrappers in your bed, you may be experiencing a sleep disorder known as sleep-related eating. This is where sleepers get out of bed, make their way to the kitchen, and fix a little something to eat, all without waking up. That may be okay for skinny people, but for most of the population, not so much.

While sleep eating may be annoying, more perilous than overeating is sleep-driving, when a person slips out of the sack, grabs the car keys, and goes for a cruise on autopilot, completely unconscious of driving, oblivious to any danger.

Probably the best-known parasomnia (doing weird things while asleep) is sleepwalking or somnambulism. People who suffer from this disorder sometimes engage in very complex and dangerous actions. They may even appear wide awake to witnesses, suddenly sitting up in bed and looking around in a confused state of mind before slowly walking around the room. I've always heard to let them be, that it's not a good idea to wake them.

Sometimes people do other crazy things while sleeping. I include myself in this group and must take credit for inventing what I call "leaping while sleeping." I once took a leap from a top bunk in the middle of the night for no reason at all during the middle of some crazy dream. I landed face-first on the hard wooden floor and went to school the next morning with two blackened eyes, a crooked nose, and a busted lip. Of course, I caught up with my lost sleep during class.

Smile for the Selfie

Whether they admit it or not, a lot of people seem to be mighty pleased with their appearance. This is evidenced by the vast number of selfies I see posted daily. Of course, there's nothing wrong with snapping a group shot selfie when your friends and family are gathered around one of those large tables at Sol Tacos & Tequila on your birthday night. Those are treasured moments that should be posted for the world to see. Especially when the Taco Team shows up to sing a rousing chorus of "Happy Birthday" while you're wearing a sombrero, which is surely embarrassing enough to be put on anyone's Instagram account.

Some social media selfie posters will go to great lengths to draw attention to their well-timed poses. Sadly, sometimes these stunts lead to tragic ends. For instance, a 29-year-old pilot of a Cessna 150 and his musician passenger were happily smiling into the lens just before they crashed into the middle of a Colorado wheatfield on a dark, cloudy night. It was noted that the pilot had activated the flash, which may have improved the photograph but did little to help his navigational skills. You know how annoying that post-camera-flash blue dot in the middle of your vision can be. NTSB investigators said the camera didn't capture the looks on their faces during the crash itself.

And it's also never a good idea to take a selfie outside during a thunderstorm, as a man from Wales would tell you if he could. But he can't. His selfie stick acted as a lightning rod during his perfect pose, not only ending his life but also ruining the shot. Some people have become quite famous for traveling the world and posting pictures taken in extremely hazardous conditions or dangerous places. Recently, a social media influencer died at the young age of 32 after she tragically slipped and fell from a Hong Kong waterfall.

Fortunately, most people have survived the art of taking a selfie, like the San Diego man who survived being hospitalized for 5 days after taking a selfie with a rattlesnake that smiled for the camera before biting him. Adding to this lucky list is a woman who was gored by a buffalo while taking a well-posed selfie with the herd gently grazing in the background. I can only assume she was so fixated on putting the proper pout on her lips that she didn't notice a one-ton beast charging up behind her. She was treated for her injuries and released.

In 2014, which is known as the "year of the selfie," the United States Department of Transportation estimated 33,000 people were injured while using a cell phone while driving. People are charging down the road, talking, listening, texting, and taking selfies. An insurance group survey discovered that 4% of all drivers admit to taking selfies while driving. I would bet those are also the drivers who focus the rearview mirror on themselves rather than on the road behind them.

Around 100 million selfies are taken worldwide every day, with 82 percent of people aged 19 to 34 taking them. Some of them post up to 8 selfies a day. Many admit that every third photo they take is a selfie. Selfitis is the word used for this compulsive need to take a picture of your face. That seems to fit.

Although it may seem like a recent development, the selfie trend began in 1839, when a Philadelphia amateur chemist and photography enthusiast, Robert Cornelius, set up his camera in the back of a chandelier store and then stepped into the frame for the first-ever selfie. During the Gemini 12 mission in 1966, astronaut Buzz Aldrin took a famous picture of himself while floating around in space. The first-ever selfie beyond Earth's gravitational pull. Since then, NASA's Anne McClain took a 2018 selfie from 418 km above the Earth while on a spacewalk. The most popular location to take a selfie is standing in front of the Eiffel Tower.

An Australian man was celebrating his 21st birthday in 2002 when he got drunk and coined the word "selfie." After posting a photo of a stitched-up lip, he added the caption, "Sorry about the focus; it was a selfie." Only twelve years later, it was named Word of the Year by the Oxford Dictionary.

A female Celebes crested macaque, which is an Old World monkey that lives in the Indonesian Islands, grabbed a camera left behind by a nature photographer in 2011. The monkey, named Naruto, showed off her strikingly reddish-brown eyes by taking a selfie. The image was promptly placed in the public domain because the courts said a monkey cannot hold a copyright.

I'm looking forward to seeing y'all's smiling faces on Facebook on "National Selfie Day" on June 21, also the first day of summer. But you won't be seeing my monkey face smiling in the sun; someone might be using those photos for some secretive face recognition technology.

Never Snore While Snoozing in Church

Some people can sleep through anything, and getting sleepy in a church is not uncommon. Especially when it's warm, and the preacher drones on in a monotone voice, and you have no idea what he's talking about. I've caught myself catching my chin from bumping against my chest more than a few times while I suffered through those sermons.

In the little Oklahoma town where I spent my boyhood years, an old man we all called Old Jack was well known in the Tabernacle Baptist Church for sleeping through Sunday morning sermons while sitting next to his kindly wife Emmeline way up on the front pew. I think he sat in the front because he thought no one would notice he was passed out from the back. Everyone did.

He was a cotton farmer and would drive to church in an old beat-up Ford pickup truck, always wearing starched overalls over a white shirt. Emmeline never failed to pretty herself up in a fancy dress on Sundays and even used makeup, even though she was getting a little long in the tooth. They were a hard-working, good-hearted country couple and always made it to church, even on the Wednesday night prayer meetings. After all, Old Jack needed his rest.

It wouldn't take long after all the singing was finished, and there were no more calls to rise to our feet when Old Jack's eyelids would flutter for a couple of seconds and then slam shut. For the remainder of the service, he would be out like a light. Pastor Lemmon would step up to the pulpit and shout out his sermons, frequently punctuating his messages by slamming his Bible against the top of the lectern, but that never mattered to Old Jack. He would just sit there like a statue, getting in some good Z's. The deacons always used to mess with him after church, asking him what he thought of certain parts of the sermon, and he'd respond by quoting the scripture. He knew the deacons would never argue with any of the scriptures.

But even while in such a deep sleep, Old Jack always kept his head perfectly level and straight, sitting in a tight, erect position, and if it wasn't for his closed eyes, you would have never known he was snoozing. My grandma once made our family sit on the second pew directly behind him, and I watched a fly land on his neck, and he never once budged.

Not even a flinch, much less a swat, even after the fly went exploring down behind his collar.

Old Jack had already been comatose for a solid fifteen minutes one Sunday morning when Pastor Lemmon raised his old black Bible high over his head, looked up to Heaven, and suddenly ceased shouting his warnings of fire and brimstone. A hush fell over the congregation for a full two minutes as they contemplated a sinner's reward and were thankful, for they were serving the Lord.

It was during this lull in the preacher's rantings that Old Jack suddenly let out a loud, abrupt snort that was followed by a snoring that sounded like a train coming down the tracks. For the first time ever, we saw that his head was bent down, and his chest was heaving with every ominous wheeze. We had never seen him in that position before, and no one certainly had ever heard such a horrible racket. We all thought he might be having a heart attack, but when the poor, embarrassed Emmeline nudged him in the ribs, he immediately jumped to his feet, mistakenly thinking he had been called on to pray to the Lord on behalf of the Tabernacle Baptist Church.

He stood there in front of us and cleared his throat, with the whole congregation looking on, wondering what was going on. He then bowed his head and, in a bellowing voice, prayed loudly, "Dear Lord, I want to thank you for letting us come here today and…" He never got to finish his prayer because the congregation immediately erupted in a spontaneous shout of laughter, and there wasn't a dry eye in the Lord's House. Folks were sliding off benches and onto their knees, praying for relief. The choir ladies were holding on to each other, trying not to fall back into the baptismal pool. Even the stern Pastor Lemmon was gripping both sides of his lectern to keep from falling off the pulpit; he was laughing so hard. Meanwhile, poor Emmeline was sobbing as she tugged on Old Jack's overalls, trying to get him to sit back down, but instead, Old Jack swatted her hand away, turned around, and faced his fellow parishioners and quoted some verse from the Book of Revelations that went unheard. We were still laughing over the fried chicken at Grandma's house later on, and I was definitely looking forward to the next Sunday meeting.

Reunion on Burnt Mountain

Once a year, on the last Sunday of June, a large gathering of the Reece and Haygood families converges for a reunion on the top of Burnt Mountain, ten miles up a steep, curvy road from Jasper, Ga., which is well known as the First Mountain City. Usually, the day is miserable, with rain blowing across Sequoyah Lake and into the open shelter where mouth-watering covered dishes are spread across plastic tablecloths covering a 30-foot-long concrete table. Casseroles of every sort are always popular, each one including the required ingredient of a can of Campbell's Condensed Cream of Something Soup.

There is always a spot reserved on the table for a small wicker basket for donations to help with the upkeep of the old church and cemetery, and there's a book where we sign in and record the births and deaths that occurred during the previous year. This year, I sadly added the name of my younger brother, David, who died in early April. I turned back a few pages and found where I had entered my dad's name a few years ago. My father loved the reunions and always told me how important it was to make sure my children continued the tradition. Fortunately, my youngest daughter always attends.

The Reeces and Haygoods are distantly related by the marriage of distant cousins, and we all get along just fine, but the Haygoods always have their place at one end of the table and the Reeces on the opposite. Still, after a lengthy blessing said by an elderly member of the clan, we all shuffle around the table, loading up paper plates as friendly as we can be. Everyone then retreats to their usual locations, sitting in folding chairs grouped together by families next to the lake, chatting about old times with country cooking balanced on our laps.

My dad's youngest brother, Uncle B.R., always brings books and photos filled with family history. He is a proud expert on the subject and even more proud to be a Reece. I like to get him riled up from time to time by mentioning how much of a fan I am of President Abraham Lincoln, whom he considers our worst president ever, while I argue he was the best. He told me Aunt Mildred couldn't make it because of a medical issue I'd never heard of.

My Aunt Shirley is getting along in years now and has to use a walker to reach the grave of my Uncle Lesley, who has been cracking jokes with my old man up in Heaven for over a decade. I've always considered my Aunt Shirley to be the best cook in the mountains, but Cousin Yvonne had to cover for her mother this year. Her mama taught her well. Poor Aunt Shirley scolded me for not introducing her to my daughter, whom she has known since she was a baby over 30 years ago.

The Burnt Mountain Baptist Church was established in the 1850s, and, as far as anyone knows, the Reece Reunion has been held there every year since. My ancestors used to own the entire mountain, but now it's mostly divided up amongst folks from up North who stay in beautiful cabins next to a nice lake situated at 2,769 feet. Golf carts are a popular mode of transportation.

The church and the cemetery are all that remain of our family, and there is a danger that we may one day lose it all as the older ones pass away and the younger ones lose interest in family traditions. We feel that if we continue to maintain the church and grounds, pay taxes, and have meetings, no one can touch it. But every year, fewer and fewer young people show up for the reunion and Decoration Day held in October. Decoration Day is pretty much the same as a reunion, except it's dedicated to cleaning graves and tidying the cemetery. Real estate companies are licking their lips, waiting for the day they can get their hands on prime real estate.

In the cemetery lies Isaac Burlison, my great-great-great-grandfather, who died in 1856 and was reportedly the earliest settler on Burnt Mountain. Also in the cemetery are my numerous cousins, aunts, and uncles, including my grandfather's twin brother, who died at the age of 22 from a whiskey still explosion.

I never met my grandfather, who perished in prison at the age of 33, leaving my grandmother destitute, living in a dirt-floor shack with six hungry children. My dad was the oldest at 12 and quit school to become the man of the house. My grandfather was in prison for running moonshine.

There is a little spot just on the edge of the woods beside the old cemetery I've often thought would be a nice place to go when it's my time, but it'll probably be sold one day, and they'll just have to dig me up and plant me somewhere else.

Being Poor Has Its Upsides

Sometimes it can be good to be poor. If I had been born into a rich family, I might have missed the great pleasures of a bowl of pinto beans served with a slab of hot cornbread. I might never have learned to hunt or fish, not just for sport but for survival.

My dad might have bought me a late-model car if he had been blessed with a lot of money. Instead, he sold me a piece of junk Ford Pinto for $1 and taught me how to take it apart and put it back together again in excellent drivable condition.

If my parents had been wealthy, I would've been enrolled in some high-class private school and taught to conform to the "proper" way of learning. Instead, I became an independent thinker and gained most of my education through trial and error, learning from the same mistakes over and over.

Being poor as a child was a lot of fun on rare occasions. My two barefoot brothers and I never encountered any rich boys wearing high-dollar shoes when we spent the occasional Saturday afternoon having a great time in the junkyard of our little Oklahoma town: that's for sure. We never had the money to go to the Saturday-afternoon Western at the movie theater, but winning an imaginary race behind the wheel of a wrecked, parked car more than made up for it. My brothers and I never crossed paths with any kids from privileged families when we went on long hikes down long dirt roads, sometimes climbing on the backs of bored cattle

and having a mini rodeo of our own.

Cigarettes were only 25 cents a pack back then, but even at that price, they were way too expensive for three young, eager-to-learn-how-to-smoke poor boys. We learned the evil vice by rolling our own tobacco using whatever thin paper we could find. Maybe paper ripped from a page from a schoolbook or the local newspaper, which was always sure to send us into a coughing fit. No one in our group smoked fat cigars or those fancy marijuana cigarettes. I remember once we got our butts torn up because our old man caught us with his pipe trying out his Prince Albert tobacco behind his upholstery shop. Unfortunately, I turned into a pretty good smoker who now buys overpriced store-bought premium brand cigarettes.

If my family had had a bigger budget, I probably would never have gotten a job at 12 delivering newspapers, walking from house to house for the Altus Times-Democrat. I would never have had the experience of inhaling that wonderful smell of the ink as I stood at the loading dock of the circulation department waiting for my papers. I remember watching that huge, magnificent printing press churn out newspapers faster than I could count. And I would never have met those wonderful characters who lived along my paper route and who I now sometimes use as models in my stories.

One Christmas, my dad waited until Christmas Eve and had to rush to the thrift store to buy enough presents for his wife and six children. He had been working all day, and it was already late in the evening, but he made it into the store with just minutes to spare. His Christmas budget was tight, so he had to take his time to pick out things he could afford, keeping a running tab in his mind and dropping previously owned gifts into his basket as he went along.

The manager of the store locked the door behind the last remaining customer of the day, except for my dad, who was still pondering and doing his math in the toy aisle. My dad looked up from a baby doll he had picked out for my sister and saw the manager standing at the end of the aisle, arms crossed in an impatient stance. My father stammered and said, "I'm sorry. I had to work late. I'm almost finished. I know you want to get home. It's Christmas Eve."

The manager smiled at my old man and replied, "Yes, sir. It sure is. How many children are you buying for?"

My dad gave him the number, and the manager told him, "Look, I've had a really great year, and you're my last customer on Christmas Eve. You just take your time and pick out whatever you need, and take it home. No charge. Merry Christmas to you and your family."

Of course, my dad was a Reece man made of proud stock and refused the man's generosity. Instead, he gave the manager all the money he had in his pocket, which the manager reluctantly accepted.

That year, my present was a used rubber printing kit that was missing a few letters. Still, I was able to create my own little newspaper, which I filled with local gossip and sold to our neighbors for a mere 5 cents per copy.

Grandma Nash Was a Flapper

She lived through two world wars, the Korean Conflict, and the Vietnam War. During that time, she raised a son without a father, who became a Marine, and a daughter who became my mother.

Our cowboy president, Theodore Roosevelt, was in office when my grandmother Tettie Mae Nash was born in Oklahoma on Oct. 6, 1903. The first-ever World Series was played during the week of her birth, and just over two months later, the Wright Brothers took flight for a few seconds at Kitty Hawk.

When Grandma Nash passed away 84 years later, two days before Christmas 1987 in North Carolina, she had lived through 20 presidents, had seen a man walk on the moon, and had watched the Challenger explode over Florida.

She was born into the aptly named Greatest Generation and saw hardships few can imagine today. She told me she once escaped the Oklahoma dust, hitchhiked all the way to Chicago, and tried life as a flapper. For all you non-boomers, a flapper was a fashionable young woman during the 1920s who flouted conventional standards of behavior. She said it wasn't for her and soon returned home. I can't begin to tell you how difficult it is to imagine my grandmother as a stylish woman.

When I first met Grandma Nash, she was already ancient at 60. In all the years I knew her, I never saw her appearance change even a little. Hard work in the cotton fields had hunched her over and given her deep wrinkles on her face. She was prone to wearing shawls, homemade clothes, and old-lady stockings that always seemed to sag. She was so old-fashioned that she even made her own underwear by hand. I know this because my brothers and I used to throw them at each other when we occasionally saw them drying in the sun on her outdoor clothesline. She was stooped over and small, but she was mean and was quick to grab a switch and use it on my brothers and me.

When my dad married my stepmother, who eventually adopted his five children as he adopted her daughter, Grandma Nash came with the package. After my parents' marriage, she moved from Olustee, Oklahoma, a little town of less than a thousand inhabitants, to nearby Altus, where my dad was stationed at the local Air Force base. Always the dutiful son-in-law, my dad enlisted his three oldest sons (I was the eldest) to help haul all of grandma's junk to her new digs just a few blocks from where we lived.

It continued that way from then on. No matter where we moved, Grandma Nash was always close at hand. Whenever my old man found us a better place to live, he always made sure she had a suitable place nearby as well. He probably thought it preferable to have her living with us.

Grandma Nash couldn't do many things for herself, so my brothers and I would take turns staying the night with her to do her dishes and chores, like removing the pile of newspapers from beneath her bed, where she threw them every night after reading before going to sleep. The bad part about that job was that her big six-toed cat, whom she called Boxer, thought the pile of newspapers was a better place to use than a litter box. Grandma couldn't reach her toenails, so we took turns with the nasty chore of trimming them.

She was terrified of tornadoes. Many times, the sky would turn green, and my dad and I would rush to pick her up, bring her home, and hunker down in the backyard storm cellar. During one particularly active storm, I was helping her down the front steps to my dad's truck, where he was waiting with the engine running. It was raining so hard it hurt my skin. She suddenly stopped on the last step.

"My cat! You forgot Boxer!" I finally got her to the truck and ran back for her stupid cat. Lightning was popping.

I went inside, found Boxer, and just as I was struggling to lock the door with a huge cat in my arms, lightning struck a transformer directly across the street. The boom was enormous, and Boxer lost it. All 12 claws of his two front feet repeatedly slashed through my wet shirt, deep into my chest. Finally, he bounced off me and ran under the house, and I stumbled back to my old man's truck a bloody mess. When I got in and closed the door, my grandmother asked me, "Well? Where's my cat?" My dad took a puff on his pipe and said, "Better go get him, boy."

We left Oklahoma when my dad was transferred to North Carolina. He drove 1,440 miles in an old Oldsmobile packed with a wife, six kids, his mother-in-law, and her fat cat, who slept on his lap the entire distance. Still, he guided us halfway across our nation to do his duty to his country, his family, and Grandma Nash.

You Can Run, but You Cannot Hide

If Waffle House is closed, something bad must be going on.

The End Is Coming, but When?

If you knew the world was to end tomorrow, what would you be doing tonight? Putting panic and hysteria aside, you are left with three sensible choices: praying, making survival preparations, or partying like it's 1999. Nearly a quarter of the US population believes the world will end during their lifetime, so I am not alone in my concern.

Eight years ago, there was a widespread notion that the Earth's final day would occur on December 21, 2012. This date was chosen by ancient Mayans who studied astronomical alignments and complicated mathematical formulas and were able to create the "Long Count" calendar, which ended in 2012. The Earth was to end by being swallowed up by a massive black hole or by a collision with a mythical planet named "Nibiru." For some odd reason, a large portion of the population actually believed this prediction. So many that a Hollywood blockbuster named 2012 made a whopping $791.2 million that year.

Scholars and scientists dismissed these predictions of cataclysmic events. Mayan scholars insisted no Mayan accounts forecasted doom, but despite these assurances, doomsayers on street corners remained convinced the end was nigh. One wild-eyed man with long, unkempt hair said,

"I'm not really sure what nigh is, but I'm fairly sure it's coming."

Due to the popularity of this prophecy, early on in 2012, I created a temporary online store called 21dec2012.com. Embedded in the header of my website, there was a countdown clock ticking away the seconds to that dreaded day. The header background had an exploding planet.

I established accounts with drop-shipping companies, and in the left column of my home page, I had a selection of religious items. Crosses, Bibles, candles, etc. In the center column, I had everything you needed to survive any apocalyptic event. On the far right, I listed items that you could use to party down. Quite a few folks took advantage of my "End of Days Sale," and I made a few bucks. My party items far outsold the other two categories.

We've been hearing doomsday predictions all our lives. My first realization that we could go up in a ball of fire at any given second was while I was enrolled in Will Rogers Elementary School. We would practice ducking under our desks whenever we heard the big yellow siren blast its warning in preparation for the impending nuclear war. We never knew if it was a drill or the real thing. If it were real, the drills wouldn't have mattered anyway. It's entirely possible that one day we'll feel the same about the shields and masks kids are currently wearing to class.

My fear of nuclear fallout paled in comparison to the nightmares I would have on Sunday nights after listening to Brother Lemmon's fiery sermons from the Book of Revelation on Sunday mornings down at the Tabernacle Baptist Church. If the bomb didn't get us, I was sure the good Lord would. There didn't seem to be much to look forward to back when I was a boy, but still, we're here against all odds.

People have been predicting the end of time for a long time. I found nearly 200 documented doomsday predictions made by various groups and individuals since the year AD 33. Not surprisingly, 22 predictions for the Day of Reckoning have been made for the year 2020 alone. One of the earliest predictions of doom was for the year 100, as it marked 100 years since Christ's birth. When that date passed, it was changed to the year 133, which was 100 years after His death. Date revisions seem to be the norm for doomsday predictors.

A famous psychic, Jeane Dixon, prophesied the world would end on Feb. 4, 1962. Several Indian astrologers also believed this, and mass prayer meetings were held in India. When the world survived, she then predicted Armageddon would take place in 2020. I've yet to see her prediction posted on Facebook.

Notable predictions include one made by Camille Flammarion, who said that the 1910 appearance of Halley's Comet "would impregnate that atmosphere and snuff out all life on the planet," but the planet itself would remain intact.

"Comet pills" were sold to people who believed they were protection against toxic comet gases.

And then there was Mary Bateman's prophetic hen, which in 1806 began laying eggs on which the phrase "Christ is coming" was written. It turned out to be a hoax when it was discovered that the sly Mrs. Bates had written on the eggs with corrosive ink and reinserted the eggs back into the poor bird, after which the hen would re-lay the eggs before a patiently waiting audience.

Except for God, no one really knows when the holocaust will come, but as the old song goes: "It's better to burn out than to fade away."

Virus Scatters Homeless

On any given night across our great state, there are 10,500 homeless people sleeping in tent camps, under bridges, or in their vehicles. A few will secure a bed in a shelter, but during these scary times, a shelter may be more dangerous than sleeping outside. The beds are too close together. Privacy is minimal. Only a few have masks. Social distancing is much easier outside. After this great economic downturn, these numbers will no doubt rise. $1,200 will only go so far.

One definition of a homeless person is someone who has exhausted all his friends and family. But many factors can put a person on the street. Alcohol and drugs are high on the list. Most people think if they give money to that person holding up a cardboard sign, it will probably be spent on booze or maybe just one more hit. And the odds are high that it probably will be. Loss of income, domestic abuse, divorce, affordable housing, lawful eviction, post-traumatic stress disorder, foreclosure, fire, natural disasters, mental illness, and physical disability are other reasons a person can find themselves without shelter. The list is long.

According to the CDC, people who are homeless are at higher risk for severe disease than the general population. Many of these are older adults or have underlying medical conditions. It is difficult to follow stay-at-home orders when you have no home. There is no quarantine when you are homeless. Toilet paper is a small concern when you have no toilet. The places where they used to find bathrooms, like fast-food restaurants and stores, are closed. They cannot panhandle when the streets are bare. Soup kitchens are out of food and out of workers. It was tough to be homeless in 2020.

It can cost taxpayers up to $50,000 per year for each chronically homeless person on the street due to the costs of jailing them or putting them in treatment facilities, institutional care facilities, or hospitalization. I know quite a few folks who make less than that with roofs over their heads and food in the cupboard.

Early this morning, I went to visit some of these displaced folks to see how this pandemic has affected their already miserable lives. I found a small crowd waiting for a soup kitchen to open. That it would be a four-hour wait was no concern to them as they had little else to do.

I met a lady named Michelle. She was prettier than most homeless women. She said that her looks were her curse. She had spent the night walking the streets, trying to avoid a man who had been harassing her. Whenever she found a place where she could wrap herself in her thin blanket and try to sleep, he would wake her by trying to crawl under her blanket. She told me this happens frequently. I asked if she had ever reported any of this. She said that the police think she is a prostitute and have no pity. She said that it was cold last night and the night before. She has no checking account.

No mailing address. She does not expect a stimulus check. While a lot of us were waiting on our checks, she was just waiting for something to eat.

While I was speaking with her, a gentleman introduced himself as Hector, walked up, and asked if I had an extra mask. He said there was a job opening down the street, but he had to wear a mask, or they would not even talk to him. I was tempted to give him mine, but I didn't. It didn't seem sanitary. I'm so sorry.

Nearby was Jerome and his friend, who did not want to give me their names. They both looked like they had a hard night. These were old men. High risk and vulnerable to dangerous diseases. I asked them where they slept. Had they tried the Salvation Army? They said that the Salvation Army had been filled for weeks. So, they sleep wherever they can. In the woods. Under an overpass.

But the saddest of all was a little girl who I found sitting alone on a piece of concrete next to my truck as I was getting ready to leave. She was around nine years old, and her parents were nowhere to be found. She said she wasn't supposed to answer questions and wouldn't tell me her name, but she said she didn't go to school and didn't have a computer to do schoolwork. She said that where she used to live was locked, and now, she couldn't get in. She wouldn't tell me where she slept now. That was a secret she was supposed to keep. I went back to Michelle and told her about the little girl. She said that she'd keep an eye on her and tell the people who work in the kitchen. I told her I would call child protective services. That organization didn't seem to be in a big rush to address the problem, but they took down the information.

These people need help. These people need prayers.

A Waffle House Disaster

Late Friday night, I was at my keyboard when I suddenly had a craving for one of those delicious Patty Melts they serve down at the Waffle House on Tift College Drive. Oh, and throw in a side order of hash browns with cheese, please. Scattered, smothered, and covered.

Due to my skinniness, it's always too cold in Waffle House for me to sit at a table for too long, so my habit is to call in a take-out order and chow down at home while watching Perry Mason or Gomer Pyle on Me-TV.

So, I punched in Waffle House on speed dial and waited until I got the message I always get when they're too busy to answer. After five minutes, I tried again with the same results. By this time, I was too hungry to wait another 5 minutes, so I put a leash on Muchacho, and we jumped in the car and cruised over there. Imagine my surprise when I found my favorite 24-hour restaurant closed! Was there a disaster happening? I didn't receive a notification from my CodeRED app. It was eerie seeing a Waffle House closed.

I didn't even consider going to the one on North Lee Street because that one isn't my Waffle House. It's a fine restaurant as far as Waffle Houses go, but it doesn't seem the same to me. They don't know me there.

I sadly walked back to my car and let Muchacho out to use the grass next to the parking lot. While standing there, pondering the situation, I realized I was resigned to eating a bowl of Rice Chex because I sure as heck wasn't going to cook anything.

The next morning, I skipped breakfast, and by 2 o'clock, I started thinking about Patty Melts again. Thankfully, this time they answered the phone, took my order, and said that it would be ready in 10 minutes. Now that's what I like to hear. Muchacho and I again loaded up and took off.

Naturally, while paying for my order, I asked the lady what had happened the night before. She said that there hadn't been a natural disaster; the problem was that they had to close because they had no employees to work the shift. She said they had only two employees at that store, and the one on North Lee Street had only three, so to keep at least one store open, they closed shop. The two employees who went to work at North Lee Street were the complete crew.

She went on to say that employees are being offered a $100 bonus for any new employee they can get to sign on. I asked her if I showed up with a pickup load of applicants, how much would I get? She said she doubted I could find even one.

If a Waffle House is closed, there's something bad going on. They have a good reputation for disaster preparedness, and as a result, even FEMA uses a metric known as the "Waffle House Index." The restaurant is known for staying open in the worst of weather, and if they do have to close, they reopen quickly to serve the public. But this is an unnatural disaster that doesn't seem to be going away. The managers blame it on the stream of stimulus and unemployment checks. No one wants to work, and why should they?

Waffle House is an icon of the South and a source of pride for Georgia. The brand began on Memorial Day in 1955 in Avondale Estates, near Norcross, when two neighbors, Joe Rogers Sr. and Tom Forkner, opened a 24-hour sit-down restaurant for their friends. Their success came quickly because they focused on folks on both sides of the counter. There are currently 439 locations in Georgia.

Waffle House has its own lingo, like "scattered," "smothered," "covered", and "chunked," to name a few. You've heard these terms shouted out by servers. The cooks have a code using jelly and mayonnaise packets, pickles, cheese, butter, and hash brown pieces. For example, a jelly packet at the bottom of the plate signifies scrambled eggs. A pat of butter is a T-bone, and its placement on the plate determines how the steak is cooked, from well-done at the top to rare at the bottom.

Both customers and employees alike are loyal to the company. Many locations are manned by families, including parents, children, and their extended family. Employees say Waffle House not only gets in your blood but also in your genes, and you pass it down to your children. The company has a high employee turnover rate, but many who quit eventually return for the pay and benefits. Apparently, that isn't enough these days.

For the time being, Waffle House #809 offers only takeout service from 8 p.m. to 6 a.m. due to an employee shortage. That's fine. It's too cold in there for me anyway.

The Post-Pandemic World

We were living in prison without bars, trapped behind masks, looking for some path that led to escape, wary of our fellow inmates standing a guarded distance six feet away.

The strict rules we were given for our own good did little for the nearly 1 million Americans who succumbed to the horrible disease they said came from China. There were many of those who died who followed all their rules, and yet they are gone. While hiding in our homes, we wondered who would be next and whether it would be us.

I was lousy at following the Centers for Disease Control and Prevention's rules, which changed almost daily. How I survived the COVID crisis without becoming "tango uniform" (toes up), I'm not sure, but I'm certain the Good Lord must have had a little something to do with it.

You might have seen me in Ingles and Walmart, wandering around, wondering what happened to all the toilet paper, while wearing an 89-cent mask clinging to my face back in the early days of the pandemic, when face coverings were required. What you saw me wearing was very likely a dirty mask I dug out from behind the seat of my pickup, lying on the filthy floorboard, before going inside the store. I still possess a large collection of those particulate-filtering facepieces hanging from a hook on a hat rack in my house. I never saw the point in paying \$2-\$5 for one of those fancy N-95 jobs, and I have never purchased a fashion mask. Not even one emblazoned with a Georgia Bulldogs logo. If you want to know the truth, I never saw the point in wearing a mask at all. I know from experience using them while spray-painting and sanding sheetrock joints that they really aren't much good. No matter how snug my mask was, my nose always became extremely clogged by day's end. I also shelled out good money on a 100-count box of those latex gloves they said that we should wear whenever we were touching things, but I only used one, which I used to blow up and freak out my cat.

Not once did I go around with a chemical-laden sanitizing cloth, rubbing down every shiny surface in sight. I can barely wash my clothes and the dishes, let alone all that deep cleaning the CDC recommended. I'm sorry; I just don't have all that much OCD.

I didn't sing "Happy Birthday" while I washed my hands for 20 seconds, either. I must admit there were times when I didn't wash my hands at all because some of the sinks at many of the gas stations I frequent are much too nasty to touch. And I've never once included one of those handy little bottles of hand sanitizer along with the other junk I lug around in my pants pockets. And yet, somehow, so far, I've survived. Thank you, Lord!

I must also confess that during the height of the pandemic, my good buddies and I continued to shake hands as good buddies do, not doing that elbow bump thing because real men don't like bumping any part of their bodies on each other. Elbows are not excluded. And that foot bump was too much like dancing with each other.

The social distancing part never bothered me all that much, though. I don't mind it at all if y'all stay over there six feet away, not breathing on my back while we're standing in a long line of strangers waiting for some yahoo to decide this week's Powerball numbers. As a matter of fact, I wouldn't mind in most cases for the required distance to be extended to eight feet. The only downside is that it makes it harder to read the phrases tattooed across the necks of some of my fellow convenience store customers.

Because of my procrastination, it took me forever to get vaccinated. I was one of the last in line. Only after my doctor frightened me into rolling up my sleeve by telling me that if I caught the virus, I was sure to die, did I break down and find my way to those scary needles waiting for me down at the CVS. I also figured that after all the poison I've put in my body over my lifetime, I might as well put something into it that just might save my life. The shots never made me sick, thank you very much. Just like I didn't get sick when I received all those vaccinations with my fellow boot camp recruits at Fort Jackson, S.C.

It seems we are finally approaching the end of yet another difficult period in history. We can now travel, go out, go to church, get together, and party hearty, and I'm "school's out" happy about all that. Of course, I'm sure we're going to emerge from this pandemic straight into some new catastrophe. Well, I say bring it on. Airborne!

The Abnormal New Normal

The world we now live in is known as "the new normal." This means things that used to be accepted are no longer socially tolerated. Here is a list of things we may never see again, even after the pandemic scare is over:

• The handshake. The simple handshake is a tradition most of the world once shared. Now it has become almost a rude way to say hello, express gratitude, offer congratulations or complete an agreement. A little over a year ago, we were advised to use elbow bumps, fist bumps, the well-known high-five, or the ridiculous foot-tapping instead. Plain old foot shaking was also suggested.

Try to imagine President Joseph Robinette Biden Jr. giving a fist bump or a high-five to another world leader after signing an important, history-changing treaty. Somehow it doesn't seem to fit the occasion, but I'm guessing you can still easily imagine it. By contrast, President Theodore Roosevelt once set a record at a White House New Year's Day reception on Jan. 1, 1907, with 8,510 handshakes. We've come a long way in the White House.

When two people grasp each other's right hands and briefly engage their arms in an up-and-down movement, they are showing trust, respect, balance, and equality. Part of forming an agreement usually involves shaking hands at the end of negotiations, and the contract is not considered official until the hands are parted. Now I guess it's okay to just shake a leg and move on. No one knows what has replaced the secret handshake. That's being kept a secret.

• Dates. Blind dates and one-night stands are also on their way out. People are afraid that the person at the end of the bar might have a fever or have had contact with someone with the dreaded COVID. It's considered extremely risky nowadays to hook up with strangers. The coronavirus has succeeded where the danger of STDs never could. I've never been on a blind date myself, but I have been on a couple of dates that made me wish I were blind.

• Playgrounds. Those ball pits they used to have in fast-food places like McDonald's and other scary places haven't been seen in a long time, either. Even though they were fun for the kiddies, we all knew they were nasty long before the pandemic era. Kids slobber in those pits, and worse, for heaven's sake. Good riddance, I say.

• Buffets. Not surprisingly, some buffet chains have had to close because they couldn't muster enough cash to hire a staffer to handle the tongs and put food on plates, which is now the proper way to do it. I admit I still do the buffet line down at Shoney's on Hwy. 18 occasionally. The fried chicken is more afraid of me than I am of it.

• Birthday candles and microphones. Birthday parties also now have a whole new look. Our epidemiologists say that blowing out candles on a birthday cake can be risky and cutting that cake and passing it around to revelers can have devastating consequences. They suggest placing the candles in individual cupcakes, so each participant can blow out their own. Okay. Let's all take off our masks, give a good blow, and quickly put them back on before taking the next breath. Also, if you really must sing karaoke at your party, Lord forbid, make sure to wear a mask while singing and wipe down the mic between singers. They also advise us to go outside to sing "Happy Birthday," which poses an even greater risk than blowing out candles by spreading droplets that could carry the novel coronavirus. "Birthday spankings" are out of the question unless you use a six-foot-long paddle.

• The office. Working in an office has also become a thing of the past for many workers. Businesses have learned that they save money and stress when they allow employees to do their duties from home. Overhead is lower, and employees call in sick less often and are less likely to quit when they can work in their pajamas.

At the beginning of the year, nearly 42% of the American workforce continued to work remotely. Just a year ago, few of us had even heard of Zoom meetings, but now it's a part of our lives, however sketchy the technology may be. Even weddings, funerals, and city council meetings are taking place on Zoom. There are drawbacks, of course. More than once, an employee's scantily clad partner has been seen prancing in the background of some important business meeting with a cup of coffee and a piece of toast in their hands, unaware he or she was live on a webcam.

This "new normal" way of doing things is a direct result of our widespread fear of disease. None of us wants to get sick or die, so we must be fanatical for our species to survive. Please excuse me while I wave goodbye from a distance.

Hard To Resist the Lure of Lotto

Normally, I'm not a gambling man, but once that Powerball or Mega Millions jackpot starts creeping up to that billion-dollar mark, I can't help but give in to the temptation of greed and plop down $2 on a Quick Pick. Even though it's only one shot in 302,575,350, what's a $2 investment for a chance to be a billionaire? And that's when I start dreaming about what I'd do with all that loot: My closest friends and I would be residing at my new compound on the fabulous Isle of Steve. There will be a Trump wall encircling my luscious tropical island, and helicopters will bring in weekly supplies like toilet paper, hand sanitizer, and 2-piece snacks from the Big Chic. I won't be quitting my job, though. I'll be working remotely and taking my Learjet back to Forsyth on Tuesdays to help with proofreading.

But the chances are that fate will smile upon some lucky Yankee living in a trailer park somewhere up in Indiana, and their life will be forever changed. Well, probably not forever. According to reports, around 70% of all big jackpot winners eventually end up broke, and 44% of lottery winners will have spent all their winnings within five years. People get into more financial trouble after winning than they were before. If you don't play, you can't lose.

Nearly two-thirds of adult Americans gamble in some fashion or another. Playing the State Lotto is by far the most popular, at 49% out of nearly 140 million gamblers. Visiting a casino is a distant second at 26%. Only 10% have bet on a professional sports event. The common conception of gamblers as lower-income and less educated has been proven to be untrue. Gallup studies show that 47% of those with a high school education or less say they have purchased a state lottery ticket, while 53% of people with a college degree have shelled out money for tickets within the past year.

In Georgia, the retail establishment that sells a winning Mega Millions or Powerball jackpot ticket receives a $50,000 bonus, regardless of the prize amount. Winning stores also usually experience a spike in sales from new customers wanting to buy tickets from a lucky store. This has only happened six times in our state since Governor Zell Miller bought the first Georgia lottery ticket on June 29, 1993, and didn't win anything. Retailers receive a flat 6% commission on all Lottery product sales. Some think it isn't worth all the hassle. Nothing can hold up a line of customers like an indecisive lottery player.

The mission of the Georgia Lottery is "to maximize revenues for specific education programs," such as HOPE and

Georgia's Pre-K Program. They tell us that "as nearly as practical," 35% of proceeds will go toward educational programs. "Nearly as practical" can mean anything. They say $3.3 million (on average) is raised every day for the kiddies. You'd think that by now, they would all be walking around in the latest style of tennis shoes, carrying brand-new laptops, and having steaks for school lunches.

Alabama has no lottery due to religious objections. But the good Lord knows, when that jackpot gets close to a billion, a lot of our Alabama neighbors will say, "to hell with all that," and cross the state line to join in the fun with us greedy Georgia sinners.

Georgia is one of the states that requires big jackpot winners to disclose their identity. Only in eight states can you remain anonymous. If you're a winner in Georgia, your right to privacy will be gone. Information regarding the prize amount, name, hometown, and the store where the lucky ticket was purchased is easily available to anyone who's interested in hitting you up for a few bucks. After a required news conference, you'll be all over the news, and you will suddenly be meeting relatives you never knew you had. Your friends and friends of friends will all be hitting you up for a share. There will be no escape from all the needs and greed. Even the people you thought loved you deep down will turn into vampires. It would be hard for me to say no to a distant cousin who says he can't work and he's about to be evicted along with his wife and four kids.

Even so, I'm still going to throw away $2 every few months when the huge jackpots roll around. It is true that money can't buy happiness, but it's gotta be better to be unhappy and rich than to be unhappy and poor.

My Ride Along with Cpl. Justice

One of my duties at the Reporter is to pull news from the Monroe County Sheriff's incident reports in the "Cops and Robbers" section of the paper. Twice a week, I'm sent reports typed out by deputies, and I rewrite in layman's terms exactly what happened. Some reports are easier to decipher than others.

While writing the reports, I'm often amazed at what our deputies go through. So I decided to find out firsthand and filled out the necessary paperwork for a ride-along. A few days later, I was told that Cpl. Jacob (Jake) Justice would meet me in front of the sheriff's office on Saturday at 9 a.m.

I was advised not to bring my weapon, and I felt a little underdressed when I showed up that morning.

"Fiat justitia ruat caelum." This is a Latin phrase meaning: "Let justice be done though the heavens fall." These words are on a sign above the entry doors at the Monroe County Justice Center. I know the meaning of this phrase because I had time to Google it while waiting for my ride-along. After 30 minutes, I called dispatch, and they said Cpl. Justice was on a call and would be there soon. I later learned he had been responding to a call regarding the death of an elderly woman in her home. Sadly, death is something deputies must deal with often.

A few minutes later, he stepped out of the front door and said, "Let's go, Mr. Steve." I was ready and excited. I've known Cpl. Justice for a few years due to my stint down at the Rumble Road BP. He would sometimes stop in for a can of dip, maybe something to drink on a hot day, and we'd chat for a moment or two, and we became friends. He always wanted to know if there were any problems and if everything was ok with the store. We always felt safer when deputies drove through our lot.

Justice was born and raised in Monroe County, graduated from Mary Persons, and joined the sheriff's office in 2013. He said that law enforcement is his life's work and that he considers himself fortunate to have found his calling so young. I consider us all fortunate to have him working in our community.

He led me around the building, and we entered through the side door of the complex using the special passkey that he waved over a high-tech reader. As we walked down a long corridor and past the evidence room, I got a good whiff of what must have been an enormous amount of evidence stashed away behind a heavily secured door. Halfway down the hall, we entered a small office where the deputies typed out reports. I immediately recognized the form.

Deputy Dalton Mosely was working on an accident report and had a question for Justice regarding the incident. The corporal pondered for a couple of seconds and came up with the answer. Done deal. I was impressed from the start.

With the possibility that a court hearing or trial may take place, I'm forbidden to discuss details of any case or incident in this column for obvious reasons. They even made me sign a form saying I wouldn't, but you can always read about what went down in our "Cops and Robbers" section.

Justice told me he had to catch up on his own reports, but he barely had started typing when his radio squawked, and he informed me we were on our way to a domestic issue in the southern part of the county. We quickly loaded up into Justice's patrol vehicle, joining his K9 partner, Gustaw, who had been waiting patiently. Justice calls his dog "Goose" for short. I don't have to tell you how smart Goose is. I am convinced he even knows the police codes. I could barely understand a word that came over the radio, but when he got excited, I knew something was up.

For my own safety, regulations said I couldn't get out of the patrol unit during a call, so Goose and I would wait while Justice stood in littered yards, surrounded by irate residents, and somehow calmly and patiently settled issues without anyone being arrested. After a few minutes, we were on patrol again.

Other than another domestic squabble and a couple of traffic stops, the day was pretty much uneventful until near the end of his shift, when Justice received a call of an accident involving a fatality on Hwy. 41 just outside of town. It was a horrible thing to see, and I had trouble getting it out of my mind when I went to bed that night. I can only imagine how many nights Corporal Jake Justice and his fellow deputies have had the same problem.

Printed Newspapers Are Worth It

ere we are, well into the year 2020, alive and well during the digital age, and yet in nearly every convenience, grocery, or drug store, you can still find a Reporter sitting in its old familiar rack. It catches your eye with its bold headlines as you wait patiently to pay for your diet drink and chips, standing in line six feet back behind an indecisive lotto player. You have an impulse to buy one. But you don't. Why would you? You get all the news off your phone.

Not entirely true. You might be reading it, but you're not getting it. According to studies, people read digital formats faster but with a major loss in comprehension. Some studies say you retain up to 49% more knowledge when reading in print as opposed to digital formats. Speed is usually associated with skill, but this isn't always the case. You may glean the main idea from the digital text, but absorb fewer details. Maybe we should all slow down and smell the ink.

Our generation has been hearing about the demise of printed newspapers since the invention of the Internet. Some of us may remember the same thing that was predicted with the invention of television and, before then, the radio. Old Walter Cronkite was rather good, but apparently not good enough. Facebook is interesting and fun and has its place, but you can't touch it. You can't feel it. You can't hold it in your hands, raise it to your nose, and smell it. Thank goodness for that.

If you come across an interesting article on your phone and you want to reread it later or maybe show it to someone, you must bookmark it. Personally, I've done this maybe ten times in my life, and not once have I ever used any of those bookmarks. I don't even know where they are without a search. It is nearly impossible to revisit where you've been once you have left a post and moved on. If I want to show you something interesting in the Reporter, all I need to do is turn to the Incident Reports page, and there it is.

We live and learn digitally in the 21st century. It's obviously cheaper to use computers in the classroom than those expensive, bulky books I used to have to lug around. Now, even kindergarten students have laptops on their desks. Most two-year-olds are highly skilled with their mommy's phone. I've seen them sit contentedly in their baby seats, moving those cute little animals through obstacles quicker than I ever could. This seems to keep them quieter than that old nasty pacifier they used on me to shut me up.

There is no denying that the newspaper industry has taken a beating. Advertisement revenues are down. Circulation has dropped drastically while delivery costs have risen.

Craigslist has all but wiped out classified advertising. Hundreds upon hundreds of hometown newspapers have vanished. Leaving a void in our culture. Hopefully, some will be able to recover after the economic lockdown.

I have hope. Newspapers have been in this country since their first appearance in Boston in 1609. Even that little paper was suppressed. Its publisher was arrested after only one issue. People in the newspaper industry have always been hardworking visionaries. Guardians of our right to free speech, and without them, this country would not be what it is. Help support this tradition and buy a hard copy of the news occasionally. It's still only a dollar. (Note: The Monroe County Reporter is now $2 a copy due to rising inflation, etc.)

Social Distancing at Home

On March 11, 2020, the World Health Organization (WHO) declared the novel coronavirus (COVID-19) outbreak a global pandemic, and the whole world got all weird and went into hiding. We are still living with the extraordinary inconveniences that have become a part of our daily routines. We are experienced with Zoom meetings, mask-wearing, and extra hand washing.

We can't go out, and even if we could, there's nowhere to go because so many businesses have closed. We've spent a long time in lockdown, and being of a curious and nosy nature, I decided to research what y'all have been up to behind all those closed doors, and I am more than just a little bit shocked.

I found in my Googling that some couples seem to be making a little more love than usual due to all the extra time at home with nothing much else to do. Back in the day, we mainly just played Monopoly or sat on the couch watching TV when there was nowhere else to go. That just goes to show TV programs were much better back then.

An online poll of 1,200 participants conducted from May 2 - May 22 showed a strong increase in COVID-induced sexual activity, with 54% of surveyed couples reporting they were being more adventurous and spending more time in bed. There has been an increase in sales at adult stores, along with a strong growth in the demand for dating apps. There has also been a 30% spike in pregnancy test sales.

For a lot of couples, sex has proven to be an excellent way to make the lockdown more bearable, not to mention more enjoyable. 44% of these frisky folks say they must make love more quietly so as not to disturb housemates.

Well, that's considerate. Who wants to listen to all that racket?

It's not all fun and games for everyone, though. Familiarity can breed contempt, and a little bit of some people can go a long way.

Around 32% of couples say the heightened stress from the lockdown has led to more arguments and fights with their partners. Also, of those couples isolated, 19% aren't having any sex at all. Even further isolate themselves by sleeping alone in separate bedrooms.

By April of last year, people thinking about divorce had already increased by 34%. Surprisingly, newlyweds are the most likely to file for divorce.

It has now been ten long months since the WHO announced the pandemic was in effect, and many speculated a large crop of new babies would be showing up last month. They were disappointed since there will be significantly fewer newborns this winter and for the rest of 2021.

Social distancing has forced some romantic partners (but not many) to avoid cuddling and the things that go with it. Financial pressures and childcare issues have led many families to delay having kids.

According to the experts, there has been a decline in both planned and unplanned pregnancies due to the coronavirus pandemic.

The baby boom idea is based on popular urban myths about birth spikes that happen nine months after major electricity blackouts, hurricanes, and blizzards.

But after studying statistics, I found these stories were exactly what I thought they would be: myths.

But the COVID-19 pandemic has become much more than a temporary stay-at-home order. It has led to widespread economic loss, uncertainty in the future, and insecurity. Therefore, birth rates are declining.

If there is a "silver lining" to the COVID-19 pandemic, some consider it to be that many babies' lives have been spared due to the fact that several Republican officials and anti-abortion advocates argued that abortion should be considered non-essential, leading to orders in several states prohibiting the procedure so that medical resources such as personal protective equipment (PPE) would be preserved.

Of course, human rights groups and several medical organizations released statements criticizing the restrictions.

Other procedures, such as elective dental work, were also suspended.

Of all pregnancies, only 62 percent end in a live birth, 16 percent end in a miscarriage or stillbirth, and sadly, 22 percent end in abortion. Of the over half a million teen pregnancies in the United States in 2011, 75% were unintended. Unplanned pregnancies are the leading cause of abortions.

Even so, unwanted pregnancies continue. The government says sexual activity without the use of contraception is the primary cause of unintended pregnancy. Fears, anxieties, stress, and isolation all come with unplanned pregnancies. This rate has also spiraled to an all-time low.

I've always wanted to ask my parents if my birth was an accident. Since my mother was barely 17 years old at my birth, I'm sure they were quite surprised to learn I was on my way. I like to think I was the result of an accidental pregnancy. It's the first trick I ever played on someone and probably my best.

You Can Run, but You Cannot Hide

As I go through the weekly process of converting the Incident Reports and Arrest Summaries from the Monroe County Sheriff's Office into news stories, one thing stands out: the frequency of fleeing incidents. During the week of April 27 through May 3 alone, there were seven separate chases reported. All told, there were 70 pursuits involving our deputies last year.

The common denominator of most of these cases is that the offender gets caught. Usually, they don't have experience handling a vehicle at high speeds and eventually crash into a guardrail, another vehicle, or end up upside down in a ditch. Sometimes these crashes are caused by a P.I.T. maneuver (pursuit intervention technique). The police car rams into the rear of the fugitive car, sending it spinning out of control and crashing to a stop. Occasionally, these wrecks end in tragedy. There were only three reports of drivers escaping deputies in Monroe County last year. Two of the fugitives were driving Dodges, a Charger, and a Challenger. According to carmaker Dodge, a Charger has a top speed of 204 mph. The other escapee was piloting a 2019 Mustang GT 5.0, hitting speeds of 170 mph. He got off the interstate, turned right onto North Lee Street, and went through town at 140 mph. FPD officers quickly gave up, but Cpl. Thomas Haskins stayed hot on his tail until the runner vanished somewhere near Lamar County.

Running from the law is an American stereotype. From Steve McQueen's famous 1968 chase in "Bullitt" to O.J.

Simpson's real-life slow-speed pursuit in Los Angeles in June 1994. The bad guys always think they can get away, but the police keep catching them.

Police have tools that go beyond firepower and horsepower. They often throw spike strips to flatten the tires of a fleeing vehicle. Sometimes, they box in a suspect with a rolling roadblock, where police vehicles move into the suspect's path and slow down to stop the suspect. Roadblocks aren't used often due to the obvious risk of injury to officers and damage to equipment. The technique requires officers to position themselves in front of a fleeing suspect, and police vehicles are used to block the oncoming offender.

The Bureau of Justice Statistics revealed that from 1996 to 2015, over 7,000 deaths were from fatal crashes in police pursuits. That's an average of about one pursuit-related fatality per day. From 2014-2018, fifty-six percent of people killed during police pursuits were someone other than the fleeing driver.

Some of these folks were fleeing vehicle passengers and police officers. Many were innocent people minding their own business in uninvolved vehicles or pedestrians just walking down the road.

In 2020, there were 68,000 vehicle pursuits nationwide. Atlanta Police Chief Erika Shields announced a year ago that her department would adopt a zero-chase policy effective immediately. Shields said, "The department is assuming an enormous amount of risk to the safety of officers and the public for each pursuit, knowing that the judicial system is largely unresponsive to the actions of defendants." She went on to say, "When I look at our greatest successes, it's not through our car pursuits."

In October, after Monroe County deputies chased an Air Force cadet who wound up being killed near Rumble Road, Sheriff Brad Freeman told the Reporter that he thinks the increase in fleeing incidents is a direct result of the refusal of certain leaders across the U.S. this year to enforce the law and bring them to account. "We've basically got a political party that condones breaking the law," said Freeman. "These criminals are not in a bubble. They see the news and what's going on. They see a party that's not gonna enforce the law, and it emboldens them to break the law."

There is a nationwide debate about whether police chases should end altogether. I think it's scary that a criminal knows he only needs to run to probably get away with a crime.

Another problem on our local streets and highways is the high number of DUIs. In 2020, 159 people were taken to

Monroe County Jail for being too plastered to operate an automobile. Keep in mind, these are the drunks who got caught. Around one million drivers were arrested in 2016 in the United States for drunk driving. That comes to less than one percent of 111 million self-admitted alcohol-impaired drivers.

Mothers Against Drunk Driving (MADD) was founded on September 5, 1980, by a California mother whose daughter was killed by a drunk driver. Forty-plus years later, even after widespread media coverage against drunk driving and increased laws and penalties for the offense, there are a lot of drunks still weaving down the road. Some of them will even make an alcohol-influenced decision to flee a police officer.

It's dangerous out there. Y'all be careful.

Riding Night and Day

Springing ahead and falling back.

Time Is on Our Side, or Is It?

The first American alarm clock was created by a 26-year-old clockmaker known as Levi Hutchins in 1787. His clock was a timepiece with an alarm that went off only at 4 a.m. There was no way to change the alarm time, and it was set at 4 a.m. because that was the time Levi put on his boots every morning, which was way too early for respectable roosters. Fortunately, "daylight savings time" had not yet been invented, or he would've been getting up late half the time. Levi was just 14 when he was present at the Battle of Bunker Hill while serving as a fifer in the Revolutionary War.

It was nearly a century after Levi's ingenious creation before the familiar windup alarm clock would begin to replace roosters. Seth Thomas, whose company created the famous clock at Grand Central Terminal in New York City, patented his adjustable clock in 1876. People used to get up at the crack of dawn and work until dark thirty. Along with factories with time clocks, Seth helped change all that. In defiance, proud roosters to this day continue with their God-given duty to welcome the day.

In modern industrialized America, nearly all of us rely on alarms. Researchers report that 85 percent of working people use an alarm to wake up on time for work. They never mentioned what the other 15 percent use. Today's wake-up alarms aren't like your daddy's old noisy alarm clock, though. Americans used to wake to bells clanging each morning and usually knocked the annoyance to the floor while trying to shut off the racket. There was no snooze button. It was rough then as it is now, but back then, we got up to dawn streaking through the window and birds chirping outside, and we eventually got moving and feeling pretty good about the world. Now we shut off our phone alarm, then hit the snooze button a few times, and finally check the news. There's never any good news, so then we go to Facebook or wherever. Not much good on those sites either, and before our feet even touch the floor, we're already in a bad mood. When we wake, we quickly grab our phones to see what new meme slogans, harsh accusations, and fighting words have been added to our pages during our few short hours of oblivion. No wonder people are tussling on planes. And now, just in time to make people even more grouchy by adding yet another change to their lives, it's "fall back" time. This is the opposite of "spring ahead," thank goodness. I like "fall back" better for that extra hour of sleep that I usually appreciate only on the first day. By the second day, I'm already used to the time change and back to my normal grumpy self. It takes me a bit longer to readjust in the Spring.

Benjamin Franklin started all this daylight savings time (DST) nonsense as a joke in a satirical letter to the editor of a French publication in 1784, suggesting that if Parisians got up earlier in the summer, they would not use as many candles and thus save a ton of francs. He also proposed taxing window shutters, rationing candles, and waking the public by ringing church bells and firing cannons at sunrise in the satire.

The first to use DST were residents of what is now Thunder Bay, Canada, who turned their clocks ahead by one hour on July 1, 1908, thus starting the world's first attempt to squeeze an extra hour out of a day. In the United States, it was introduced in 1918 by a Pittsburgh industrialist who called it "Fast Time." His idea didn't last long at first; only seven months later, it was repealed, then later made a strong comeback.

Most of my clocks will reset themselves back an hour at 2 a.m. this Sunday and ahead an hour in the Spring without any help from me, and I guess the clocks on my stove and microwave are easy enough to correct, but my body has its own clock that it likes to follow. I can't just turn a little knob and suddenly be in sync with whatever new time the government says it is.

It has been found that "springing ahead" and "falling back" can have serious consequences on our health. One study has found that the risk of having a heart attack increases during the first three days after a switch to DST. There are also more traffic accidents and workplace injuries on Mondays following a time change, and losing an hour of sunlight in the fall can trigger mental illness symptoms. They call this "seasonal affective disorder" (SAD), otherwise known as winter depression.

There is a growing movement around the country to make DST permanent. So far, 19 states, including Georgia, have enacted legislation or passed resolutions to provide for year-round daylight saving time. It seems that whoever first came up with the concept of clocks was off by at least an hour.

Back to Mayberry

In the year 2020, we have a surplus of trouble and a deficit of solutions. Back in the 1960s, we merely had the Vietnam War, antiwar protests, a slew of political assassinations, hippies, and the "generation gap." Times were simpler in those days. It was a sweeter place.

By the time 1960 rolled around, I had already accrued three younger brothers and a sister. With five unruly brats, my worn-out mother always made sure we were tucked into bed by 7 p.m., and many evenings she'd have us in the sack even before the sun went down. I was never sleepy at that early hour and would amuse myself by tying knots in a string or counting the number of blades on the Venetian blinds my mother closed to simulate nighttime. Then she'd relax, watching black-and-white TV with my old man.

Back then, 7 p.m. was when the best TV shows aired, such as "Lassie" and "The Rifleman." My favorite was always "The Andy Griffith Show," which premiered on a Monday night at 9:30 p.m. on Oct. 3, 1960.

Even though it was well past my bedtime, every Monday evening, I would wait to hear that familiar whistle during the opening credits. I'd creep out of bed and sneak down the hallway with my skinny little legs dangling from loose-fitting, worn-out whitey-tighties and peek around the doorway at the show behind my folks' backs. I once nearly got busted when I snickered out loud at one of Barney's antics, but I quickly ducked back. My dad thought the cat sneezed.

Tonight, I'm sitting at a table in the kitchen of Andy Griffith's mother, writing about her son while spending the night in his boyhood home. When Andy lived in this little house at 711 East Haymore Street, in Mount Airy, N.C., from the time he was in the first grade until he graduated from high school, it had only two rooms. He had to sleep in this very kitchen next to a pot-bellied stove. The small family had an outhouse out in the backyard, but I found no sign of its former location. I assume they bathed in the kitchen sink. The house is now a pleasantly remodeled bed-and-breakfast you can rent at any time except for the week of Mayberry Days, when it has been booked for the next 17 years by some Hollywood bigwigs. Griffith more than doubled the size of this house for his parents after he moved to California. They eventually moved out west to be with him.

Mount Airy is an interesting town, but don't expect it to resemble Mayberry because it doesn't, even though there are numerous references to the town's street names, places, and even people in several "Andy Griffith" episodes. For instance, Pilot Mountain, with a beautiful state park just down the highway, became Mount Pilot on the show.

There is a section of town with a Mayberry set that has the courthouse, Darling's place, and Wally's gas station. The sheriff's Ford Galaxy, used as their squad car, is there and available to rent for a tour of places like where Andy went to church and where he learned to play the trombone. The last stop on tour was at Andy's house, and the driver told me he had never been inside, so I gave him a little surprise when I unlocked the front door and took him on a little tour. The car is also a nice prop for a photo in which you can pretend like you're being arrested by Deputy Fife.

Mount Airy is also home to many notable people besides Griffith, including Donna Fargo, a country singer, and Anna Wood, a well-known television actress. Betty Lynn, who played Barney's girlfriend, Thelma Lou, made her home there and, until the Covid-19 pandemic, made monthly appearances signing autographs at the wonderful Andy Griffith Museum. She also takes part in the annual Mayberry Days weeklong event held in September.

After touring the United States and Europe performing in "freak shows" during the nineteenth century, the original Siamese Twins, Chang and Eng Bunker, amassed considerable wealth and settled near Mount Airy, living in two houses after marrying sisters and fathering 21 children between them. Their first two children were born within six days of each other. It must have been quite the honeymoon. Today, over 200 years after their birth, their many descendants from all over the world gather there once a year for a large reunion.

When Andy Griffith passed away, he was quickly buried on the grounds of his home in Mateo, N.C., within five hours of his death. I thought this was odd and a bit too soon, but locals explained he wanted no fanfare and few tears at his graveside. Isn't that just like the Andy we loved?

A Call to Greatness

There are striking similarities between now and 100 years ago. A century ago, the Spanish Flu, or H1N1, took the lives of 50-100 million people worldwide. Of those, 675,000 were American citizens who now lie mostly forgotten beneath crumbling headstones. This is more than five times the total number of American soldiers who died during the four years of World War I. The death rate for Spanish Flu was 10 percent worldwide.

On April 29, nearly 60,000 U.S. citizens succumbed to coronavirus. This number is 12,000 more than the total number of soldiers who died during the Vietnam War. Experts estimate a death rate of 1-3 percent for the coronavirus. This is due to research and modern healthcare. The public policies in place then and now are almost identical. During the Spanish Flu pandemic, state health officers advised local officials to close schools and local citizens to avoid large gatherings, and as the disease progressed, so did the government-imposed measures. The disease put a stop to political campaigns, rallies, and stump speeches. Churches and schools were closed. Photographs from that era show worried citizens wearing masks, fumigating public transportation vehicles, and sheltering at home. They, too, were told to wash their hands and not touch their faces.

During the 1920s, for the first time in history, the number of Americans living in cities exceeded the number living on farms. This caused a considerable cultural backlash. Popular trends shifted away from religion and ruralism toward entertainment and pleasure. People were listening to Jazz and going to movies. Movements began for the equality of minorities and women. Women gained the right to vote in 1920. Many people started to hold more liberal views on sexuality and drug use.

Now it is more difficult to define the boundaries of our cultural war. We have more of a generational divide than a geographical battlefront. Older generations get their perspective through television and film, while the younger generation turns to digital media. There is still a rural-urban divide on the political landscape, but with modern technology, that line is fading with each succeeding election. And still, women and minorities are fighting for equal rights.

I will not even mention our views on sexuality compared to those of a hundred years ago. I will leave you to your own.

The passing of the 18th Amendment caused the ban on the manufacture and sale of intoxicating liquors on January 29, 1920. We all know alcohol did not go away; it went underground. Transporting and selling hard stuff was handled by criminal organizations, as well as prostitution and gambling.

Today, recreational marijuana is legal in 11 states, with 22 states saying it is okay for medical purposes. More states are expected to follow suit with this year's elections. Even though 55 percent of its citizens support legalization, Georgia is not on this list. Transporting and selling marijuana in Georgia is controlled by criminal organizations. There are seven generations of Americans alive today.

The oldest is known as the Greatest Generation, whose members were born between 1901 and 1927. The youngest are now well into their 90s. They lived through the Depression, fought in the Second World War, and built this country into the richest and most powerful in the world. The youngest generation, known as Generation Alpha,

are those born from 2010 to 2025, largely children of Millennials. So far, they have lived through a technological revolution and, more recently, the coronavirus pandemic.

The oldest and youngest generations have a lot in common. Knowing some of these young people, I have faith they will also overcome impossible odds and possibly become even greater than the Greatest Generation, but they must make good use of what has already been built for them.

From Pony Express to Porch Pirates

If I were able to travel back in history, I would set the date on my time machine to April 3, 1860. I'd then put the GPS on St. Joseph, Missouri, and after landing in another world just before the Civil War, I'd apply for a job as a Pony Express rider. An advertisement in a St. Joseph newspaper at that time supposedly read, "Wanted: Young, skinny, wiry fellows not over eighteen. Must be expert riders, willing to risk death daily. Orphans preferred". Sign me up.

To be a rider, you couldn't weigh over 125 pounds, and at only 114 pounds, including my belt buckle, I could easily fit that requirement. The average age of the riders was around 20, but if I could go back in time, I'd make myself a little younger while I'm at it. The youngest rider employed by the company was reputedly only 11 years old. The oldest was 45, who not only rode but also worked as a station keeper. The famous frontier showman William "Buffalo Bill" Cody claimed he served as a Pony Express rider at the age of 14, but it is believed he was stretching the truth when he wrote about his adventures in his autobiography. But truth or fiction, he epitomizes the legend of the Pony Express.

Riders were paid a rather handsome sum for the time, receiving up to $150 a month ($5,023.16 in today's dollars) for riding a galloping beast nonstop for 75-100 miles a day. During emergencies, they would have to pull a double shift and ride 20 hours without stopping. I'm not sure if they received overtime or bonuses for beating deadlines.

They rode day and night and delivered mail from St. Joseph to Sacramento, California, or in reverse in just ten days. A feat many said was impossible before being proven wrong by the brave young riders who became heroes and icons of the American West.

The route was 1,966 miles long, with stations every 10 miles for riders to change horses. At some riverbanks, riders would dismount to swim across to a fresh horse waiting on the other side. They dealt with extreme weather conditions, hostile terrain, and the always-present threat of attacks by bandits or Indians. It has been documented that during the 18-month existence of the organization, four riders were killed by Indians, one was found guilty of murder and hanged, one died in an accident, and two froze to death. Station keepers had an even more dangerous job as they were sitting ducks for any bad guys that happened along.

The opening of the transcontinental telegraph on October 24, 1861, signaled the end of the Pony Express. Sending a telegraph was much cheaper and a whole lot faster than even the fastest ponies, and the delivery service rapidly became outdated technology. Sadly, the Pony Express completed its final delivery two days later, on October 26, 1861.

In this age of same-day delivery, we take for granted the packages that are delivered directly to our doorsteps. Men in brown shorts, or maybe USPS final-delivery agents, rush up to our front doors, dropping off something we ordered the night before while drinking a cup of hot cocoa. Soon, drones will be taking over a lot of these deliveries. Amazon Prime Air says it is "committed to making our goal of delivering packages by drones a reality." They say they can deliver packages up to 5 pounds in 30 minutes or less using small drones. I can easily imagine porch pirates hiding in the bushes, knocking package-loaded drones out of the sky with a marble or a rock loaded into a slingshot. Seems less risky than sneaking up to someone's porch, where there's a chance of being seen by a homeowner's Ring camera.

Package theft has become a huge problem, especially during this year's holiday season, when online sales are expected to reach $207 billion. Twenty billion parcels were sent during 2020, and a survey reported that 43 percent of Americans have had a package stolen. Law enforcement suggests using a pickup locker where available or giving special instructions to hide the package behind your house or under a bush. Another suggested idea is to have packages delivered to a place where people are present. Also, security devices and cameras are extremely helpful to police investigators.

Even with these safeguards, your package might not make it to your porch. Just last month, a property owner in Blount County, Alabama, discovered packages strewn about his land. A 22-year-old former subcontractor for FedEx later admitted to dumping 400 packages into a ravine five separate times between Nov. 17 and Nov. 24. After days in the weather, 247 packages were undeliverable due to being unscannable or without a legible address, messing up people's Christmas to the tune of $24,700. A Pony Express rider would never have done something like that.

The Forgotten Art of Hitchhiking

Enter a southbound on-ramp of I-75, and you might see a person holding up a cardboard sign, hitchhiking their way to a better life. It's rare that someone will stop and give this person a ride other than a deputy or the GSP. These are scary times, and giving a stranger a ride is not advisable unless you are a Lyft or Uber driver, that is. The commercialized version of hitchhiking.

These drivers are not taxi or limo drivers who are required to carry a Class B Carrier Certificate. They're just regular people with a valid driver's license who passed a background check and own a smartphone. No special training is required. We're taught it's dangerous to catch rides with strangers, background checks or not, but we think nothing of getting into their cars because other people give them good reviews.

Hitchhiking was once common. During the Great Depression, hordes of out-of-work people were searching for opportunities, and those with automobiles often stopped to help a fellow who was looking for employment. After World War II, many servicemen traveled from bases to visit their families using the cheapest means possible: their thumbs.

And then, when the 60s arrived, hippies across the nation were thumbing their way to rock festivals and San Francisco, spreading peace and love. This hippie fantasy of cooperation faded in popularity during the 80s, as people became more self-interested. The economy was good, and suddenly everyone had transportation. Those without vehicles were the homeless who stood in the way, and no one had the time to stop and give them a lift.

Hitchhiking is legal in the United States except for five states, provided that the hitchhiker is not on the road itself or hindering traffic. Hitchhikers can use on-ramps, sidewalks, and shoulders, but not interstates. A 1974 California study found that hitchhikers or drivers were not disproportionately likely to become crime victims, but some local governments have outlawed hitchhiking in the interest of public safety.

Although hitchhiking originated in the United States, the practice is worldwide. In Cuba, it is mandatory for drivers of government vehicles to pick up hitchhikers if space is available. People wait in designated areas to be picked up on a first-come, first-served basis. On May 4, the price for a gallon of gas in Havana was $3.03, which seems like a deal to us, but to the average Cuban citizen who makes only $43.66 a month, it's astronomical.

When I was just fourteen, I was ready to take on the world and did a little hitchhiking myself. My dad had recently been assigned to Pope Air Force Base in North Carolina, and we lived in base housing on Ft Bragg. Early one cold morning, while everyone was sleeping, I put on a sweater, grabbed my guitar, slipped out the back door, and headed for the West Coast, ready for stardom.

I soon discovered what it is to walk for miles, stumbling in roadside gravel with semi-trucks sending blasts of cold wind down my neck. I experienced the disappointment of running to a stopped car only to have it drive off just as I caught up. I know the fear of having a carload of yelling rednecks chasing me into a ditch.

My first night on the road was very cold, too cold for just a sweater, and in the darkness, I noticed I was standing across the road from an auto salvage yard. It was late, and there was no fence, so I found an old, wrecked pickup and crawled in for sleep. Lying on the seat was an old, torn coat that fit me perfectly. Not only was I cold, but I was also starving, and when I stuck my hands in the pockets of the coat, I found a candy bar. The Lord was watching out over a young boy that night. Looking back, the most surprising thing is that even though I was only fourteen years old and looked much younger, I was never stopped or questioned. No one asked who or where my parents were. No one cared; I wasn't in school.

It took me a little over two weeks until I hitched to western Oklahoma, and I thought it would be cool if I stopped in to visit my best friend, Kirk, and show off a few new chords, but Kirk's parents were aware that I had run away and were waiting for me. Soon, I was in Jackson County, Oklahoma, jail behind bars as a runaway. The big man's jail, as there were no juvenile facilities in that area at that time. My guitar and I were incarcerated for two weeks while my old man requested time off from his company commander and drove 1,384 miles to bail me out and take me home. I know this to be the exact distance because I received a good butt-whooping for every mile marker we passed along the way.

The Hard Life of a Poor Sharecropper

The life of a sharecropper wasn't much of a life, but it was the only one available to many poor Georgian folks for nearly a hundred years, from Reconstruction until the 1960s. When African Americans were finally freed after the Civil War, many ex-slaves took off in search of new lives, but an even greater number had no idea of where to go when they were told they were free to do whatever they wanted, whenever and wherever they wanted to do it.

At the same time, the former slave-owning landowners suddenly found themselves with hundreds of acres of land with no one to work it. And with the destroyed economy, there was no money to pay the people now referred to as "freedmen" and "freedwomen."

From this troublesome dilemma was born sharecropping and tenant farming, which effectively replaced the bondage of slavery with the yoke of serfdom for both blacks and whites alike. The landowners supplied workers with housing, often no better than dirt-floor shacks, tools, and seeds, to the people who toiled in the fields from daylight to dark, from planting time to harvest time, with no assets of their own and burdened with the need to feed their families. After the crop, mainly cotton but also tobacco, rice, and sugar, was brought in from the field, the landowner would claim from one-half to up to two-thirds of the harvest as his share and always kept the upper hand in the business relationship.

From the tenant farmers, who provided their own upkeep and tools and thus received a greater share of the crop and were considered slightly higher up on the social ladder, deductions were made for things the landlord had supplied them with, so that they could survive during the hard months. Also, merchants selling food and clothing to the tenants and sharecroppers would extend their credit and then place liens on their anticipated crops to secure their debts.

It has been estimated that the average tenant farmer paid an annual interest rate of 59% in 1880. Contracts were renewed yearly, but since the workers were perpetually in debt to the landowners and merchants, they had no legal choice other than to sign that piece of paper year after year. Also, landowners would often threaten not to renew the lease at the end of the season, applying even more pressure.

Landowners forced workers to grow crops that generated profits, and the land was too valuable to allow most sharecroppers to have personal gardens for their daily food. This created even more business for the greedy merchants. It was considered an exceptionally good year when a tenant farmer or a sharecropper broke even.

Sharecroppers' children were taken from their schools to assist in growing and harvesting cash crops, and few had. Owen, the track-and-field athlete who embarrassed Hitler by winning four gold medals and breaking two world records at the 1936 Olympics in Berlin, was the grandson of slaves and the son of a sharecropper. As a child, Owens was often sick with chronic bronchial congestion and pneumonia, but still, he was expected to help his family by picking 100 pounds of cotton a day at the age of seven.

Although sharecroppers were largely African Americans after the Civil War, by the Depression Era, two-thirds of the impoverished workers were white, and both groups were considered about as low as you can go socially. Sharecropping peaked in the 1930s, and the practice began to decline as workers left rural areas for industrial jobs in cities. Some became migrant workers whose lives were even more miserable. John Steinbeck's famous story "The Grapes of Wrath" is the tale of a family of sharecroppers who were forced to leave their home in Oklahoma during the Dust Bowl years and head for the Promised Land in California, where they were exploited even more. Many southern families joined others in the backs of packed work trucks traveling from farm to farm across state lines as the seasons advanced, following the crop. Once common, migrant workers have now declined in number, making up only 5% of farm employees.

Sharecroppers formed a union in Alabama in 1931, with an initial membership that was exclusively African American. The union, known as SCU, demanded the continuation of food advances and the right to sell their surplus crops directly to markets rather than relying on the deals the landowners made. They also demanded the right to grow their own food.

By the 1960s, sharecropping and tenant farming had largely disappeared from America's fields, although it has been reported that a small number of Georgia farmers still toil under the miserable conditions of a tenant arrangement.

The Youngest Soldier

The Civil War should've been named the "Boys' War." During the conflict, between 250,000 and 500,000 underage soldiers were enlisted in both armies. There were 100,000 boys under the age of 15 marching off to war in the Union Army alone. After the fall of Fort Sumter, President Lincoln initially asked for 90-day enlistments, but after the Yankees were driven out of Richmond and the Rebel Army set its sights on Washington, D.C., Lincoln called for 300,000 volunteers to enlist for three years.

Young boys on both sides of the conflict were eager to join up. The Northern boys thought it their duty to discipline the South, and the Southern boys joined the Confederate Army to repel the Yanks, whom they considered to be hostile invaders. Boys on both sides saw the war as a chance to escape boring life on the farm, and all had visions of marching back home as heroes.

In 1861, the minimum age to enlist was 18, but it was easy to fool recruiters who needed to meet quotas, especially given the war's urgency. The easiest way to get around the age requirement was to lie, and many recruiters turned a blind eye even when it was obvious that some boys hadn't even reached puberty. Some underage recruits wrote the number "18" on the soles of their shoes so they could honestly say they were over 18. Other underage boys were able to join up with the endorsement of an adult. If a boy's father vouched for his strong work ethic and shooting abilities, he was in.

Forty thousand non-combat positions, such as buglers and drummers in the Union Army alone, were filled by young boys who signed up legitimately. Other positions included assisting surgeons with wounded soldiers and carrying stretchers into the battlefield. They also would relay orders, and some even picked up rifles alongside grown soldiers.

These boys suffered during the war as much as their older counterparts. Food was always scarce, and at times the boys would sneak out of camp to gather berries or steal crops from nearby farmers.

This practice was frowned upon at the outset of the war because it violated one of the Ten Commandments, but as the war dragged on, it became clear that stealing from the enemy weakened it and thus helped the cause. Usually, the commanding officers forbade foraging even though they shared in the spoils of war.

It didn't take long for the excitement of going to battle to diminish for the young soldiers. Camp life was boring, and marches were long and dusty, and after experiencing the horrors of war, their fantasies of glory quickly faded.

The youngest of these brave troops, David Bailey Freeman, hailed from Georgia. He was born in Ellijay in 1850, one of ten children of well-to-do, religious, and prominent citizens of the community. His brother, Madison Freeman, was a patriotic Southerner and became a lieutenant in the Confederate Army even though he was burdened with the debilitating disease of phlebitis. Madison wasn't sure if he would be able to serve with his disease and asked his mother's permission to take along young David as his aid, and they ended up at Camp Felton, near Cartersville, where David enlisted in the 6th Georgia Cavalry on May 16, 1862, barely two weeks after his eleventh birthday.

He began his military career serving under "Fighting Joe" Wheeler and saw action at Resaca, Kingston, Cassville, and

Kennesaw Mountain. And he was even with General Joseph E. Johnston when General William Tecumseh Sherman took Atlanta. When the war finally ended for the boy (Johnston surrendered on April 26, 1865 – the same day John Wilkes Booth was killed), the boy was barely a week shy of his 14th birthday.

When Freeman turned 21, he began a newspaper career as the editor of the Cartersville Courant, which he bought only two years later and renamed the publication to Cartersville News. A few years later, he also bought out the Cedartown Advertiser. He eventually also owned the Cartersville Courant-American newspaper, which he renamed the Cartersville News.

In 1875, when he was 24, he met and married Callie Dudley Goodwyne, whose great-grandfather was a minuteman in the Revolutionary War. Callie was born in Forsyth, Monroe County, Georgia, in 1857.

The following year, Freeman was elected mayor of Calhoun, and his first son was born. He went on to become the mayor of Cedartown and Cartersville. His writing career included co-authoring "The Wizard of the Saddle."

The Civil War's youngest soldier died from a heart attack at the age of 77 in his Atlanta apartment on the evening of June 18, 1929. His body was taken by train to Cartersville, and David Bailey Freeman answered his last muster call to his place in Heaven.

Nancy Hart, Frontierswoman

She was a big, muscular woman who stood six feet tall, with cross-eyes glaring out from a face scarred by smallpox. Her bright red hair was piled high above a woman not known for her beauty but rather for her temper, bravery, and her passion for getting even with anyone dumb enough to offend her, her friends, or her family.

She was born as Ann Morgan sometime around 1735, either in Pennsylvania or North Carolina, and some say there's evidence she was related to the famous frontiersman Daniel Boone. When she got older, everyone called her "Aunt Nancy." She became Nancy Morgan Hart when she married Benjamin Hart at the ripe old age of 36. She never had formal schooling and couldn't read a word, but she more than made up for it by learning everything about how to survive on the American frontier. She had extensive knowledge of the healing properties of herbs and plants and was a skillful rifle hunter, despite her wild eyes looking in all directions.

Back in those days, if you wanted to experience the frontier, all you had to do was move to Georgia. In the case of Nancy and Benjamin, they chose to settle beside the beautiful Broad River in Wilkes County in 1771. There was no doubt she was the undisputed boss of the family with two daughters and six sons, and often managed the family farm while her husband was away fighting the British during the Revolutionary War.

While her husband was away, Mrs. Hart managed their farm, but she would often sneak off to spy on the British. Dressed as a man, she would enter British camps pretending to be feeble-minded but would overhear and steal information, which she handed off to the Patriots. Hart also engaged in combat during the war and may have been present at the Battle of Kettle Creek on February 14, 1779, a brief battle in North Georgia that lasted only four hours, in which Loyalists to the king suffered around 300 casualties and the Patriots lost only about 32 men. It is also believed by some that with her shooting skills, she served as a sniper, picking off Tories as they made their way across the Broad River.

With such a reputation, the British naturally kept an eye on the patriotic woman. Once, a Tory was spying on her family through a hole in a wall while Nancy was making a kettle of lye soap. After her daughter alerted her to the soldier in their yard, she took a ladleful of the boiling-hot soap and tossed it into the spy's eye, scalding him. He was turned over to the Patriots after the women tied him up.

Her most well-known feat was when five or six British soldiers showed up on her farm, killed her last turkey, and then made the mistake of demanding that she cook it for them. While she was cooking, she did the polite thing and passed around her corn liquor, getting the redcoats smashed. While they were enjoying themselves, gorging on turkey and getting drunk, she sent her daughter to get some water and told her to use a hidden conch shell to signal their neighbors of the British presence. She then began sneaking out the weapons they had stacked next to the door through a hole in the wall.

She was able to sneak two weapons outside, but then was caught red-handed holding the third, so she threatened to shoot them all. One of them stupidly made a mad rush at her, and she shot him dead and wounded another, who also made a sudden move. The remaining soldiers quickly surrendered. When her husband finally returned, Nancy was still holding the Brits at gunpoint. Legend has it that they, along with their neighbors, hanged the soldiers from a nearby tree. The neighbors and her husband wanted to shoot them, but Nancy insisted on hanging. Adding credence to the story, six bodies, believed to be those of the soldiers, were found buried near the Hart home in 1912 while construction crews were grading a railroad site around a mile from the old Hart cabin. The necks of a few of the skeletons had been broken.

Nancy Hart and her husband moved to Brunswick, where he died around 1800. In her grief, she wanted to move back to the banks of the Broad River, but sadly, her cabin had been washed away. She then moved to Henderson County, Kentucky, to be near one of her sons until she died somewhere around the age of ninety-three.

It is impossible to know how much is true about old Aunt Nancy. Rough-hewn in appearance and mannerisms, she wasn't much to look at, but she more than made up for it with her fierce American patriotism. The local Native Americans knew her as "Wahatche," which translates into "War Woman." Hartwell, Georgia, and Hart County to the north of Elbert County were named for her, as were Lake Hartwell, Hartwell Dam, and Hart State Park.

A 400-Year Span of Monroe County

As I was hanging out on the Square this past weekend during the Bicentennial Celebration, I started imagining how my surroundings must have looked 200 years ago. The Creek Indians had been living here for hundreds of years and had left the area in pristine condition when General McIntosh of the Creek Nation signed the Treaty of Indian Springs, which caused their rapid eviction. Soon afterward, many walked the Trail of Tears to Oklahoma.

Standing on the corner of West Johnston and North Jackson, I could visualize standing in the middle of thick woods with a special kind of beauty. Such beauty would cause the earlier settlers of Monroe County to chase away all the animals, cut down the woods, and carve out a square in the center of the new county. For a moment, I felt sad that they had removed what had been here since the dawn of time, but then I raised my gaze to our amazingly beautiful courthouse. The earliest citizens of our area had a vision, and as I looked around at my friends, neighbors, and a whole lot of strangers, I was proud that they were celebrating that vision. I felt as if I was standing in the middle of something important. And when I heard Tony Orlando was coming and the governor showed up to give some speeches, I had no doubt this was a big day. Real big.

And then I started thinking about how the streets and buildings surrounding the Square might look 200 years from now. After the job Larry Evans and his crew of Monroe County workers did on remodeling the courthouse eleven years ago, we can all rest assured the most beautiful courthouse in the State of Georgia (and I dare say the entire country) will still be admired (and in use) in the year 2221. I also feel confident that, with interest in history among our local citizenry, the other beautiful structures standing in the shadow of the clock tower will be preserved. When I look to the future, I see everything in downtown Forsyth will probably be pretty much the same. The major difference is, of course, that instead of gas-burning cars driving around the block looking for a place to park, there will be autonomous vehicles hovering over the Courthouse, waiting for a vacant landing pad.

There are also many other historic homes and structures throughout the county that are so beautiful and full of history that I just know will be well preserved for many generations to come. Well, I can hope, can't I?

Of course, I'm less sure about the future of the areas that border the interstate. Who knows what commercialism will bring? The new QuikTrip they're rushing to build on Harold G. Clarke Parkway might be an indication of what lies ahead. We'll see. I'm also waiting to see if they'll be able to find any clerks on-site to run the registers, stock the shelves, and sell lotto tickets. Or if they will be able to keep their fuel tanks full due to the lack of tanker truck drivers. Although by the time 2221 rolls around, I doubt that will be much of a concern.

There's a lot of history along both sides of that 8-lane concrete slab; we can only see much of it in old photos stored in the archives of the Monroe County Historical Society Museum in the Forsyth Train Depot. Now, that's a place y'all should check out if you are ever free on a Wednesday or Friday from 9 a.m. to 4 p.m.

I can envision hungry Interstate 75 travelers of the distant future taking the exit to what is now known as "Hamburger Hill" but labeled with a new moniker such as "Vegan Valley" or the like. There, they will be lined up in the drive-thru much as we do now, but in some sort of hovercraft. All fast-food joints will be using the method pioneered by Chick-fil-A, except employees won't be telling you to have a blessed day; it will be robots. There won't be a minimum wage issue because there won't be a need for minimum wage employees.

Everyone thought we'd be buzzing around in flying cars by 2021. Well, some companies have already invented autonomous flying vehicles. Aeromobil is planning on releasing a model to the public as soon as 2023 for a mere $1.6 million. Prices will no doubt one day fall within the reach of the common working man.

In my imagination, I can see criminals fleeing from Monroe County deputies crashing to the ground rather than just crashing into an ordinary ditch. Our deputies and officers will still be saving lives even in the sky. But there is no doubt, even two hundred years from now, certain local Facebook users will still be complaining about our sheriff's office's efficient "chase and catch" policy.

Sometimes You Just Need to Hunker Down

Back on November 22, 1992, Bobby Perkins, who lives out on Dames Ferry Road, witnessed the biggest tornado he'd ever seen. He was relaxing on his front porch swing when I stopped by to talk to him about it recently, and didn't get up when I pulled up in the yard. "What is it?" He's a pretty good guy, but he just tries to appear unfriendly. I told him I was interested in the storm shelter he built just after that big storm so many years ago, and what prompted him to build such a structure.

Old Bobby stood up and pointed across his yard, "I was renting a trailer right out there while I was building this house. And, uh, me and the wife and the boy there, he came into the trailer and said, 'What's that noise?'

"I went to the door, and there was the biggest tornado you have ever seen coming across yonder. It came across behind the BP over there, came across the chicken houses on Edge Road. It just picked them up and flattened them out. Chickens everywhere. And we didn't know which way to go. I said, "Doggone; I don't know which way to go."

"So, we got in the car and took a right. If we had taken a left, we would've been alright, but we ran right into it about a mile down the road, and it totaled the car out with us in it. It just slammed trees down on us. It slammed a tree down on us and totaled the car. Glass everywhere. It's a wonder it didn't kill us."

I told Bobby he should've taken a left instead of a right. "I didn't know which way to go. It was scary. It went over it and tore a house up, up there somewhere. Then it went through the Piedmont Reservation, up there across the river in Jones County; it looked like a giant lawnmower cut down all them pine trees up there. It was a big ol' tornado. It went on up to Oconee and picked a house up with a man and woman in it and threw it out in the lake. Killed both.

"That's why I built that shelter out yonder. But I didn't do that until '98."

Bobby's little storm shelter is an impressive bunker just the right size for him and his wife Carol Ann, but it ain't nothing like the underground shelter that was repurposed from a previous US Army Base in South Dakota, outfitted with 575 concrete and steel bunkers. That shelter can house 5,000 people and provide food, water, fuel, and hygiene supplies for a year or more. If the zombies are still pounding on the door after that, I guess you can forget it. If there are any spots left, you can lease one with a $25,000 upfront deposit and $ 1,000 per year for 99 years. The company that leases the 80' x 26 ½' bunkers capable of supporting up to 24 people says that only the prepared will survive.

During the Cold War, the U.S. government built a secret underground facility beneath the beautiful Greenbrier Hotel in West Virginia to house members of Congress and their staff during the aftermath of a nuclear holocaust. The government never acknowledged its existence but kept it well-stocked with supplies from 1961 until 1992. Of course, if a congressman happened to be on the golf course when a bomb was dropped, I guess he was out of luck. Today, for

$39, you can take a tour of the massive bunker that, fortunately, never had to be used.

If you're a billionaire "prepper" (what people who prepare for doomsday are called), you can wait out the zombie Apocalypse in real luxury style. While the rest of the world is burning to the ground, the superrich can simply retreat into what's known as "Doomsday Luxury bunkers." These bunkers are designed with military-style fortifications that are guaranteed to protect the chosen few and their valuables. In Kansas, there is a structure known as the Survival Condo that extends 15 stories beneath the topsoil. It features a community swimming pool, a rock-climbing wall, a store, and even a dog park. Penthouse units start at $4 million, full-floor units run $3 million, while half-floor spaces cost a mere $1.5 million. The property owners like to brag that the structure has the protection of a nuclear-hardened bunker with the facilities of a luxury condo. Nice. But where's the sunlight? Where do we fish?

I've lived with the threat of a nuclear holocaust since my birth, as most of you reading this also have. I don't have a lot of protection here in my little house on the edge of the woods on Lee King Road. I guess I'll just have to put my head between my legs and… well, you know the rest.

The Trouble with Laws

Keep an eye out for state legislators.

There Ought to be a Law, or Not...

For the most part, most of us are good citizens and try to stay out of trouble with the law. No one wants to go through the hassle and embarrassment of going to jail, gathering bail money, and hiring an overpriced, underhanded lawyer. And don't forget the court process where, depending on the offense, you could end up with even more jail time, not to mention a financial blow and all the shame.

And yet, there are few of us who haven't broken some law at some point in our lives. There are so many rules it's nearly impossible not to. Maybe it was just an infraction as minor as driving 5 miles over the speed limit. Or perhaps you innocently threw out some junk mail addressed to someone else that came to your house, committing a federal offense that could land you in prison for 5 years. Or maybe you put your donkey in a bathtub which is a crime in the state of Georgia.

I know it sounds crazy, but I can understand someone wanting to lather up a stinky donkey. However, it's perfectly legal to let your dirty burro stand in your tub in Arizona if you don't let them go to sleep. That makes good legal sense because a donkey nodding off in a bathtub could lead to disastrous results.

Up in Massachusetts, people don't allow donkeys in their tubs because it's illegal in their state to go to bed without taking a bath. Donkeys are allowed in bathtubs in South Carolina, but your horse must take his bubble bath elsewhere unless you want to be hit with a large fine accompanied by a criminal record.

There have been many seemingly ridiculous laws passed by various legislators across the nation over the years. Most of these weird statutes made sense and seemed necessary at the time and place of their passing. Although archaic, many of these laws are still on the books, so you might need to watch your step.

For example, in Alaska, there's a state law that prohibits the awakening of any sleeping bear with the intention of photographing them or posing with them for selfies. Bears don't look their best after just waking up. A protest was made, and a bill was subsequently passed.

Leave your blindfolds at home if you're driving through Alabama, where it is a punishable offense to be caught driving blindfolded. Now you've been forewarned and can't use ignorance as an excuse. A safer place to drive would be the town of Dunn, North Carolina, where it's illegal to play in the traffic or to drive on the sidewalk.

Back home in Georgia, be sure to keep an eye out for any state legislators that might whiz by at 90 mph. It could be a representative who helped pass a law allowing state legislators to speed without fear of being ticketed during the legislative session.

If you're walking in Georgia, be aware that it is illegal throughout the state to walk around with an ice cream cone in your back pocket. This statute is only enforced on Sundays, so I'm not really worried about this one. I wouldn't want to mess up my nice Sunday britches anyway.

In 1961, in Gainesville, the poultry capital of the world, the city council passed a measure requiring chicken to be eaten only with fingers. A 91-year-old woman was arrested for breaking that law in 2018, but fortunately, the mayor was standing nearby, and she was quickly pardoned. While we're discussing chickens, you probably know it's illegal in Quitman for any chicken to cross the road. Leaving us still without an answer to the age-old question regarding why.

In Dublin, Georgia, it remains illegal to wear a hood, but a mask is required in certain establishments, which should please our newly minted president, Joseph Robinette Biden, Jr., who, during his inauguration festivities, took a short break to sign a flurry of executive orders. Among these orders was a mandate requiring face masks to be worn during interstate travel aboard all trains, planes, or buses.

This requirement is also enforced inside federal buildings and while on federal land. As you know, federal land also includes national parks. This means while walking on narrow trails and participating in other outdoor activities, you must keep your mask on, along with social distancing, of course. This law may or may not be good. I don't know. I'm not a scientist. I just hope they remember to take it off the books after all this is over. But like a lot of the other crazy laws I mentioned above, I doubt it. I think I'll just stay in my tent.

And in Kennesaw, there is a requirement that heads of household keep a firearm in their homes to protect their families. Well, now maybe that's a law that isn't so crazy…

Jaywalking at the Crosswalk

Some people are fortunate enough to work remotely. I am one of those. It isn't necessary for me to get up at any set hour, shower, shave, and use up gas to get to the office. In the morning, I stumble just a few feet into my home office and start typing away with Muchacho in my lap.

But Tuesdays are a different story. Will requires me to show up in the afternoon because the paper goes to press that evening, and it's "all hands on deck." Sometimes it can get hectic at 50 North Jackson Street on Tuesday afternoons, but somehow, we always pull it off.

For some reason, a couple of hours after I'm into my weekly proofreading session, I always have a need for a sugar rush and let Will know I'm headed to the Dev Foods store for a Twix bar. He never wants me to bring him back anything, but I always bring back a small bag of chips for Tammy, which I feel helps keep me on her good side.

Dev Foods is on North Lee Street and just a block from the Reporter's office. I always cross North Lee Street at the Forsyth Welcome Center, directly across from Castleberry Drug, which seems to be the part of town with the most traffic at that hour. For two and a half years, I must admit I have been illegally jaywalking to satisfy my afternoon craving for something sweet solely because I'm too lazy to walk all the way up to Johnston Street, down to the crosswalk, then back down to Dev Foods. Besides, on Tuesdays, I don't have time for all that.

Then, lo and behold, back in 2020, the good old Georgia Department of Transportation engineers proposed a crosswalk on North Lee Street with a flashing pedestrian light. They said it would be 65 feet north of the intersection with Adams Street and would line up with the Castleberry

Drug Store Parking Lot and Lee Street Park behind the Forsyth Welcome Center. The Forsyth City Council approved the proposal at its Nov. 2, 2020, meeting.

When I first heard the news, it seemed like they were doing it just for me. Wow. My own personal crosswalk. The DOT said the new crosswalk would include a rectangular, solar-powered, rapid-flashing beacon to slow drivers when pedestrians press a button to cross the street. The DOT also said the project would cost about $46,000 to install. That seemed like a chunk of change to me, but I sure appreciated the thought. I read a little flak about it on Facebook, but of course, someone always must stir the pot about something.

And then, sometime in the middle of September, a worker from the DOT parked a nice white work truck on North Lee Street with an electrical sign attached to a trailer that said the crosswalk would open on Sept. 24. It seemed like the sign was there forever, and I was getting anxious to see it happen. For some reason, the truck remained attached to the sign. Parked there like it had nothing better to do.

As I mentioned, I felt the new crosswalk was mine, and I wanted to be part of Forsyth's history by being the first citizen ever to use it. No one seemed to know when on the 24th the crosswalk beacon would be activated, so I called Mayor Eric Wilson. Surely, if anyone knew, it would be him.

Nope. He did have a number for me to call in Thomaston for the DOT people who oversaw the project, though.

After being on hold for a few minutes, the nice lady at the DOT informed me that she had spoken to the supervisor of the crosswalk department, and he said no crosswalk openings were scheduled for that day, and no one was sure when it would happen. Later that day, I noticed the date on the sign had been changed to Sept. 26. I called the DOT again that morning of the 26th, but no one could tell me what time the magic would happen, though I was assured it would for sure happen that day.

I rushed over to my crosswalk and got there around 9:45 a.m. and found it ready to go. Now I can't say for sure I was the first one ever to use the gadget, but I can at least say I was one of the first. I was amazed at the technology. The beacon started flashing immediately, just as promised, when I pressed the button. I congratulated myself on living in these wonderful times and felt confident as I stepped off the curb. Then suddenly, a car swished by without even slowing. Then another and another. I finally made it to the suicide lane and waited while one car slowed but never stopped.

I felt much safer back when I was jaywalking.

What Planet Are You From?

omen may be from Venus, and men may be from Mars, but suddenly there wouldn't be enough planets in 7 solar systems to cover all the genders that are now identified by various groups and online news websites. Facebook claims there are 58 different genders, while some medical sites say there are as many as 77.

You've probably never even heard of most of the new ways people identify themselves nowadays. Names like "androgyne," which is a person who is either both masculine and feminine or somewhere in between. "Agender" is a person who does not identify with any gender. Or the all-encompassing "omnigender," which is a person who possesses all 77 genders rolled into one. Now that one could be a little confusing. You could never figure out what to wear. During my research, I learned that I identify as AMAB, an acronym for "assigned male at birth." I'm glad someone got that right.

There has always been a battle between the sexes. It has been waged for a long time, when we thought there were only two. Now, with all the different options, it has turned into an all-out war with no way to tell who's winning or even who is on which side. There are many new battle flags.

Back in the day, all I had to worry about regarding what was then known as the "fairer sex" was not to buy her clothes as a present or give her a gift certificate to Jenny Craig or Weight Watchers. I also knew enough not to buy her any appliances or sharp objects on her birthday.

There were simple but easily recognizable differences between men and women back then. Such as if a woman said, "Smell this." You could be sure it would smell nice. If a man walked up to me and said that, I'd immediately back away as far as possible. Also, it is well known that men will spend $2 for a $1 item if they need it, but women will spend $1 for a $2 item if it's on sale, even if they don't need it.

It also seems that men need women much more than women need men. Eighty percent of American men say they would marry the same woman if they had to do it all over again, while only fifty percent of American women say they would marry the same man. They learned their lesson. Also, only fifty-eight percent of men say they are happier after their divorce or separation, while a whopping eighty-five percent of women say it was the best thing they ever did, and they'd do it again by golly.

They say men think, women feel. But at the same time, they also say the "male intellect" is an oxymoron. It has been shown by decades of research that men and women have equal intelligence quotient (IQ) levels, but women score higher on emotional quotient (EQ). Scores show that women are more self-aware and know what to do with their emotions once they become aware of them, whereas some men will throw a hammer all the way across the yard if they smash their thumb. Score one point for the ladies' side.

Also, contrary to popular belief, judging by the number of deaths they cause on the road, women are better drivers than men. And although men insist they have more skill, male drivers have twice the rate of fatal accidents per mile driven compared to women. They also cause 80 percent of pedestrian accidents. Reasons given for this are that men feel like they "own the road," and women drive with the nurturing instincts they were born with. Women are more defensive drivers, have longer attention spans, and are more careful to avoid accident-causing behaviors. Apparently, good mothers also make good drivers.

More proof that women are smarter than men is that they live longer. Of those who live beyond age 100, 85 percent are women; many men would live much longer if they weren't so stupid on the road and elsewhere.

I couldn't find any numbers on the intelligence level (if any) of the remaining 75 genders. It might take years to figure that out. By then, there will probably be 75 newer ones. I'm sure someone has already secured a government grant to conduct research on that subject. The gender-apathetic people who don't care what gender they are seem to be smarter than others. They just live their lives, don't bother anyone, and don't even think about it because they don't care.

I'm not here to offend anyone or to judge anyone's lifestyle. And if you think I am, you're wrong. I realize what a sensitive subject it is to certain people, but I'm merely reporting on what's going on in the world around us. Don't blame me for all the craziness. I'm just an AMAB reporter doing his job.

We Love a Good Conspiracy Theory

Americans love conspiracy theories, and believers don't always wear hats made of wrinkled tinfoil. Maybe it is because of our own humdrum reality or a time of paranoia, but these whoppers have grown in the count and in the level of ridiculousness, such as the persistent local rumor that there exists a gas mafia in Monroe County. The truth is, our gas prices are determined by giant corporations out in Oklahoma and elsewhere. That little independent station down the street from the Quik Trip sets its pump price accordingly. That station's owners hope that people will come inside to buy beef jerky, boiled peanuts, and drinks, where the real profits are.

Conspiracy theories are not a recent creation. An early one was when Andrew Jackson left a congressman's funeral in 1835, and a would-be assassin, Richard Lawrence, an unemployed housepainter, pulled out a pistol and pointed it at the president's back, but the weapon misfired. Lawrence then quickly pulled out another weapon, which also misfired. He was then subdued by Jackson's cane and several nearby bystanders, which included Rep. "Davy" Crockett, thus creating a theory that Jackson had staged the assassination attempt to gain support and show what a strong man he was by soundly beating his attacker with his walking stick. And some said that Sen. John C. Calhoun of South Carolina and Mississippi Senator George Poindexter were involved. Lawrence was later found "not guilty by reason of insanity."

Presidential assassinations have always been a good source for those who indulge in believing in wild ideas. Although it is widely believed by scholars, historians, and the general public that John Wilkes Booth assassinated Abraham Lincoln, there were folks back in 1865 who thought that the deed was too great a project for a lowly actor and found it difficult to believe he was able to lead his band of 8 fellow conspirators to murder the president and attempt to kill cabinet members, Vice President Andrew Johnson and Secretary of State William H. Seward simultaneously. Not surprisingly, suspicion immediately fell on Confederate President Jefferson Davis and Confederate Secretary of State Judah P. Benjamin, who allegedly had connections to the Rothschilds' banking empire that was concerned about Lincoln's trade policies. And since Mary Surratt and other convicted and hanged conspirators were of the catholic faith, suspicion was cast upon the pope or, at the minimum, high-ranking church officials by many skeptics. Supporters of that crazy theory point out that John Surratt, Mary's son, fled the United States and, strangely enough, was located later at the Vatican.

President John F. Kennedy was murdered on the morning of Nov. 22, 1963, in the streets of Dallas, Texas. Six decades later, Americans remained fascinated by the events that followed. Even after the Warren Commission was established to investigate the assassination and found it to be the act of a lone gunman, Lee Harvey Oswald, many scoffed at the findings and said, "The president was killed by CIA agents acting either out of anger over the Bay of Pigs maybe at the behest of Vice President Lyndon Johnson or by the KGB or by mobsters mad at Kennedy's brother for initiating the prosecution of organized crime rings," according to Time magazine.

Another presidential conspiracy theory is one by "birthers" who say President Barack Obama wasn't eligible to be president as he was born outside our borders. They make this claim even though his birth announcement was published in two Honolulu newspapers given to them by Department of Health officials, and state officials such as Gov. Neil Abercrombie and the former director of Hawaii's Department of Health say that they have both seen Obama's birth certificate.

Of course, conspiracy theorists have many alternative explanations for the horror that happened during the September 11 terrorist attacks, including that the United States government plotted to take down the World Trade Center so that the country would be taken into war in the Middle East. Some of these nuts say a missile was fired at the Pentagon rather than a commercial airliner nosediving from the sky. Others present an unconvincing argument that United Flight 93 didn't crash and burn in a field near Shanksville, Pennsylvania, after brave passengers stormed the cockpit but were blown out of the sky by an Air Force jet. All these claims are easily debunked with real evidence and common sense, but that won't stop some people from truly believing in such crazy ideas.

Even our money can't escape the scrutinizing eyes of conspiracy theorists. Many point to the secret messages hidden on the back of the lowly dollar bill, such as the Eye of Providence gazing out from a triangle set above an unfinished pyramid with 13 steps, saying it symbolizes Big Brother watching us or has ties to the Freemasons and the Illuminati.

In this age of fake news, we need to take all unsupported claims with a mountain range of salt.

Confederate Gold Still in Georgia?

Folks say there's Confederate gold hidden in our state, a rumor that has persisted for over 150 years. The story goes that when Confederate President Jefferson Davis was chased out of Richmond as the Union Army was closing in on him in April 1865, he was carrying a considerable amount of Confederate treasure. Much of it disappeared somewhere in Georgia. When he was finally captured near Irwinville, Georgia, on May 10, 1865, the former president had only a few dollars in his pocket. There was no explanation of what had happened to the fortune.

The legend of lost Confederate gold began in Richmond, Virginia, on Sunday morning, April 2, 1865, when President Davis's prayers were interrupted during a church service as he received an urgent message from General Robert E. Lee. Lee advised him that he needed to immediately mount his pony and get out of town, or risk doing time in a Yankee prison.

Davis quickly said his amens, and his fellow Confederate officials wasted no time loading up two southbound trains. The first train carried the nervous heads of the rebel government along with the most important documents needed to run a country.

Whatever loot they could grab from the vaults of Richmond banks and other hiding places throughout the city was loaded on the second train. This included all of the Confederacy's cash reserves, meaning gold and silver. They also boxed up a large amount of jewelry that had been donated by trusting, patriotic Confederate women to the cause. The trains then sped south in the dead of night straight to Georgia.

The amount of fortune on the second train was estimated between $500,000 to millions of dollars. To generate more interest in Davis's capture, Union officials generated rumors that the train left the Confederate capital with cargo rich enough to fund a nation. Even among Confederate veterans' groups, stories were told that their leaders shamed the South and fled in fear while carrying Confederate treasures worth millions of dollars. The true amount will never be known, but the rumors continue to this day. Supposedly, some of the Confederate treasury was hidden to wait for the South to rise again.

Davis arrived with the loot in Washington, Georgia, in early May. It had been an expensive trip. The fleeing Confederates had to pay $108,000 to soldiers to escort them near the Savanah River, and to buy supplies in Augusta, and Washington took $40,000 (nearly $667,000 in today's money) from the strongbox.

More money disappeared on May 4, after Davis and his few remaining advisers decided to disband the CSA government and entrusted $86,000 from the treasury to two naval officials who were to take it to Britain. The bankroll never even made it on the boat. Some say the money was spent by one of the naval officers on a love affair with the widow of President John Tyler, Julia Tyler. Others say it was buried. When Union troops captured Davis less than a week later, he was flat broke and rumored to be disguised in women's clothes. He spent the next two years in a Yankee prison.

Macon was also a Confederate depository, second only to Richmond. When the war ended, a Union general was sent to Macon to oversee $275,000 ($4.5 million today) in confiscated gold and silver, including that which was plundered from civilians by Union soldiers. Some of this total included $35,000 of gold coins and bullion that had been earmarked for hungry rebel soldiers trudging back home. The general also grabbed $188,000 from the Central Railroad Bank. The Georgia State Bank had $200,000 in gold coins hidden in Macon that he had never found. An often-repeated story states that Confederate gold was stored in a hidden room at the Hay House on Georgia Avenue. The federal government also confiscated more than $500,000 from Augusta. Remember, those were 1865 dollars.

Some leftover funds from the Richmond banks had been left in vaults in Washington, Georgia. This sizable sum was to be taken by a detachment of Union soldiers to a railhead in South Carolina, but bandits attacked their wagons, which had camped for the night in Lincoln County, and got away with $251,029. Some of the stolen money is said to have formed the basis for several local fortunes around Danburg in Wilkes County.

Other gold in Georgia came when the Confederates hastily transferred millions of dollars of gold from New Orleans when the Union was on the verge of invading, to what they thought was a more secure location in Columbus.

Confederate General P. G. T. Beauregard was ordered to take the gold to Columbus, but somehow it was misplaced. He wrote in his biography, "What became of that coin is a mystery." I'd love to find just one of those coins. Just so I can hold a piece of history in my hands.

The World's Most Exclusive Home

Before the Civil War, the home at 1600 Pennsylvania Ave, NW, Washington, DC 20006, was the largest house in the United States. It currently has 55,000 square feet with 132 rooms, including 16 bedrooms and 35 bathrooms. To give you a better idea of its size, it takes about 3 tons of white paint to cover the exterior. Known as the White House (since 1901 when Teddy Roosevelt first used it on his stationery), it has 412 doors, 147 bulletproof windows, 28 fireplaces, 8 staircases, and 3 elevators. The structure is situated on 18 perfectly manicured acres maintained by the National Park Service.

The residence isn't up for sale, but Zillow.com says it is valued at $423,594,800, and if you were able to rent it, you'd have to cough up around $1,663,119 a month. It cost $232,372 to construct in 1792, which translates to $329,239,992 in today's money.

President George Washington chose the site of the home, strongly influenced its design, and it has housed every president except for him. In a grand Masonic ceremony to inaugurate the construction of the building, Washington laid the cornerstone on October 13, 1792. Behind the stone, they placed a plate of polished brass on which they inscribed the words: "This first stone of the President's House was laid on the 12th Day of October 1792, in the 17th Year of the Independence of the United States of America".

After the ceremony, the participants met at a local tavern and drank toast after toast to their ambitious project. Unfortunately, their hangovers were so bad the next day no one could remember where they had placed the cornerstone, and since construction had already begun, it was buried under something or possibly stolen. To this day, no one knows what happened to it, and it remains one of America's most persistent mysteries. If you have any idea where it may be, the History Channel is offering a cash reward to anyone who finds the stone so they can feature it on one of their shows.

America's second president, John Adams, and his wife, Abigail, were the first residents of the presidential mansion and found it cold and damp during the five months they lived there. Abigale said that the structure was tolerable only "so long as fires were lit in every room" and was more than happy to return to her farm in Massachusetts after Jefferson defeated her husband in 1801.

After his swearing-in ceremony, President Andrew Jackson continued a tradition started by Jefferson and hosted an open house at the White House. He went to his new home to meet and greet a crowd of celebrities, politicians, and upstanding citizens, but instead found a boisterous mob of 20,000. Soon, the once-dignified mansion became the scene of a rowdy, drunken party. Folks were dancing on fancy furniture with muddy boots while others wandered through the many rooms looking for the new president, grinding cheese into the carpet and breaking expensive crystal and dishes while they searched. The White House staff finally had to resort to setting up washtubs filled with a mixture of juice and whiskey on the White House lawn to lure the raucous partygoers out of the house.

In more modern times, our oldest living president, Jimmy Carter, recently revealed in a documentary "Jimmy Carter: Rock & Roll President" that his son James Earl "Chip" Carter did a little partying on the White House roof when he climbed the stairs with Willie Nelson until they reached the top, leaned against the flagpole, and fired up "a big fat Austin torpedo" back in 1980. President Bill Clinton also did a little partying with Monica Lewinsky in the Oval Office between November 1995 and March 1997. Lewinsky stated she "partied" with Clinton a total of nine times.

Twelve babies have been born in the White House, with only one as the child of a sitting president, Esther Cleveland, daughter of President Grover Cleveland. Most babies who took their first breath within the walls of the presidential palace were either grandchildren or children of nieces or nephews of the sitting president. In November 1801, a fourteen-year-old enslaved cook, Ursula Granger Hughes, left Monticello to work in Thomas Jefferson's presidential household, arrived heavy with child, and gave birth to the first baby born in the residence in March 1802. Sadly, by late summer, the child had died, and she returned to Monticello.

On January 17, 1806, Jefferson's daughter, Martha Washington Jefferson Randolph, gave birth to his grandson, James Madison Randolph, in the executive mansion. Then, exactly one hundred and nine years to the day, on January 17, 1915, the grandson of President Woodrow Wilson, Francis Bowes Sayre, Jr., also entered the world at the White House.

Nowadays, to tour the president's house, you must submit a request through your Member of Congress, and tours are scheduled on a first-come, first-served basis. Since I'm one of the landlords of the place, I should do that one day.

No Handouts for Adam

When Adam and Eve were evicted from the Garden of Eden and found themselves homeless, they needed not only a place to stay but also food and something to wear other than those scratchy fig leaves. Unfortunately for them, no government assistance was available. No EBT cards to apply for. No grants, student loan forgiveness, or PPP loans. Poor Adam had but one choice in life: go to work. There was also no such thing as childcare assistance, so once Cain and Able came along, Eve also had her hands full.

Adam's employment was easier during his brief residence in the Garden. According to the Book of Genesis, he was appointed by God only to dress the Garden and keep it. After the Fall of Man, he was sent out to "till the ground." That is nearly an impossible job for one man without tools. Adam must've been exceedingly intelligent and creative, as well as hardworking.

Like everyone on their first day starting a new career, the world's first worker was probably quite nervous and unsure of himself. Unlike us, he had no one to explain his duties, and there were no how-to YouTube videos to help him get started. The only good thing he had going for him was that he had no boss except for his wife. I imagine when Adam returned home after working that first long day with meat under his arm and maybe a new dress for Eve, he must've felt pretty good about himself. No doubt he was still remorseful for his great sin, but at least he felt the satisfaction of a job well done.

Mankind was forced to follow Adam in this life of labor, but we became inventors to make our work easier and more efficient. We still must till the earth, but we went from wooden plows dragged by domesticated animals to heavy machinery such as John Deere tractors pulling tempered-steel plows. We found ways to build great cities made of reinforced concrete, with wide highways connecting them. Goods and products of every kind from around the world are easily accessible to nearly everyone. Each generation has worked hard to make life better than the one before it, getting us to where we are now. Advancement has occasionally sputtered, but humanity has always managed to move onward. It was either that or all of us would have surely starved and died.

For a variety of reasons, some are unable to work and depend on others just to survive. They can be sick or disabled in a way that, sadly, forces them to miss the blessings that come into a person's life when they are productive.

There were many social programs in the U.S. before the Great Depression, including church charities and some state-supported programs that helped needy people with basic needs like food, clothing, and shelter. There are still many churches and groups, such as the local Circle of Care and the Anchor of Hope, that continue to help those less fortunate. During the 1930s, private charities and local communities were overwhelmed by the growing need among the American public. The great poverty of the masses made it necessary for the Federal Government to act quickly. First came loans, then grants to states to pay for direct and work relief. Cash payments were made to those in immediate and desperate need. (Much like the PPP loans, so many businesses, not all legitimate, recently received.) Later, government projects were initiated through a program called the Civilian Conservation Corps, or CCC, and hundreds of thousands of young men were put to work on environmental conservation projects, regaining the dignity of putting on their boots and working for a wage.

In Georgia, according to my online research, in 2021, there were 1,308,264 food stamp recipients, which equaled 12.44% of the state's population carrying an EBT card in their wallets. The amount spent using EBT cards came to close to $2.5 billion of taxpayer money in our state.

Most of those receiving the benefits qualify for assistance legitimately. Others abuse the system. Around

In 2019, Georgia investigators spent $7.2 million to investigate fraud claims and found that $8.4 million in food stamps was improperly obtained in 2,985 cases. Offenders can receive up to a year in jail and pay a hefty fine. Retail stores, as well as private citizens, were among those caught abusing the system.

I've spent a fair amount of time processing EBT cards while standing behind a convenience store cash register. Nothing bothers me more than a person paying cash for a handful of scratch-off tickets and then buying an armload of junk food with an EBT card that was obviously fraudulently obtained. I can only shake my head as I watch them drive away with a tankful of expensive gas in a car much nicer than mine.

The Right Size for the Job

According to the National Center for Health Statistics, in 2019, nearly 33% of adult Georgians were obese with a BMI of 30.0 or higher. This is above the national average of around 31% of

American adults in this condition. Even President Trump is considered obese, with a BMI of 30.4 and weighing in at 243 pounds. Last May, Nancy Pelosi called President Trump morbidly obese. Although he doesn't quite meet the requirements for that description, he's getting there.

In the early 1960s, the average American man over 20 weighed about 170 pounds. Today, the average American man tips the scales at nearly 200. I'll leave the weight increase over the last 6 decades of the average American woman out of this discussion for obvious personal and politically correct reasons.

The reason behind this extra poundage is that the calories we use day-to-day have changed little since 1960, while the calories we consume have risen dramatically. We have a great love for fast food and little love for exercise. In the sixties, families cooked their own food and ate it at home. And it wasn't French fries and pizzas, but real food. After the lengthy lockdown, with a rise in home cooking, a few curves may be flattened.

There are many health issues associated with obesity. Most of them are major. It is also expensive. The current estimated annual healthcare cost of obesity-related illnesses is $190.2 billion in the United States. Childhood obesity alone carries a $14 billion bill.

Overweight people spend a lot of money to get back into shape. There is no limit to books, DVDs, apps, exercise equipment, diets, pills, and prepackaged meals guaranteed to help you lose weight. 45 million Americans will go on a diet this year, spending $33 billion on weight loss products. You can't blame them for trying, but if weight-loss products really worked, wouldn't these companies be putting themselves out of business?

But I'm not here to talk about being fat. I want to tell you about being skinny. It's easy to underestimate my skinniness. I've gotten so skinny that my legs resemble chopsticks and are just as hard to use. I think it is probably time to put on a few pounds, but for people like me, that's more difficult than losing them. I'm in the 1.5% of the American population that is underweight, and also in an unhealthy condition. It has been reported that being underweight leads to increased mortality at rates comparable to those of morbidly obese people. That scares me a bit. I blame it on my metabolism. Just as a lot of overweight folks do.

Just about everything in my life is small. I have a small dog, a small truck, a small house, and a small girlfriend. Maybe it's my Napoleonic complex, but the only time I notice I'm little is when I'm shaking the hand of a man the size of Shaq O'Neal or when I'm buying clothes.

There aren't any clothes on any rack my size except for the garb in the boys' department, and I'm not going to be seen sneaking into the dressing room carrying an armload of those duds. I'll just put an extra hole in my belt to hold up these baggy britches before I resort to those fancy skinny jeans. I don't really mind it, walking around in britches too big for me. I consider myself to be a trendsetter. Look around at all these young men with baggy pants, and you'll agree. But I don't show my boxers. I'm too shy for that.

Apparel companies are more concerned with producing clothing for the 31% who comprise the obese population than they are for us in the 90-pound weakling group. I understand this makes good business sense, but maybe if y'all lost a little weight, marketing strategies would be revised more in my favor, and I would be able to find some long johns that fit.

My biggest gripe is the fairness of the cost of my size "S" shirt compared to the cost of the size "XXXXL." All the material needed for that larger shirt is at least 5 times as much as what's needed for my little shirt. And surely the time it took to put all those stitches in that plus size had to have taken at least a few minutes longer. Still, the price is the same for the smaller shirt as it is for that bedspread size. And it's the same story at the cleaners. I don't get it. It's not fair, and if I were bigger, I'd do something about it.

I've had a lot of folks tell me they wish they had my problem. I always tell them being skinny ain't all that, but when you need someone in a tight spot, I'm the right size for the job.

Nerds Need Love, Too

If you think I'm a nerd now, I was nerdy back when nerdy wasn't cool. My glasses were too thick, my body too thin, and my unstylish corrective shoes did little to correct my pigeon-toed feet. I once masked off and spray-painted those ugly shoes white on the toes and black on the sides to resemble the saddle oxford shoes that were so popular with all the cool kids in my high school.

My "new" shoes fooled no one. I got some good laughs, though. I also thoroughly ticked off my dad for ruining a pair of specially made shoes that were more expensive than his spit-shined Air Force boots. My old man was a sergeant in the daytime, but when he pulled into the driveway in the evening, he became a general. Not a smart thing to tick off a general.

The girls in my school had never given me a second glance until that day when I showed up in those ridiculous kicks. After that, they would snicker as I clopped past them in the corridor. It didn't take long for my custom-painted shoes to begin fading and peeling, and there was no way my dad was going to replace them until I wore them down to my socks.

Still, all this embarrassment didn't stop me from falling in love with the impossibly beautiful Michelle Hollingsworth. Smart, witty, and completely out of my league, she sat next to me in Mrs. Brewer's 10th-grade English class, and she was the reason I had to take the class again during summer school. How could I be expected to concentrate on sentence diagrams and prepositions while inhaling the fragrance of a goddess?

I sat next to her, trying to hide my shoes under my seat, and pretended I was sincerely interested in what the teacher was trying to teach me. Behind such thick lenses, it was easy to look like I was getting it, but Michelle was heavy on my mind.

There was no way I could reveal my affection for her, but I had to tell somebody. I told Turkey Belknap, who happily spread my deepest secret to my classmates with a handwritten note. I thought they were laughing at my shoes, but they were laughing at the absurdity of the goofiest kid in class being in love with the hottest girl ever to grace the halls of Altus High School.

Valentine's Day was just a day away, and our class planned a Sweetheart Banquet at the classiest place in our town, the Cattleman's Cafeteria. I had no plans to attend until Turkey gave some astounding news. He said that, as a friend, he thought he should tell Michelle how I felt, and that if I asked her to the banquet, she would go. He gave me a small slip of paper with her phone number.

I dug deep for the courage to dial her number. I rehearsed my speech. I didn't give in to the impulse to hang up when I heard her angelic voice. I stammered out my prepared words, and she said, "Yes!"

My mom always bought the same style of shirts for the three oldest boys, just in different colors. My color was green. All my shirts were green. David's color was red. John, blue. At that time, we were all the same size. David loaned me his nicest red shirt, and I thought I looked spiffy except for my shoes. But it would be easy to hide my feet beneath a table.

We had two sets of surplus military bunk beds in a room of four boys. My bunk was the top one next to the window. I had a fitful sleep that night. I dreamed crazy wild dreams of dancing with Michelle, and for some reason, I leaped high out of my bed and landed face-first on a bare floor. I didn't realize I was screaming until my mother switched on the light, and I was staring into a pool of blood.

She took me into the bathroom and cleaned me up. I looked into the mirror at two busted lips and two black eyes. I was hurting so bad the next morning, and my face was so disfigured I couldn't go to school, let alone some fancy banquet. I called Michelle and let her down easily. It took a few days before I was able to return to school, and my black eyes looked worse than they were behind the magnification of my glasses. There was no way a girl like Michelle would be interested in me in my condition, so I didn't even try.

I still think of her from time to time, and if she weren't as old as I am, I might consider looking her up.

Slap Happy Hollywood

It was the slap heard around the world. I'm referring to Oscar Night 2022 when Chris Rock insulted Will Smith's wife by joking about her shaved head (she is bald due to alopecia), and Smith sucker-slapped him on stage. Smith then returned to his seat and shouted out some strong curse words, saying, "keep [my] wife's name out of your f***ing mouth." Shocked, Rock whimpered to the audience, "Will Smith just smacked the sh*t out of me." All this action was live on the ABC network during prime time when all the kiddies were still up, hoping one of their favorite stars would receive the cherished Best Actor Award, which he did later in the show.

The uncut, uncensored versions of the clips we've all seen on the internet came from far away, where they are much more broadminded about such matters than we are. American censors could never allow such language to go out over the air, and the standard 20-second delay is always in effect for any live show, so the bleeps were loud and clear. There was one small glitch, however; apparently, someone forgot to bleep the closed-captioned dialogue scrolling across the bottom of the screen, and I'm sure there was more than one shocked prude in the American television audience. Before the story nosedives into obscurity, I have a couple of thoughts about the incident: What surprised me most about that night was that Rock was slapped rather than punched. If any man insults my woman and I think he should be slapped, then I would send her to do the job because if I'm stepping up, I'm doing so with closed fists. And they would be up and ready as I invite him to go outside. Only a coward would sucker punch someone. And only a sissy coward would sucker-slap someone. There are just some things real men don't do. It's not something Clint Eastwood would've done; of that, you can be sure. Even at his age, I'm sure he would go into a fighting stance. I'm no advocate for violence, but there are times when a man's gotta do what a man's gotta do. Another great surprise is that Smith wasn't arrested right there on the stage. I see incident reports on the public records page in this publication every week involving much less violence than was displayed at the Dolby Theater in front of millions of witnesses, and the perpetrators are always handcuffed and placed in the rear of a patrol car. And you know where they go after that.

But Will Smith didn't get arrested for punching Chris Rock onstage. The Los Angeles Police Department explained that "LAPD investigative entities are aware of an incident between two individuals during the Academy Awards program." The incident "involved one individual slapping another." The individual involved, Chris Rock, "has declined to file a police report." However, if Rock chooses to file a report later, the LAPD "will be able to complete an investigative report." Most victims in Monroe County usually don't have such a choice. If someone gets hit around these parts, someone is going to the Monroe County Justice Center. And rightfully so. If Smith is charged, it will be for a misdemeanor battery count, which carries a penalty of up to six months in jail. Merely a slap on the wrist.

Another point I'd like to make is that if another man slaps me, we're probably both going to be rolling around on the floor immediately. Those who know me know that I'm just a bit smaller than the average guy, and I'm no threat to anyone, but a man slapping my face is one thing I'm not going to allow. Whoever does something like that to me will not turn his back on me and walk away to take a seat, even if I do get my little rear end stomped in the process (which I am pretty sure would happen) I have been slapped by a few ladies, but even though I never deserved it, I let those incidents slide.

All this makes me wonder if the whole Academy Awards ceremony was staged. Although the show's viewership was up somewhat this year compared with last year, it has been in steady decline since 2014. What better pathetic attempt to get folks to tune in next year than to create a little controversy? After all, Hollywood is the world's illusion factory. To most viewers, it was real anger and violence being played out on the stage by two of the industry's most popular actors. I'm not so sure. Maybe it was the way Rock arched his back, the way it's done in a staged fight, or the exaggerated way Smith moved during his follow-through like an actor would do. On the world stage, their little spat is insignificant other than to show how gullible we all might be.

When Men Wore Bellbottoms

And why do we have warnings on

wheelbarrows?

Fashion Started in the Garden of Eden

It took the power of Satan to tempt Eve to taste the fruit from the Tree of Knowledge in the Garden of Eden but only the beauty of a woman to take down Adam. What if, when Eve offered the forbidden morsel to Adam, he refused to partake in that sinful harvest? What if he had done the smart and correct thing and resisted the temptation of his beautiful wife? He could've walked away from the whole ugly affair, and he would've lived forever.

But I'm not sure how that would've worked. Would we be living in a world full of old holy men with sinful wives who keep dying off? As it turns out, we are all sinners. Not just half of us.

Most of us think it was an apple that was eaten, but I tend to believe it was a fig. Immediately after committing that first sin, they realized their nakedness and were ashamed and adorned themselves with loincloths made from leaves pulled from a fig tree. An odd thing about the material used in this wardrobe choice is that fig leaves are very irritating to the skin and can cause itching and even blisters. These rashes aren't pretty. With no anti-itching cream available in

Paradise, it must have been extremely uncomfortable. Thus, began the woes of mankind and the beginning of fashion.

Adam and Eve were cast out of Paradise immediately after committing the original sin, but God soon took pity on them and gave them garments He Himself created from animal skins. They wouldn't be considered fashionable in today's world, but the descendants of the world's first couple continued wearing animal coverings for many generations.

Then the fashion scene slowly started to evolve. One tribe noticed another tribe wearing some nice animal skin suits made from striped raccoon skins. Not to be outdone, they made a real fashion statement as they strutted around their campfires, showing off their homemade, stitched-together skunk skins pieced together for the nice eye-catching, contrasting black-and-white effect.

Skip ahead a few thousand years, and we find the Romans and Egyptians taking great interest in their appearance. Especially those in important positions who could afford fancy duds. Rulers thought it necessary to distinguish themselves from the common working man, and Roman emperors wore only the most expensive, made from the rarest and finest materials. The emperor was always instantly recognized by what he wore. He was also the only one in the empire allowed to wear purple.

Around the same time, pharaohs were making a big splash among their subjects by wearing half-pleated kilts wound around their waists, leopard skins over their shoulders, and lion tails hanging from their belts. They capped off this regal look with a fancy crown that featured a golden cobra as a centerpiece.

During the Middle Ages, clothing began to take on what we think of today as fashion. It began slowly at first. We watch fashion change from season to season, while their clothing designs change from generation to generation. When the Crusades came along and Marco Polo started bragging about his adventures and introducing new cultural influences and fabrics, great technological advances in medieval European garments followed.

The handheld spindle was replaced by the much faster spinning wheel and horizontal foot looms with treadles, and soon textile and clothing production exploded. Attractive garb became more affordable and within reach of the emerging middle class, who began to emulate the styles of the rich elite.

In modern times, an Englishman named Charles Frederick Worth moved to Paris in 1858 and established a fashion salon that soon attracted European royalty. He was an innovative designer and adapted his 19th-century dresses to make them more suitable for everyday women. He was the first to use models to showcase his creations and the first to sew branded labels into his clothing. Suddenly, simple dressmakers became arbiters of what women should wear, and fashionistas came into being.

Then came the twentieth century with the flappers in the 20s with their bare shoulders and sleeveless dresses. This was the time women started shaving their armpits as well.

The miniskirts of the '60s caused quite a stir, and men's styles raised some eyebrows as well. Men started wearing bellbottoms and beads and growing their hair long. I happened to be around during that time, and my military dad wore me out more than once for coming home looking like a hippie.

In his later years, my hair was much shorter, and his was much longer. Way longer than mine ever was in 1969. Matching his hair was a long gray beard. I once gathered up enough courage and approached him, "Daddy, don't you remember you used to whoop my butt for looking the way you do now?" My old man looked me straight in the eye and said, "Boy, I'll still whoop your butt!"

Ignorance Can Be Dangerous

Ignorance, while blissful, can be very dangerous. For instance, if you don't know how to drive, you'll probably wreck if you get behind the wheel. Ignorance of the law can land you in jail with no excuse. And if you mix ignorance with stupidity, there can be a significant impact on happiness and well-being. A person can accidentally kill themselves.

This is exactly why we have warning labels on wheelbarrows that let us know they are not intended for high-speed highway use and why we are advised not to hold the wrong end of our chainsaws while in use. Another sticker might say never to use a match to check its fuel level.

There is a bright warning label stuck on the handle of a fancy cordless drill hanging in my tool shed that advises the tool wasn't designed for drilling out cavities in human teeth. I must disagree. A drill is a drill and can sometimes even be used as a hammer. It is a tool helpful for numerous projects. Just ask the drunk Juliette man who, last July, held a battery-powered drill with a ½" wood bit in the chamber to his head while threatening suicide before he tossed the tool and hit a deputy on the leg. Soon, drill makers will issue advisories not to try that at home.

Mothers are warned against folding up strollers before removing their children and not letting them play in the dryer while the dryer is in use. On our coffee cups, there is a printed advisory that tells us to avoid pouring the hot liquid into our crotch areas. I have never needed this bit of advice. Due to my passion for reading the warning labels on packages and my shirt labels, I know that I am not supposed to iron my shirts while wearing them. I also know that an egg carton may contain eggs, that pepper spray may irritate eyes, that a hair dryer is not intended for use while sleeping, and that a scooter moves while in use. Luckily, I read that a fishing hook is harmful if swallowed.

I made a mental note of that good advice.

There is a reason for all these warnings that most consider ridiculous. We all have the sense to remove that folding windshield sunshade before driving. Still, some manufacturers feel compelled to put a sticker in direct view of the driver stating the obvious danger of operating a vehicle with the apparatus in place. The sticker is there simply because one bright day, a not-so-bright driver didn't like the sun in their eyes and took a spin, dependent only on GPS directions.

You can't fix something if you don't realize it is broken. If you are ignorant, you can't prepare for what you can't see coming. Your choices are limited. We have never had so many people with so much access to endless knowledge, yet who refuse to learn much of anything. Most of these people are ignorant of their own ignorance.

Some of this resistance against knowledge can be blamed on the influx of fake news. Fundamental rules of real evidence are rejected, and few make logical arguments. This is seen every day on all news channels. Other than the Bible, no one knows what they can truly believe anymore.

Of course, no one can know everything. Fortunately, we don't have to. I don't have to know how to set a broken bone, drill out a nasty tooth, or get myself out of jail. I simply call a doctor, a dentist, or a lawyer who hopefully isn't too ignorant to correct my legal problems because I'm too small for prison.

Sometimes a lack of knowledge can be justified by a person's age and circumstances. While a toddler can probably show you how to use your cellphone, we can't expect them to know the rules of the road and trust them to drive.

Sometimes ignorance can be a lot of fun for those in the know. It's much easier to pull a prank on someone who has no idea what's going on. Victims must stay on their toes and be ever vigilant.

If you're ignorant, you simply don't have knowledge or understanding. If you're stupid, you might be educated, but for unknown reasons (again, ignorance), you still do stupid things. The mistakes I've made due to stupidity far outnumber the mistakes I've made due to ignorance. I've even repeated the same mistake more than once, expecting a different outcome. They say that's insanity.

The simple cure for not knowing something is to learn it. We all begin with a blank slate, and it is up to each one of us to fill it with as much knowledge as possible. Whenever I see someone walking around smiling for an unknown reason, I wonder what it is that they don't know.

Self-Made in an Educated World

A great deal of importance is placed on college education. A degree can provide greater access to job opportunities and higher earning potential. Higher education can open doors, help with personal growth, and pave the way to a better career. There are 20 million students currently going to college in the United States, and 44 million student loan borrowers who owe a collective debt of over

$1.5 trillion. Some argue that the debt is too high. They say that students who go to college are delayed from buying homes and getting married. They contend that many jobs do not require degrees, and many successful people never graduated from a higher institution of learning.

It's true that some of the greatest men in history came from nothing. Starting with Benjamin Franklin, known as our country's first self-made man. He was born the 10th son of a soap and candle maker who had 17 children. By the age of 10, his formal education had ended, yet by the time he died, he was one of the most famous men in the world, known as a printer, publisher, author, inventor, scientist, and diplomat who helped draft and sign the Declaration of Independence.

Franklin's list of inventions is impressive. He is famous for his experiments with electricity, such as his kite experiment, which we all learned about in elementary school. After he accidentally shocked himself in 1746, he turned his attention to inventing the lightning rod. As an avid swimmer, Franklin invented swim fins at age 11. As he grew older and his vision worsened, he invented bifocals, an invention that is helping me tremendously as I write this. It was so cold in Pennsylvania that he invented the Franklin Stove and gave away all rights for public use, saying, "As we enjoy great advantages from the inventions of others, we should be glad of an opportunity to serve others by any invention of ours; and this we should do freely and generously." A full list of Benjamin Franklin's accomplishments is impossible in this space.

A lesser-known self-made person is Madam C.J. Walker, recorded as the first self-made female millionaire in the Guinness Book of World Records. She was born in Louisiana as Sarah Breedlove in 1867, just after the Civil War, as the first member of her family to be born free. She started out on the same plantation where her parents had been enslaved, and both her parents had died when she was

7 years old. She married at 14, had a daughter 3 years later, and, 3 years after that, became a widow. She then moved to St. Louis to start a new life where her brothers had gone a decade earlier as part of the African American exodus from the devastated South.

She became a member of a church where the women there told her she was more than just an illiterate washwoman, even though she was completely uneducated and only knew how to pick cotton and wash clothes. Her life began to slowly improve. But tragedy struck Sarah's life when both of her brothers died in 1894, and she went through a disastrous marriage. The stress became so much that her hair began to fall out, and she became ashamed of her appearance.

Then one night, Sarah had a dream where a big man appeared to her and gave her the formula to repair her balding scalp. Some of the ingredients had to be shipped from Africa, but after mixing everything together and applying the mixture to her scalp, her hair began to grow back rapidly.

She moved to Denver in 1905, married a newspaperman, and soon started running ads in a local black newspaper selling her product under the name "Madame C.J. Walker." She thought since the French used the term "madame," it would be considered fashionable. Even so, it was difficult to sell her product to black women in a state with so few black residents, so she went on the road to Texas, Kansas, Oklahoma, Mississippi, and, where it all began, Louisiana.

She visited towns, giving demonstrations and recruiting sales agents along the way. She was the first in history to propel sales in this manner. Long before Mary Kay.

In 1909, she moved to Indianapolis and started advertising in the nationally distributed Indianapolis Freeman. Her ads included testimonials from women who were sales agents proclaiming how much better their lives had become from selling Madame Walker's products. She soon trained thousands to be sales agents and created an army of black women who gained economic independence, became rich in the process, and became well-known as philanthropists. She worked hard all her life and once said, "When I was a washerwoman, I was an excellent washerwoman."

Education is wonderful and necessary, but we don't have the same opportunities. Sometimes we must make do.

The Demise of One More Old-School Skill

In the National Archives Museum in Washington, D.C., is a document written over two hundred years ago that continues to inspire: the Declaration of Independence. Although Thomas Jefferson is credited with writing this priceless instrument, now faded and barely legible, it was a Pennsylvania brewer named Timothy Matlack who took a quill pen and set Jefferson's words across a piece of parchment using an elegant script.

If you view a copy of the document, you can see that Microsoft Word couldn't have formatted it more perfectly. The margins are exactly centered and aligned. Every line across the page is perfectly straight. If you take the time to read these lines, you will have no difficulty reading each word clearly. Every letter was painstakingly formed with precision. I did notice an early-day typo on the 16th line, however. The word "Representative" is misspelled "Represtative." A correction is neatly made with "en" inserted in the correct spot above the misspelled word with a tiny arrow below, but it was done so perfectly that it doesn't bother my OCD issues in the least.

Writing with a quill pen is messy. You dip the feather of a goose or a swan into a bottle of ink and let the excess ink drip back into the bottle before scratching out a couple of words, then repeat. The ink dries slowly, and you must be careful not to smear. It took Jefferson 17 days to pen the Declaration of Independence. I couldn't find any documentation on how long it took Matlack to write the document, but it was an effort of love. Not only should Jefferson's work be considered a masterpiece, but so should Matlack's penmanship. His work is pure art.

The first signer of the declaration was John Hancock, who made a bold statement by placing his signature in the exact center using an extremely large script. When later asked why he wrote his name so large, he answered, "so that the fat old king can read my name without spectacles." Some say it was because he was so egotistical. His historic autograph is so famous that many still use it as a noun synonymous with "signature," and National Handwriting Day is observed on Hancock's birthday, January 23.

According to the Georgia Department of Education website at www.gadoe.org, the State Board of Education adopted the Common Core State Standards (CCSS) in July 2010. The new guidelines were implemented in Monroe County during the 2012-2013 school year, and under the new rules, schools are not required to teach cursive writing. Among the reasons cited for the change were the increased use of technology for communication and feedback from teachers themselves. A longtime Monroe County educator, now retired, told me every teacher she knows supports teaching handwriting and that any average student can learn the skill in just one semester. She also said that time and budgetary constraints made penmanship a low priority. Some conspiracy theorists believe cursive handwriting was stopped from being taught in public schools so that the general populace wouldn't be able to read the Declaration of Independence, the U.S. Constitution, or the Bill of Rights. They seem to ignore the fact that the documents can easily be found and read online in good old Helvetica font.

The legibility of handwritten words can be an extremely big deal. According to a shocking 2006 report from the National Academies of Science's Institute of Medicine, doctors' sloppy handwriting skills killed more than 7,000 Americans every year. The report also said that unclear handwriting on some of the 3.2 billion prescriptions issued annually injured more than 1.5 million patients. Thanks to computers, the internet, and call-in prescriptions, this serious problem is rapidly being resolved.

My own handwriting is a mess, I must admit. I am not sure why, as I remember being an excellent student during my penmanship lessons. I enjoyed the way my letters looked so nice and neat and lined up in those perfect rows. That was then. I now write nothing like the letters I used to trace in my little workbook. At some point, I deviated from making the fancy loops in a capitalized S and ended up just making a simple printed-style S. I do that with nearly all my capitalized letters. My educator friend said students begin to develop their own styles almost immediately after learning cursive.

You would think that demand for ink pens would be practically non-existent in today's digital world, but writing instrument sales are growing, especially in Asia, Latin America, and the Middle East. In the U.S. and Europe, luxury pens are in high demand as gifts that go mainly unused.

It used to be said that "a good hand was the sign of a good man." This was back when people believed that good handwriting showed discipline and integrity. Penmanship: one more old-school skill we can write off.

A Regrettable Turn of Events

What began in 2016 as a platform for short, humorous clips is now better known for its viral online challenges. Some of these challenges will solidify my argument that humanity has finally hit rock bottom. For instance:

A female TikTok poster recently wound up in the hospital after styling her hair with Gorilla Glue. She smeared the adhesive onto her scalp, and within 15 seconds, she was sporting a nice "permanent." After 4 hours of surgery, she raised $20,000 in donations and hundreds of free hair products, prompting several imitators.

Another use for super-strength adhesive you shouldn't try at home is to glue fake vampire fangs to your teeth. Clips of geniuses struggling to remove the plastic choppers from their incisors the morning after Halloween garnered over 9 million TikTok views.

And a 14-year-old Monroe County boy suffered second-degree burns to his face and eyes and had to be life-flighted to a hospital after reportedly trying to create a video for social media early in the summer of 2021. The boy apparently was lighting a fire with rubbing alcohol, trying to replicate a video challenge he had seen on TikTok.

If there had been social media when I was a boy, my brothers and I would've gone viral. All boys do things considered borderline dangerous, like climbing trees or skateboarding tricks, but we went above and beyond. Unfortunately, none of our shenanigans were ever videotaped.

One summer evening, my dad brought home a used dartboard set and hung it on the paneled wall on the back porch. He stuck a piece of tape on the concrete floor a few feet back, taught us how to keep score, and proceeded to impress my brothers and me with his throwing skills.

It turned out to be a great diversion for three young boys. We spent hours practicing on hot summertime days and got pretty good at it. The competition was fierce, of course, and although the arguments were frequent, the game kept us somewhat out of trouble.

Maybe it was because my old man was in the military, but our favorite activity as kids was playing war games. Either with other neighborhood kids or wage battles among ourselves. We had many different weapons at our disposal.

A long stick was a rifle. A short stick was a knife. Dirt clouds were always cool because they exploded into a puff of dust upon impact, and it was easy to imagine they were hand grenades. A piece of gravel or a chunk of rock was less dramatic visually but much more effective. I still carry a small scar on the left side of my left eye from one of David's lucky shots. Sometimes we used BB guns or bows and arrows. When in season, Black Cat firecrackers or bottle rockets were our weapons of choice.

One day, we chose the darts my dad got for us. We got bored with the limitations of throwing darts on the back porch and discovered that darts would also stick in trees, wooden fences, the doghouse, and the roof. I can't remember what started the battle, but soon we were throwing darts at each other.

I was hiding behind my dad's work shed, vigilant with three darts ready to fire. I spotted John low crawling across the yard, and I jumped out with my arms high for the throw, but John was quicker on the draw. He did a quick roll in the grass and threw his dart at me in the same instant. His weapon found its mark exactly bullseye center in my navel. I don't remember any pain, only the horror of looking down and realizing there was a dart hanging out of the middle of my shirtless tummy. John was proud of his incredible shot and jumped up with a cheer, pumping both fists in the air. David tried to take advantage of his sudden exposure but missed by a mile. I ran into the house crying for my mama.

Mama was sitting on the couch, drinking sweet tea and watching "Dark Shadows" when I ran in screaming, "He got me!" Without looking up from the TV, she answered, "Please don't shout while I'm watching my show." So, I stood before her, patiently squirming in my bare feet, waiting for a commercial. Finally, she turned her gaze toward me and noticed the dart dangling from my belly button. "Oh, my lands!" A trickle of blood had started to slowly ooze out.

I had never seen her so shocked. We both looked away as she grabbed the dart and gave it a hard yank. When I looked back, she was holding it in her lap with her head lying back on the couch with her eyes tightly closed. And on the TV set that dominated our living room, I heard Barnabas Collins solemnly say, "Well, that was a regrettable turn of events."

We Like to Be Liked

My first computer was acquired in the early '90s when I did some carpentry work for a man who couldn't come up with the $600 he owed me and offered me a slightly used Macintosh instead. The heavy, bulky device that took up way too much space on my desk was valued at $1,000 (about $2,066 in today's dollars), so I accepted the barter without hesitation and was instantly amazed by the technology. My wife at the time called my amazement an addiction because instead of sitting next to her on a sofa every evening watching Wheel of Fortune and The Dating Game, I was sitting bug-eyed at a computer monitor until long after she went to sleep learning all I could about a device I knew would change the world, which it has more than any other.

The first time I heard the word "internet" was back in 1984. I thought then it was some type of net ladies threw over their hair or maybe some fancy gadget I could use on a fishing boat to catch tuna. I learned later it was a word the military shortened from "internetworking," which was used to describe networks linking several computers. The top-secret military computers at that time were merely hypothetical, so I'm not sure why they even used the expression. Even so, it was considered such an important word that it wasn't until 2016 that the Associated Press style guide finally decided to decapitalize it.

The first experience I had on the internet was in Los Angeles when I played a game of chess with a friend who lived on the other side of town. I was checkmated within 5 moves, all sent over a phone line. Since then, I've become a bit more sophisticated with 10 separate email accounts and my own fancy personalized Facebook page, where I have been trying to amuse my friends and family for going on 13 years. I don't think many of them get my humor, though, gauging by the low number of likes I get. If you like what I post, you might be a weirdo.

We all like to be liked, especially on social media. People get a little dopamine rush when they post something that gets more thumbs-ups and hearts than they usually get. When we get a like, it's like eating a Reese's Peanut Butter Cup or winning $10 on a $5 lottery ticket. Scientists used to say dopamine was responsible for the pleasure we feel in our brains, but now they say that, rather than giving us pleasure, it only makes us crave it.

When someone posts a picture or comment on social media, they're opening themselves up to judgment, but deep inside, they're hoping for those promised fifteen minutes of fame. They get up in the morning, and the first order of business is to check their notifications to see if they have hit viral status. If the post doesn't receive the reaction they hoped for, they shrug off the disappointment and keep scrolling. Maybe if they like someone else's post, that person just might like theirs.

Due to the "follow the crowd mentality," people are more likely to react to posts that have been liked by many of their peers, so users continue to post. Grannies post pics of cuter and cuter kitties, teenage girls put more and more pout into their pouts, and gadflies never cease stirring up the pot. Facebook currently has 2.8 billion users, which is nearly 8 ½ times the population of the United States and over a third of the world's population. Of course, not all of these Facebook accounts are legit. In the first 3 months of 2018, 583 million fake accounts were deleted. I know of a local user who currently has four or five different accounts. All with phony profiles. Gives himself likes and even argues with himself sometimes.

Nearly 75% of users visit the site daily, and 51% click the link several times a day. All these users have the same goal: that rush. With each passing minute, about 400 new users sign up. That's over half a million per day. It's like legal crack. And this is the reason social media isn't going away anytime soon.

According to my Google research, the average Facebook user has 338 "friends." Of these, fewer than a hundred are people they consider to be genuine friends. I also learned that more women are on Facebook than men: 74% vs. 62%.

Every 60 seconds, 24 hours a day, 136,000 photos are uploaded, and 510,000 comments are posted on Facebook. Also included in that short minute, a whopping 4 million posts are liked. If I could get just ten of those likes and maybe a couple of hearts on one of the great pics I've posted of Muchacho flashing a toothy grin, I'd be high as a kite.

Back to Full Service

There was a time when you went shopping for groceries; you would step up to a friendly clerk standing behind a counter, who would gladly put your order together with a smile. They'd open a barrel, scoop out a few pounds of pinto beans or flour, grab some items from the shelves behind them, wrap it all up, and you were good to go. Service was everything. The problem was that all this wonderful one-on-one service was expensive. And the more customers a store had, the more clerks were needed. Then along came Clarence Saunders from Memphis, Tennessee, who changed everything. In 1916, Saunders proposed the novel idea that shopping would be much more efficient if customers could serve themselves. He proposed letting people stroll through his store and load up baskets (at first made of wood) on their own, rather than paying at a centralized location. His store would have no clerks putting together shopping lists. His workers would be busy stocking shelves, cleaning the store, and checking out customers.

People thought he was off his rocker and that his innovative business would fail, especially when they learned the name of his new establishment: "Piggly Wiggly." No one really knows why he chose such an unusual moniker for the store. He was always shy about revealing its origin. My favorite explanation is that when he was once asked, "Why Piggly Wiggly?" he answered, "So people will ask that very question." It is a name easily remembered.

Saunders achieved many firsts in the industry, including checkout stands, price marking each item in the store, and using refrigeration to extend produce's shelf life. He also put his employees in uniforms for a more professional, cleaner look.

His idea was a hit with the public, and soon Saunders was issuing company stock, which was successfully traded on the New York Stock Exchange. During the early 1920s, he had a run of bad trades and lost control of his company. Soon, he was pushed out and was no longer associated with the company he had established.

Undaunted, Saunders then opened a new chain of stores under the less colorful name "Clarence Saunders, Sole Owner of My Name Stores." At first, he made money, but the Great Depression forced him to close the doors. After the Depression, he built an automated grocery store called "Keedoozle," but the automation didn't work properly, and that venture didn't last long.

He was designing yet another cutting-edge automated grocery store when he sadly passed away in October 1953, an entrepreneurial genius ahead of his time.

Located primarily in the Southeast, Piggly Wiggly now has more than 530 independently owned and operated stores in 17 states. The company is an affiliate of C&S Wholesale Grocers, Inc., which was ranked the 10th-largest privately owned company in the United States by Forbes Magazine in 2010.

The new Ace Hardware now occupies the location where Forsyth once had its own Piggly Wiggly. That short-lived store was closed for good on July 4, 2019, after competing against the big national brands at our local Walmart proved to be too much to overcome. "It's just not working," said district manager Carl Whitaker at the time, "This town isn't big enough for three grocery stores." Maybe not, then. And maybe not today. But with all the property transfers I see every month, I believe it will be soon.

But the competition is good. Look at what's happening to our two remaining grocery stores. Walmart recently revamped its layout, and Ingles is adding a Starbucks, a pharmacy, a Chinese and sushi bar, and curbside pickup.

We can now have a friendly clerk put together our shopping list, wrap it all up with a smile, and we're good to go. We have come full circle. While this is convenient for the customer, it seems inefficient and expensive.

According to its website, Ingles charges $4.95 for curbside pickup regardless of order size. When I think of all the time I spend walking around aisles trying to find cat food and a cartload of other essentials and then having to stand in a boring line to pay for it all, I don't mind shelling out five bucks at all. But instead of buying for a single person, what if I were stocking up to feed a family of five for a month or so? No way that a fee that low will cover the labor expense of completing that order.

You will be able to purchase alcohol with the new curbside service, but tobacco, lottery tickets, and prescriptions must be bought inside the store. You also will not be able to redeem paper coupons.

It would be necessary to have a horde of employees fulfilling orders if everyone went on their apps to take advantage of this "new" innovative way of shopping. I'm not sure old Clarence Saunders would think it such a great idea.

Work Can Be a Risky Business

When I started swinging a hammer back in my Alabama days in the mid-70s, my fellow carpenters and I never gave much thought to on-the-job safety rules. We tried to have enough sense not to fall off the roof or run our fingers through the table saw on our own. Even though the Occupational Safety and Health Act (OSHA) was passed in 1970, no one ever came by to inspect our homemade scaffolding made from nailed-together 2x4s or to make sure we were protected by hard hats and safety harnesses. I never even heard of OSHA until the 90s.

Even though we always tried not to get hurt, something bad would occasionally happen. I've seen a man lose an arm and watched another cut off the tip of his nose. I've pulled long, ugly nails from the hands of fellow carpenters and thrown the offending nail as far as I could into the woods. I once had a buddy nail himself to a plywood floor with a 16-penny nail gun, and when I asked him if he wanted me to cut the plywood around his foot and take him to the hospital with the decking attached, he replied that he preferred me to remove his foot from the floor with a crowbar instead. So, I placed a crowbar under his boot, pushed down as hard as possible, and set him free. But not from his agony. He squalled like a baby all the way to the emergency room. His wife brought me a cake the next day as a reward for helping her husband.

During my carpenter career, I smashed my left thumb with a 22-ounce hammer coming down with full force more times than I can count. Once, I sliced four of my fingers open to the bone with metal flashing, stopping myself from falling off a 3-story roof. And then, one time, a ¼-inch cable snapped and hit my right eye, turning it into an ugly mess that only steroids could fix. I could go on, but this column is already graphic enough.

Although construction work is on the list of most dangerous jobs, the most dangerous occupation is logging, which is 33 times more dangerous than the job I currently have, which is only perilous when I'm trying to interview the rare citizen who doesn't care much for the Monroe County Reporter.

Both loggers and landscapers fell trees, which is obviously extremely risky work. According to OSHA's database, between 2010 and 2020, there were 314 deaths when a worker was struck by a falling tree or limb, more than likely on the head. A hard hat doesn't do a whole lot of good when you're bonked on the noggin by a limb weighing half a ton. Falling from trees was also a contributing factor in logging injuries and deaths. The death and injury rates surge in the logging industry after large storms and hurricanes, so the statistics vary greatly from year to year.

Around a million American workers have died on the job since the 1920s. Statistics from the U.S. Bureau of Labor estimated workplace fatalities to be at 30,039 during the early 20s and 75,000 railroad workers perished in the twenty-five years before World War I.

OSHA was passed by Congress after the National Safety Council reported that 14,000 Americans were being killed and 2.5 million permanently injured in workplace accidents every year. When the law was passed, more people were dying in workplace accidents than there were soldiers dying in Vietnam. Unlike the war, no one was protesting the death of the working man.

Insurance companies have also done a lot to reshape the workplace landscape. Their rules are strict for companies that want to stay protected, including drug testing workers and no-smoking clauses.

While rules and regulations meant to protect the common worker are generally good, there are times when they can get in the way. A few years back, I had a gig setting up a trade show in Orlando, and the floor was packed with carpenters, painters, and laborers getting ready for the big event. I was new on the unionized crew. A few displays over from mine, a carpenter was climbing a ladder with an armload of materials when I saw the ladder suddenly tilt to the side, and the carpenter hit the concrete floor with a thud from about 12 feet up. Of course, I immediately rushed to see if I could help him, but everyone else ran away from the accident. Fortunately, he was okay, but no one other than me cared to see if the dude was hurt or not. The reason: anyone who witnessed an accident had to be interviewed and drug tested. It was much better for them just to let him lie there and suffer than to go through all that hassle.

The Minimum Wage for Robots

The federal minimum wage was first established under the Fair Labor Standards Act on October 24, 1938, with a rate of 25 cents per hour. The amount increased over the decades, with the latest rise nearly twelve years ago, on July 24, 2009, to $7.25. The original purpose of the minimum wage was mainly to prevent a repeat of the Great Depression and to protect the nation's workers by establishing a minimum standard of living. The minimum wage can be described as the amount a worker is worth from the shoulders down. Any amount earned over the minimum wage is what the worker is worth from their shoulders up.

Most of us entered the workforce at minimum wage. There was no negotiating. If you were the newbie, that's where you started. I've never liked that concept. I don't think the government should tell us what we're worth, minimum or otherwise. What if you're worth more? What if you're worthless? I was lucky; my first job was delivering newspapers door-to-door on foot, and I got paid based on how many papers I sold. Fortunately, this was more than the government's idea of the value of an enterprising 11-year-old kid.

You may not believe it, but there are some people who are not worth the minimum wage. I know this to be true because I've worked alongside a few. Sometimes these folks cost the company more than they're worth, but they usually stay employed because they're at least warm bodies.

Large and small companies alike report having extreme difficulty finding employees, especially in the retail and hospitality industries. Of course, many companies are increasing their wages and perks to attract workers, but this isn't always easy for smaller companies. Any increases in workers' pay will be covered in what the consumer ultimately pays, so it'll all come out in the wash anyway.

Maybe robots are the way to go. Economists recently said robots could take over 20 million manufacturing jobs worldwide by 2030, and that within the next 11 years, there could be 14 million robots in China alone. They say the number of robots in worldwide use has increased threefold over the past twenty years to 2.25 million units. The rise of robots will no doubt bring about many benefits in productivity and economic growth, but, of course, there will be negative aspects as well. Millions upon millions of jobs will just disappear. This could be devastating in poorer local economies that depend on lower-skilled employees. Some say this will exacerbate the income inequality problem.

Even so, researchers estimate that global GDP would be boosted by 5.3% by 2030 if robot installations were increased by 30% relative to the baseline forecast. This equates to adding $4.9 trillion per year to the global economy. Equivalent to an economy greater than Germany's.

You may not like robots, but they're coming. Soon. To a McDonald's near you. In preparation for the anticipated $15-

an-hour minimum-wage hike, America's most popular fast-food company has been experimenting with robots to offset rising wages and labor shortages. They have recently installed automated voice ordering for their drive-thru service at 10 locations near Chicago. If all goes well, the plan is to have the units installed across the country. They also have robots for the fry pots. Cooking fries, chicken, and fish to perfection and for a whole lot less than $15 per hour. Robots aren't only under the Golden Arches, either. Fast-food companies have tried new and innovative methods to satisfy hungry customers. Domino's Pizza has rolled out its pizza delivery machine, the R2 Robot, in Houston, Texas, and it's going well. No more delivery people standing on my porch with their hands out. I'm going to miss those guys.

A Taco Bell in New York City's Times Square has no employees at all at the counter. When you step up to order, you are met with a user-friendly touch screen. You just conveniently select your items, tap your card, and it's back to the party. You may interact with the cooks back in the kitchen, but only if you shout loudly enough. Chick-fil-A is firing up its robot delivery service in California after partnering with a robotics company. They currently have three locations in Santa Monica and make deliveries with "Kiwibot," a four-wheeled autonomous rover. The company says the delivery time is around 30 minutes and the cost is $1.99. That's not bad, plus you get to see a robot.

White Castle has expanded its partnership with a robotics company to supply robots to 10 of its locations. A robot called "Flippy" has taken over the fry operations at the stores. Personally, I don't think Flippy the robot could make them any better than they already are.

I wonder if the new automated voice ordering systems will have a treat for Muchacho when we pull up to the server window. Probably not.

Hold On to Your

Biscuits and Grits

*It's just as cold if you go outside
without your britches as if you went
outside without your hat.*

Things You Know That Just Ain't So

In my little survival kit packed in alongside Band-Aids, some rusty fishhooks, and an old knife, I also have stashed a can of pork 'n' beans, some sardines, and a couple of packs of Twinkies, all waiting for emergency use. It isn't much, I know, but at least I feel a little more secure having something ready just in case some Chinese rocket crashes down on Lee King Road, and I can't get to town.

Well, I've just learned I might as well throw my aged Twinkies in the trash. I've been tricked by a myth. I've always believed those delicious golden cakes were good for decades or even longer, but come to find out, they have a shelf life of only 45 days. I was taken in by an urban legend.

The myth goes that Twinkies are made entirely from chemical ingredients and no actual food, so they will never go bad. Supposedly, they have been edible for years. I've heard it said that even nuclear fallout didn't affect the tasty treat. I used to worry a little about ingesting a bunch of bad chemicals while enjoying a Twinkie, but that never stopped me from stuffing my face with half a cake at a time. It's a real relief knowing I haven't added any extra harm to my body by enjoying my favorite sweet snack.

And hold onto your biscuits and grits: It turns out another worry I've carried for years has been debunked by new research that exposes another of the world's most widespread food myths. Forget what you've been told for years; breakfast is not the most important meal of the day. I feel better learning that, as I've been off the breakfast habit for decades and always felt guilty about it, thinking that was what was making me so skinny. But worry no more.

It seems this falsehood is so widely believed due to "research" financed by Kellogg's Corn Flakes that "proved" corn flakes as the most convenient solution for the "most important meal of the day." A recently published review finds no evidence to support the claim that eating breakfast promotes weight loss or that skipping breakfast leads to weight gain. They say all meals are created equal, so we can scratch that one off the worry list as well.

"We found that breakfast is not the most important time of the day to eat, even though that belief is really entrenched in our society and around the world," says study co-author, Monash University head of rheumatology at Alfred Hospital, Flavia Cicuttini. How an arthritis doctor in Australia knows this, I'm not sure, but his word is good enough for me if I can skip making that early-morning mess in the kitchen without guilt.

Another common misconception is that the seats of a toilet are the nastiest of all places and full of germs—after all, it's logical that we would think the least sanitary place would be a bathroom. But a recent study conducted by the University of Arizona found them to have ten times fewer germs than cell phones. Well, that's not-so-great news. I think I'll go back to doing the crossword puzzles in the Reporter. If someone sends a text, they'll just have to wait a couple of minutes.

And did you know that fortune cookies aren't Chinese? They came from Japan. Only in America do we receive fortune cookies after filling up on Kung Pao chicken. It is also a little-known fact that Napoleon wasn't short. He was tall by French standards in his era. (Which isn't saying much, I know.) And coffee isn't made from beans, either. It is made from a bean seed. And you think peanuts are nuts? Nope. They're beans, just like pintos. Have you heard you can see the Great Wall of China from space or even from the moon? Well, astronauts say you can't. Yet another urban legend.

And grandma will be pleased to know that most scientific researchers have concluded that sugar does not cause hyperactivity in children. According to them, that glazed donut all over your little tyke's face has no effect on their energy level. So, if your child is running around at Walmart, screaming and hollering, and you can't do anything with them, there could be a cause other than sugar you should explore.

It also isn't true that one human year equals seven dog years. It depends on the size, age, and breed of the pooch. And you think you lose body heat fastest through your head? Well, they say you'd be just as cold if you went outside without your britches as if you went out without your hat.

It's amazing what we believe just because we heard it somewhere. In this crazy age, with the internet, TV, radio, and even print (still), who knows what or who to believe? But still, what a great time to be alive.

Next Plane Trip Will Be on a Train

Nope. I can't take it anymore. Even though plane travel is by far the safest and quickest mode of transportation, I'd rather walk or even crawl than get in a giant aluminum tube again filled with possibly diseased, nasty strangers. I don't like driving to the Hartsfield-Jackson Atlanta International Airport, figuring out which parking lot is right, and then trying to remember my parking space. I hate putting that mask over my face when I walk through the airport doors and not being able to understand what the ticket agents and security personnel are saying to me in their strange, muffled language behind their masks.

I'm uncomfortable standing in a long line, looking at the backs of thousands of fellow travelers' heads, all waiting to be screened at security checkpoints. And I really hate it when they tell me to take off my shoes and worry that there might be a hole I missed that morning in my cleanest pair of dirty socks. And then I must go through putting my shoes back on over my now even dirtier socks. Usually, one of my shoestrings breaks because I'm so frustrated; I pull on it too hard. Besides, my feet hurt after all that standing in line.

After all those struggles, it's time to find the right train to the gate. Hopefully, I won't screw that up, so I'll be there on time for all the annoying pre-board announcements. After finding the right location to catch the right train and keeping my carry-on luggage tightly squeezed against me, I grip the cold metal bar, which I hope has been sanitized, and sway dizzily as we race down the rails to yet even more hell.

The train doesn't go all the way to the gate, so I usually must walk another 10-15 minutes, sometimes asking a stranger if I'm headed in the right direction. Finally, at the right gate, I plop my bag under the seat, take out my phone, and pass the time watching stupid videos. I always try to find a spot with a view of the tarmac. It's the only thing I like about airports. During 15-second video ads, I like to look up from the screen and watch the planes gently land and depart one after another, and there's something calming about the neatness of the planes all parked military-style, side by side, on the tarmac. At this stage of my trip, a little calm is welcome.

Finally, all the rich people are in their places in 1st class, and the special needs people are taken care of, and we regular folks are called to line up to get on the plane. I prefer to say get in the plane as I am not a wing walker and don't ride on anything unless it's a horse.

Once I'm greeted with a smile at the plane's door, I slowly squeeze my way down the aisle and wait patiently behind those who are squeezing obviously oversized packages and luggage in overhead bins and under seats.

Whenever possible, I try to get a window seat so I can watch the clouds rather than the multitude of masked faces. Faces that I don't know if they are smiling or frowning, but I'm pretty sure they're frowning. And then, if a meal is served, the masks come off, and I'm reminded of cattle chewing cud. I sometimes buy a movie to escape, but I can't stand the sensation of earbuds in my ears. It reminds me of all the wet willies I used to receive. I usually just stare out the window and try to calculate our airspeed by clocking how long it takes a car below to travel what I guess is a mile. I have other ways to pass the time while my phone is on airplane mode, but they would probably bore a more normal person.

Back in the day, a person could strike up a conversation with a fellow passenger in the next seat, but folks don't feel so comfortable doing that these days. Maybe our masks are keeping us more socially distant than we should be. But I guess other than a bunch of bad news, there isn't that much to talk about anyway.

I'm not the only grouchy person on the plane, though, that's for sure. According to the FAA website, as of Nov. 23, 2021, there have been 5,338 reports of unruly airline passengers, 3,856 mask-related incidents, and 1,012 investigations initiated. Security violations, which are handled by the Transportation Security Administration (TSA), are excluded from these numbers.

The FAA can now fine passengers up to $37,000 per violation for unruly behavior. Sometimes one incident can result in multiple violations, and stories of passengers punching flight attendants and yelling obscenities are becoming more and more common. For my next flight, I think I'll board a train.

I'm Familiar with the Taste of Soap

The average American lets loose around five curse words every waking hour. This arithmetic works out to be from 80-90 "bad words" uttered every day. Including Sundays after church. Some people never cuss. I usually watch my foul mouth around these types of folks, mainly out of respect and fear. Like when I'm around certain aunts and don't feel like getting a taste of the backhand.

Being a carpenter, I'm no stranger to cussing. That's not a 2-by-4. That's a blankety-blank 2-by-4. Sailors and carpenters use offensive adjectives all day long just to get the job done. I've often wondered what type of crew Jesus worked with when He was a carpenter. Were His co-carpenters careful to watch their language? It's difficult not to cuss after you smash your finger with a hammer. I know this from personal experience. But I'm sure He forgave them, considering the circumstances.

Like everyone, I was strongly discouraged from using bad words during my childhood. I know the taste of soap in my mouth. Unfortunately, my mother discovered that soap was also useful for discouraging talking back, not just for cursing. Looking at the way I turned out, I'm not sure the tongue-cleansing ritual really did me all that much good.

As negative as cursing is construed to be and, of course, frowned upon in most uppity polite societies, you're doing something beneficial for your body after stubbing your toe and shouting out a few favorite well-chosen expletives. Swearing has been proven to raise the heart rate, which in turn helps reduce pain. Personally, I've noticed my heart rate goes up after stubbing my toe, whether I curse or not, but usually I do.

If you're one of those folks that frequent the local gym, lifting weights and killing yourself on those fancy high-tech muscle-making robotic machines, you might want to consider that spewing out a few primitive four-letter words during your workouts will help improve your performance. Researchers had people curse out loud while pedaling a stationary bike, holding a device that measured their handgrip strength. They were not surprised to learn the volunteers pedaled faster and gripped harder while letting loose a string of dirty cusswords.

Want to reduce stress and anxiety? Shoot, that's nothing a little swearing won't help. Studies show that cursing even helps drivers avoid road rage by helping them deal with frustrations while on the road. The emotional relief swearing gives us is so common scientists have even given it a name: lalochezia. They tell us it's a safe way to express the strong emotions we feel without needing to slap someone.

Another good reason to curse is that researchers say using off-color speech can make you come across to others as sincere and the real deal. It shows that you don't care who they are; you are going to say exactly what's on your mind.

Men tend to use stronger swear words than women and use them more often. It has been discovered that women have larger areas of the orbital frontal cortex, which controls anger and aggressiveness, and that evolution has better equipped them to remain in control. Well, I've been the target of some out-of-control female cursing incidents on more than a few occasions, so I'm not sure about all that.

The oldest known vulgar word in English dates back around 800 years. It is also the first bad word learned by young first graders who still make jokes and giggle about it to this day. Due to the nature of this publication, I can't repeat the word in this space and probably wouldn't even if I could, but I can give a hint: it starts with an "f" and ends with "art."

It seems the overused word we all know as the "F-Word" has some real use after all. Researchers say this versatile word helps people who work together express politeness, alleviate tension, and bond. I'd be cautious using it around clients or the boss, though.

I was barely big enough to hold a .410 shotgun when I first heard the F-Word used. My dad and I were hunting turkeys, and while lying behind a rotted log on the cold ground, he poked his head up, spotted a big bird, and uttered under his breath to me, "There's that 'f-word-er'." My virgin ears burned red with embarrassment. I couldn't believe such a word had escaped the lips of my old man, and somehow, my innocent mind immediately knew exactly what it meant. No explanation needed. That's the type of word it is. After I grew up, my dad and I couldn't have a real "man-to-man" if any women were present.

So, if I accidentally slam the car door on my fingers or something equally as stupid and I embarrass you with my foul language, I'm sorry, I'll go eat some soap.

Blue Is for Boys, Pink Is for Girls

Back in the day, the gender of an unborn child could be predicted by many methods, such as the belief that if a woman had cravings for all things sweet, she was expecting a baby girl. If she couldn't get enough salty foods, it meant that she would be having a boy. Expectant mothers could also swing a ring tied to a string or a strand of hair over their bulging bellies. A circular motion meant a girl was on the way. Another old wives' tale held that if a pregnant woman could eat a lot of garlic without stinking, she was carrying a girl. If you wish to do the garlic test, you might want to wait for the results before venturing out in public.

Studies show that 71 to 81 percent of women want to know the sex of their unborn child. And, of course, it makes sense to be prepared for that upcoming bundle of joy. It is important to make the right color choices for nurseries and clothing. It is impossible to tell the difference between a female baby and a male baby if they aren't dressed in traditional gender-specific colors, so it's a handy tradition. As we all know, blue is for boys. Pink is for girls.

When this color tradition first started in the 19th century, it was the opposite. Blue was considered a daintier color and was assigned to girls, while pink was assigned to boys because it was thought of as a stronger color. Later, pink was deemed close to red and thus more romantic, and the color was associated with the more emotional and delicate sex.

This custom continues well into the 21st century against all odds. During the women's lib movement back in the

1960s, women tried to send gendered colors to the trash bin, but once prenatal testing became the norm, parents were able to pre-plan, and retailers quickly realized they could cash in on selling gender-specific products, and the colors are now a big part of our culture.

Gender reveal parties began in 2008 when Jenna Karvunidis, a pregnant blogger, went on YouTube and announced the sex of her unborn child with a white frosted cake that revealed pink filling when sliced. The parties became the rage, and their popularity has continued to grow through the 2010s and into the present. Extreme reveal events have become quite the norm. Mainly due to social media. Everyone needs to know, don't you know?

Some of these events have ended up in disasters, such as the nearly 23,000-acre 2020 El Dorado Fire in California, sparked by a pyrotechnical device that malfunctioned at a gender reveal party. In 2019, a 66-year-old soon-to-be grandmother was hit in the head by a piece of shrapnel at a party when a homemade gender-reveal contraption made from a metal tube exploded. A fuse was lit, a bomb went off, and the woman was killed.

Karvunidis, the woman who started it all, recently said she regretted posting that first gender-reveal video after learning how the LGBT and intersex communities feel. She said the daughter she announced back in 2008 turned out to be a gender-nonconforming individual who wears men's suits while still identifying as female. After hearing about the numerous tragedies around the world caused by the events, Karvunidis pleaded for people to stop the nonsense.

I never worried about the gender of my children with the first four. There was always plenty of time to purchase the proper-colored clothes for the newborn, and I was always able to paint the nursery before the mother and child were released from the hospital, which was usually at least a few days.

When my then-wife was pregnant with our last child many years ago, her doctor had recently acquired a new-fangled ultrasound machine that she proclaimed could predict the sex of babies with 100% accuracy, and she wanted to try it out. Somehow, I was forced to attend this session and ended up watching an assistant apply lubricant to my wife's taut belly and attach wires that ran from a small monitor to strategic points above our unborn child.

Once everything was in place, the doctor checked the monitor, let out a squeal of happiness, and announced a son was on the way. I had no idea what she was looking at. I couldn't make out the head or tail. After we left the doctor's office, it was straight to K-Mart and then straight to the infants' department. Few men care to go shopping with women, and there's a reason for that. After a few minutes of taking more than I could take of giving my opinion about baby clothes, I excused myself to the toy section and went crazy buying baby boy toys.

A few weeks later, the prettiest little girl I've ever seen came into our lives. She was even pretty in her little boy clothes, playing with her cowboy gun.

Living with Big Brother

Throughout Monroe County, 21 12-foot-tall poles equipped with high-definition cameras were recently erected in high-traffic areas. They are there for the sole purpose of catching the bad guys and protecting the public. If it seems the cameras appeared overnight, they did. It was only last month when county commissioners approved placing the cameras on county rights-of-way in a 3-0 vote. The devices were purchased using funds taken from criminals. Sweet.

Although the cameras read and record the license plates of passing vehicles as well as the makes and models, Sheriff Freeman told me a person would have to have their head hanging out a window for the cameras to see who was inside.

Well, you won't catch me doing that. Maybe Muchacho because he loves the wind in his mouth.

Even though the camera data is kept for only 30 days, it didn't take long for a few paranoid local folks to become alarmed by what they think is the latest government intrusion into our lives. I learned of their Big Brother concerns on a Facebook group page. You know, the same group that's clamoring for the use of body cameras by law enforcement.

For over 50 years, we have been shopping under cameras that record our every move. We can't even buy a tin of chewing tobacco without the transaction being closely monitored. Some stores even install fake cameras as an inexpensive deterrent to people with shoplifting on their minds. It is a necessary evil that most of society has seemingly accepted without much thought. It's something we've become accustomed to and expect as a part of our everyday lives.

The first time I encountered a security camera was inside a 7-11 convenience store just off an I-10 exit, where I had stopped while on a cross-country trip sometime in the 80s. It was a life-changing experience. While standing in line waiting to pay for my Mountain Dew and peanut butter crackers, I noticed a monitor mounted above the counter, its screen split into four views of different areas around the business. I had never seen such high technology. One camera was focused on the entry door, another on the beer cave, and another showed my car parked out front. I could see my pooch standing on the dashboard, wondering when I would return. I thought that was way cool. But there was another camera fastened to the ceiling

directed toward the checkout counter, and I saw the top of

the head of a man with a sizable bald spot. I was so busy amusing myself by watching my little dog that I didn't pay much attention to who I thought was just another customer until I turned around and realized that I was the other customer. A bald customer.

When I go to the barbershop, the barber always takes a mirror when he's finished to show me the great job he did on the back of my neck. Never off the top of my head. And I've never had a reason to use a mirror to see what the top of my head looks like. Before that moment, I had no idea that I was missing so much hair and was shocked to learn that the top of my head was as shiny as a cue ball. I had been married to a woman for eight years, and not once did she mention it. Of course, I noticed hairs in the shower drain, but I figured those came from my long-haired ex-wife.

I returned to my dog, a changed man. A changed bald man. As we sat there sharing our peanut butter crackers, I pondered what it could mean. I imagined that I had some sort of terminal illness or something. No man in my family before me had been bald on either side. I was the first and was a little upset that no one had ever pointed it out to me.

Not that it would've changed anything. I do feel a little better now because my youngest brother turned out to be much balder than I am. We both agree it is a sign of high intelligence.

When I was in high school, students were required to read George Orwell's Nineteen Eighty-Four, written in 1949. If you haven't read it, you should. Many of the things he wrote about, which seemed incredible in his story, are now a part of our daily lives. The perpetual war. The War on Terror is surely that. Newspeak. Open the messenger or social media app on your phone and scroll. If you had read that text ten years ago, you probably wouldn't have been able to understand half of it. And the increasing ability of an increasing number of people who can accept and believe fake news covers doublethink.

We may not like it, but Big Brother is here to stay. Smile for the camera.

Grew Up Poor but Well-Mannered

When I was a young squirt, around 14 years old, thin, and beardless, and the eldest of six children, my position at the family table was to the right of my dad. He, of course, sat at the head of the table. I wasn't sitting in the most comfortable seat in the house. If my old man happened to reach up and scratch his head, I'd automatically duck. If you were raised in my era, you know exactly what I mean.

My mother, who adopted my dad's five children, always sat at the other end of the table. I kept a close eye on her also. I think she sat down there so she could easily send my dad secret eye signals that would alert him that something was up with one of the children.

My brother John, who was barely a year younger than me, sat to my dad's left. He had a bad habit of always watching my dad while he ate. Always ready in a defensive mode. This bothered my dad, but mostly he let it go.

To my immediate right sat my brother David. Also, within arm's reach of my old man. He is eleven months younger than John, and during most of March and part of April, they are the same age. The three youngest children in our family never got into much trouble, that I can remember. But the trouble three teenage brothers so close in age can get into is incredible. I don't blame my folks for being tough on us. Lord knows we needed it.

My mom wasn't the best cook in the world. Her idea of a delicious supper was a deep pot with a couple of pounds of greasy hamburger meat squeezed down into the bottom. Then she'd top it off with a bag of tater tots, add a thick layer of Campbell's Cream of Mushroom soup, and bake for an hour at 350°. Another one of her specialties was sliced and fried Spam, sometimes crusted with cornmeal, served with a side of canned white hominy. We usually washed these tasty meals down with a glass of cherry Kool-Aid. My favorite meal was pinto beans. It's hard to mess up pinto beans unless you burn them.

The breakfasts she cooked for us were worse than her suppers. For example, we would eat hours-old pancakes that she had cooked extra when making breakfast for my dad around 5 a.m. We'd wash that mess down with warm Tang. We had only two manners at our table that we strictly adhered to. The number-one rule was that you were forbidden to rest your elbows on the table. My dad said the reasoning was that if everyone on one side of the table put their elbows on the table at the same time, it would tip over. Even with this danger, you'd be surprised how many times I broke that rule and got a taste of the backhand. Rule number two was don't talk with food in your mouth. Many times, my dad would wait until I forked a piece of burnt Spam into my mouth before he would demand an answer to why I fell asleep in English class or some other such question. His method always gave me time to think up a good answer while I was choking down a slab of Specially Processed American Meat (SPAM). He told me later in life that if he had known I was going to make so much money being a b.s. artist, he would have never discouraged it.

After I went out on my own at an age far too young, I embarrassed myself quite a few times because I didn't know which fork to start with or that my napkin was supposed to lie in my lap and not hang around my neck. Shoot, we didn't even have napkins at our table when I was a kid. We used our shirt sleeves. And they didn't teach manners in school back in my day, either. I learned what few fancy manners I do know mainly by following others' lead. I know how it is to feel out of place.

I learned to say "please" and "thank you." I use "sir" and "ma'am." I still open doors for the ladies, and I believe that it's "ladies first." If I'm entering an establishment, I think it's polite to wait a few seconds for the guy behind me and let him pass the door. If I say or do something out of order, I think the proper thing to do is to apologize.

Those who have good manners were taught so by their families. My dad was an Appalachian boy raised poor and fatherless. He wasn't taught much in the way of manners. And even though we had to sometimes be careful of where we took him for dinner, I was always proud to sit at his right-hand side.

My Good Friend, Cooter

The first time I laid eyes on the little dog was in the dark. It was my earliest marriage, and I had just eloped with a pretty Alabama gal in an old Alabama courthouse just at

closing time on April Fool's Day. That special date, along with the fact that she turned her head away when the judge said I "could kiss the bride," should have been clues that the relationship was doomed from the start. I can't give you her name because I've already had enough trouble.

Plans had been made for a church wedding, but for a reason I can't remember, we decided to skip that fanciness and took the big plunge on the sly. I can't remember the names of her two redneck friends she called up to serve as witnesses, either.

I had already rented a furnished house in what wasn't really the best part of town, and we decided to spend our first night together in that little love nest. It didn't matter that the electricity hadn't been turned on. I stopped by the Piggly Wiggly and picked up a flashlight and a pack of candles. We thought it would be romantic. She called her momma from a phone booth and gave her the big news, which wasn't well received. That part I do remember well.

She was a small thing back then, and I easily lifted her across my arms, stepped across the threshold, then immediately dropped her to the floor when I tripped over a small dog that previous residents had abandoned a week earlier. The dog yelped, I yelled, and my new bride screamed. After helping her to her feet, I leveled the beam of my flashlight on the sorriest, saddest-looking excuse of a dog I had ever seen. Of course, my wife immediately fell in love with it, and to her, it was a sign. Like a wedding gift from God, she said.

She was a little toy poodle that had never been groomed, with tangled, matted hair hanging in ugly clumps. She couldn't see for the hair in her eyes nor hear for the hair in her ears. In the kitchen were a couple of bowls on the floor. Both empty. There was a bag of dry dog food that the poor pooch had torn into and eaten most of it.

My wife put the remaining food in the bowl and added water to the other. She said she wished we had a way we could remove some of the hair from the dog's eyes and ears, and I remembered I had a pair of small scissors in my toolbox and rushed out to perform my first honey-do.

The scissors were dull, and my hands were blistered by the time I finally had the little whelp looking halfway presentable. My bride came up with the name "Cooter" after a character who played a mechanic on the then-popular TV show "The Dukes of Hazzard." He was her favorite actor, and even though Cooter was a man and the dog was female, she insisted on the name. I thought Daisy Duke was much more appropriate (after my favorite character), but we went with Cooter.

Maybe it was because I spent so much effort and time trimming up Cooter while keeping her calm and rubbing her soft belly that we bonded. She wanted little to do with my wife and became my constant companion. I'd carry her around in my nail pouch at work, and she stayed in my lap during lunch breaks. She especially loved sunning herself, lying in the valley of a roof while I was pounding down the shingles.

We eventually moved from that old house to another old house way out in the country and had a baby. After a while, we moved to the Atlanta area and had one more. Cooter stayed at my side as the years passed, always wagging that little stub of a tail.

Sadly, my first marriage dissolved, and she got everything but Cooter, who was by now old and blind.

I found us a room in the basement of a mansion on Ponce de Leon Avenue near Little Five Points. A fancy place for my status at the time. The landlord lived upstairs and knew every lyric of every song that Bob Dylan had written up to that point, but he sang them even worse than Dylan. Even so, I played guitar while we disturbed his uppity neighbors from his porch, and we became great friends.

One day, he was working on his car and accidentally drove over little Cooter. She died in my lap as I was rushing her to the vet. I pulled over and cried hard while the spring rain came down even harder. I then went back to my basement and built her a tiny coffin from pressure-treated pine and dug a grave so deep in the mud my landlord had to drop down a rope to pull me out.

A Tribute to an Oklahoma Woman

The first time I ran away from home, I was nine years old. My younger brother, David, and I decided we had had enough of my old man's stern discipline and decided to hitchhike from the southwest corner of Oklahoma to the northeast corner of Kansas, where my mother was living. There wasn't much to our plan. We just went. No food, no water. We walked down a hot highway one summer afternoon, sticking out our thumbs at every passing car. Back then, hitchhiking was common.

Pickup trucks sped by, blasting their horns, but none stopped. We spotted a police car approaching in the distance, so we lay down in a ditch and hid for a while to give him time to turn around and go back to town. It was getting dark as we continued north to Kansas, and I wondered why my dad hadn't driven by looking for us yet. I surmised he was probably glad to be rid of us.

We could barely see the lights of town when, finally, my dad's best friend, Miles, roared up on his Harley and pulled over on the shoulder in front of us, and gunned his engine before shutting it down. "Where're y'all headed?" He put down the kickstand, dismounted, and lit a cigarette. I mumbled my answer, "We're going to Kansas. To see mom."

Miles was a good guy. All of us, five kids, of whom I was the oldest, really liked him. "You're only going to Kansas? Shoot. Y'all get on." A ride to my momma's house on a motorcycle? Let's do it! He straddled the seat, pulled us up behind him, and slammed his boot down on the kick starter. Off we roared northbound with the hot wind beating our faces. But it was a trick. A quarter of a mile down the road, Miles did a quick U-turn and took us straight back to our dad's house, where we received yet another good taste of the discipline we tried to get away from. I probably ran away ten more times after that. I got caught every time but the last.

My parents had divorced a couple of years earlier, and it had been arranged that the children would spend the summer with our dad, after which we would return to our mother when school started. But it didn't happen that way. She showed up in early September carrying a few boxes of new school clothes for the three older boys. My younger brother and sister got baby clothes. And before the sun went down, she was gone. It was years before I heard from her again. After all this time, I still hate the smell of a new pair of Levi jeans.

We were motherless for quite a while. My dad found babysitters to care for us while he worked at the Air Force base when possible, and when he couldn't, we took care of ourselves. When you put five children in a small house with little or no supervision, something is going to happen. Something will be broken or scratched, or missing. The house will catch on fire. All kinds of crazy things. And even though my dad was only a sergeant in the Air Force, when he came home at night, he was a general. Around 5:30 in the evening, my throat would start to feel dry, and my stomach would get all knotted up. Then, when my old man pulled his pickup into the driveway, my baby brother would run through the house shouting, "Daddy's home! Daddy's home!" and we knew it was the time of reckoning.

The next year, my dad started dating. There were two women he favored, and brought them to our house, separately, of course, to introduce them to his five motherless children. A couple of days later, he sat us down in the living room, explained that we needed a mother, and asked which of the two we liked best. One of the ladies had a little infant daughter, and she won our vote.

They were married in an Air Force chapel on the first day of December in 1963, with my dad looking sharp in his Air Force blues. Guests included my new step-grandmother, my new baby sister, and the five kids.

Just two months after the wedding, my dad was transferred to Clark AFB in the Philippines, and for whatever reason, left us behind in Oklahoma. So, my new 27-year-old mother took on the job of raising six children alone for the next two years. She made sure we went to church twice on Sundays and every Wednesday night. She taught us to work and didn't put up with any shenanigans. No one else could've pulled it off as she did. She made a family. My dad chose well.

She will be buried next to him this week. I'm sure they're enjoying their reunion.

Farewell to My Brother, David

David was my guitar-playing partner and my fishing buddy. We shared songs we sometimes wrote while sitting in a wet tent next to a swamp. In the good times, we'd get together and jam all weekend. Those were good times. He was my brother.

We shared our childhoods, staying mostly in trouble and even running away together a couple of times. I was only nine, and he was seven when we decided to head to Kansas once. We walked a couple of miles out of town and hitched a ride on a motorcycle for a couple of more before a U-turn was made, and we were taken back to our dad, who was waiting with his belt ready.

We had another brother who was between us in age, but he never went along with our schemes. He had his own schemes going. We were three motherless boys who had the run of the Oklahoma countryside every weekend, swimming in nasty cow ponds, learning how to smoke nasty cigarettes, and walking for miles down long dirt roads. Once, we found a couple of electric cattle prods in an old barn and spent the afternoon using them as swords. We even staged a rodeo once, out in a cow pasture we came upon, but the cows didn't cooperate all that much.

When my dad finally remarried, he left us six children with his new bride almost immediately after receiving an assignment to Clark Air Base in the Philippines. For two years, we lived with a woman who began as a stranger to us but became our mother. She was a hard woman, as hard as our dad, but that was a good thing because she would've never survived the antics of a household full of Reece boys and a couple of Reece girls.

When we became teenagers, I got a guitar with my newspaper route money, and David and I took turns learning chords and driving the rest of the family crazy. It was a cheap guitar with rusty strings, but that didn't dampen our desire to learn. Rock n' roll was just beginning, and we were there with a little country music thrown in to keep my old man happy.

When we became men, the three of us older brothers all got into the construction business, framing new houses, remodeling, and doing a lot of roofing. David and I worked on many projects together, and he even went to Hollywood with me for a while as I was building movie sets. Only once did we all three work together, and that was a disaster for the books.

I was the oldest of three brothers, and I once had the bright idea of forming the Reece Brothers Construction Company while we were all in Atlanta at the same time. My brother John must've thought I said "destruction" instead of "construction" because he turned our first and only job into a disaster. At that time in Atlanta, all homes were built on the sides of hills since those were the only lots available. That meant every house had a deep concrete-block basement, on top of which we would build the floor system.

You may not know much about floor systems, but typically there's a heavy steel I-beam set in the middle of the structure that supports the floor joists. So, with David waiting on the concrete wall at one end of the house and me on the other, John lifts the steel beam that was chained to a forklift and swings it around in a quick swoosh and completely knocks out the concrete wall on which David was standing. I took a leap before it swung back around to me. In a panic, John pulled the handles in the opposite direction and, in doing so, rammed the beam directly into the center of a huge transformer that powered the entire subdivision. There were no cell phones back in those days, and we had to drive to the nearest phone booth so our boss could tell us to leave and never come back.

We separated for a few years after that. I lived in Los Angeles, David went to Florida, and John caught a ride to Maine. David worked as a high-rise window washer for a few years in Miami until one day a rope broke, and he fell four stories, landing on top of a concrete awning. He somehow survived the fall but spent a few years in a rehab center; he hated to recuperate, which he never fully did.

He finally relocated to middle Georgia, as I did a few years ago, and we rekindled our old jam sessions and began to play every weekend. We made many music videos during that time and posted them on Facebook. I'm so glad we did that. He was my brother, and I miss him. My childhood is truly gone.

Americans are Known
for Their Stubbornness

In 1975, the United States Congress attempted to introduce the metric system with the Metric Conversion Act. The act said adopting the metric system would be strictly "voluntary." There were no surprises when no one showed the desire to volunteer. The United Kingdom began switching to the metric system in the 1960s to align with the rest of Europe.

While the rest of the world uses centimeters, we prefer inches. They use meters, and we like our 36-inch, 3-foot yards. A foot equals 0.3048 meters. A yard equals 0.9144 meters. In 1793, the meter was defined by French scientists as one ten-millionth of the distance from the equator to the North Pole. It was a dimension that arrived at through mathematics without the aid of GPS.

On the other hand, the length of a foot was originally determined to be equal to the size of the foot of King Henry I of England. When his rule began in 1100, he decided to standardize this unit of measure by adopting the length of his somewhat oversized clodhopper as the official standard. Also, the width of a man's thumb determined the distance of an inch. This method seems a little less scientific and a lot less accurate than the metric system.

As Americans, we have always enjoyed doing things differently from anyone else. We not only don't use the metric system, but we also do weird things like write dates with the month before the day, something no one else does. After the Revolutionary War, a dictionary was published containing words deliberately spelled differently from British spellings. We also prefer a different temperature system from most of the world.

In 1793, then-Secretary of State Thomas Jefferson sent a note to some buddies in France requesting a standard kilogram to help the United States adopt the metric system. A scientist named Joseph Dombey was promptly dispatched to America carrying a small copper cylinder with a little handle on top. It was around 3 inches tall, about the same width, and weighed exactly one kilogram. However, before reaching the United States, Dombey's ship was blown off course by a storm, and he ended up captured by pirates and died while in captivity. The metric system was doomed in the United States thereafter.

There are only three countries in the world that still use the Imperial System of measurements today (inches, feet, miles, gallons, ounces, etc.): Liberia, Myanmar (formerly Burma), and the United States.

The use of this archaic system of weights and measures by the country of Liberia comes as no surprise since it is a nation created by Americans who believed black people would face better chances for freedom and prosperity in Africa than in the United States. Even their constitution and flag are modeled after those of the U.S.

Myanmar uses the system simply because it was under British rule from 1824 until after World War II, when the Brits were using imperial units. Their government says it has no time to focus on units of weight and measure due to the intense strife that has continued in their country since their independence.

Of all the industries, construction has been the slowest to adopt metric units. Two-by-fours are still two-by-fours, although they really aren't two-by-four anything. They are one and a half inches by three and a half inches. Many immigrants in the construction trade seem to have little trouble learning the increments on a 25-foot Stanley. It is obviously easier to learn to read a measuring tape than to read our language.

We may not notice it, but we all use the metric system every day. For example, we say, "He makes over $100K per year."

We use the letter "K" because it is commonly used to denote "thousand" in the metric system. Some still say "$100G," with the "G" meaning a grand, which was a code word for a thousand dollars used by the underground in the early 1900s. Shampoo bottles and other products are labeled with both ml and fl oz. Another example is the popular-sized two-liter soft drinks. The half-liter water bottle has now replaced the 16-ounce. You can't buy a quart of wine anymore. You ask for the 750-milliliter size. But Americans don't like to buy liters of milk, so we can still buy it in gallons. The same goes for gasoline, though fractions of a gallon are expressed as decimals. There's no explaining what we think is acceptable and what isn't. We are Americans.

Just like our language and our customs, Americans will use only that part of the metric system that works for us, and no one is going to make us change what we don't want to.

What Ever Happened to Common Sense?

If anything can go wrong, it will. This well-known law has been scientifically proven and attributed to Captain Edward Murphy, an aerospace engineer who worked at Edwards Air Force Base in 1949. This is the same base where General Chuck Yeager broke the sound barrier two years earlier. As the story goes, Murphy was complaining about one of the men serving under him, and what he really said was, "If there is any way to do it wrong, he'll find it." Attempts to prove or disprove this law are doomed to failure by the definition of the very law itself. Nevertheless, buttered toast knocked off a table will always land butter-side down.

I always try to prepare for anything that might go wrong, and on the rare occasion when everything seems to be going well, I know I have obviously overlooked something. Nature always sides with hidden flaws. As the military says, "No battle plan ever survives contact with the enemy, and if your advance is going well, you are walking into an ambush."

We can never tell which way a train is coming by studying the track, and that light at the end of the tunnel is usually that oncoming train. All we can do is remember that if anything simply cannot go wrong, it will anyway. We can only pray for the best and hope we don't make some foolish mistake.

Fools can be exceptionally clever in their endeavors to mess things up, so it's impossible to make anything truly foolproof, and companies will go to great lengths not to get sued. Federal and state laws, as well as insurance companies, require that consumers be well-protected against unseen hazards.

This is why we have warning labels on chainsaws advising us not to hold the wrong end while it's running, and notices on laundromat dryers saying it's hazardous for children to be inside the dryer while it's operating. Another good piece of advice I once saw posted on a Florida gas pump was not to insert the gas nozzle into your mouth or any other orifice, which I'm not allowed to mention in this space. Even though these notices seem ridiculous to most of us, there is a reason they are posted on nearly every product. There are some folks out there who really need this guidance. As cowboys say: "Never approach a bull from the front, a horse from the rear, or a fool from any direction."

According to Voltaire (1694 – 1778), French author, humanist & satirist, "Common sense is not so common." Common sense is a lot like my barber who could use some mouthwash; those who need it the most don't have it.

If everyone would just behave and use a little more common sense, we wouldn't need so many laws, rules, and warnings cluttering up our lives. Wikipedia compiled a list of more than 30,000 statutes that the United States Congress has enacted since its inception in 1789. Yet even with the listing of these 30,000 laws, this extensive list is incomplete. Add to that total the state, county, and local regulations we live under. We must truly walk straight and narrow to be law-abiding citizens these days.

Of course, we need most of these laws. This is no utopia where there is no need for lawyers. Where leaders and judges are immune to bribery because money doesn't exist. We need to keep some of these folks under control. I'm in no way advocating abolishing any of these laws enacted with common sense, except for maybe replacing the income tax laws with the FairTax law. I like the fact that it's fair and makes good common sense. Will Rogers once said, "The only difference between death and taxes is that death doesn't get worse every time Congress meets."

In Monroe County alone, around 55-60 people a week are jailed for various reasons. Sometimes ridiculous reasons. Usually, the number of incidents and arrest reports we print in this newspaper each week spills over onto a second page. Many of the people in our local hoosegow could've easily avoided arrest with a bit of planning. It doesn't take an Einstein to know you shouldn't haul butt through Monroe County at 90 miles per hour in a darkly tinted car with an illegal license plate held on with only one screw and 4 pounds of cocaine in your trunk and a stolen pistol under the driver's seat. You're sure to attract the attention of one of our hawk-eyed deputies, and common sense will tell you you're going to jail.

And it's not a good idea to leap out of a second-story window from a home you broke into and burglarized, even if your name is Byrd, because if anything can go wrong, it will. I once heard an old cowboy say, "It don't take no genius to spot a blue jay in a flock of hummingbirds." Someone had to say it.

The Great Equalizer Will Come for Us All

Your position in life won't stop the day most of us are dreading. Not your race, your creed, or your profession. Life is priceless, and your money will be worthless on the day you meet death. Death. The great equalizer. The one thing that truly unites us all.

Some of us won't go to Heaven when we die, and some of us will, but I don't think too many of us look forward to checking out of this world, no matter where we might end up. There won't be any more pain or bills, and I look forward to that part of it. I'm not afraid of dying, but it's not one of my favorite things to consider, either. Even so, after that close call with the Chinese rocket debris we had recently, I couldn't help but ponder my impending demise.

For one thing, I don't like to think of the darkness that lies six feet down in the dirt or that I'll be out in the elements during winter. I'm thin, and I get cold easily. When I'm a skeleton, I'll be even skinnier. I also don't cherish the thought of people accidentally trampling over my grave, as I've accidentally done to the dearly departed, as I've browsed around an old graveyard trying to read the names of folks long gone. I always try to step off lightly, though. And I don't care to be cremated because who knows where I might be scattered, making yet one more mess on this messy planet.

As Mark Twain once said, "No life is ordinary." Yet, according to a senior demographer at the Population Reference Bureau, roughly 100.8 billion quite ordinary people have died since the beginning of time. Most of them are soon forgotten forever. No names were remembered. No stories retold. There are around 7.4 billion folks alive today who face that same destiny. It seems such a waste, especially to a storyteller.

Deep down, we want our friends and family to keep us in their memories after we pass. Hopefully, one day I'll accomplish something people will remember me for, but just in case I don't, thankfully, there's an app for that. We now have "legacy" apps that promise to make you "immortal." These apps are used to record important information, such as your will, and to permanently store your messages and memories, such as photos and videos, for future generations to cherish. It's an ingenious way to remain a part of your loved one's life forever. Some of these apps are free. I'm dead serious. You'd think they'd try to squeeze one last dollar out of you before you go.

Some folks now adorn their tombstones with QR codes on their tombstones. This began in 2012, when tech companies started creating sites linked from a little funny-looking code on a cemetery headstone, about people who are more than just names and a set of dates. We can pull out our phones, see the faces of those below us, and learn about their achievements, passions, and disappointments.

I'd like to have a touchscreen installed on my tombstone. Touch the screen, and I'll pop up on a video and say howdy and tell you a good story or joke. Type in your name on your phone, and I will give a personalized message intended for you alone. Enter the secret password I gave you before I expired, and I might tell you where my treasure is hidden. Of course, there will also be a link to subscribe to www.MyMCR.net. That way, I can keep selling newspapers even after I'm gone.

All this gruesome technology I envision will be powered by a solar panel mounted on top of this elaborate monument to my life. The solar panel will also be the source of power for the cell phone I will be holding, forever in my hands, tight against my chest, held up so I can see. That way, y'all can send me text messages on my birthday or shoot me pics of my great-great-great-great-grandbabies 200 years in the future. Please be sure to include names and birthdates.

I'll have automated responses set up, so I might give you a call from time to time. My number will be engraved beneath my name. Be sure to add me to your contact list so I won't be blocked.

My oldest son and I once discussed planting a black walnut tree over my chest after that final shovel of red dirt had been tossed over me. Then, after 30 years or so, he will return to my gravesite and look up into that old tree until he finds my likeness hidden somewhere in its branches. He'll cut out that part of the tree and carve my bust, complete with my ballcap, glasses, and my famous big smile. After a heavy coat of varnish, it will be displayed proudly on his mantle.

Until then.